D1765760

Father of Lies

A Darkly Disturbing Occult Horror Trilogy – Book 1

S. E. ENGLAND

<u>About the author</u>: Sarah England originally trained as a nurse in Sheffield (UK), before working in the pharmaceutical industry and specialising in mental health – a theme which creeps into many of her stories. She then spent many years writing short stories and serials for magazines before having her first novel published in 2013.

At the fore of Sarah's body of work is the bestselling trilogy of occult horror novels – Father of Lies, Tanners Dell and Magda; soon to be followed by The Owlmen, out on April 26th, 2018.

You might also enjoy, The Witching Hour –a collection of some of her darker short stories; and, The Soprano, a supernatural thriller set on the North Staffordshire Moors.

If you would like to be informed about future releases, there is a newsletter sign-up on Sarah's website, the details of which follow here. Please feel free to keep in touch via any of the social media channels, too. It's good to hear from you!

www.sarahenglandauthor.co.uk

Also by S. E. England:

Tanners Dell - Book 2

Magda – Book 3

The Witching Hour – an anthology of short stories and serials

The Soprano – A Haunting Supernatural Thriller

The Owlmen – Pure Occult Horror out April 26th, 2018

ISBN: 9781517458089

2nd Edition: EchoWords

www.echowords.org
www.sarahenglandauthor.co.uk

Prologue

Something woke him. His eyes snapped open. Heart slamming against his ribcage.

Beside him, Jack's wife slept deeply, silently.

His ears strained into the darkness. Who or what was there?

Seconds passed. Nothing. It had been nothing. He slumped back against the pillows. A bad dream, then? Just a nightmare, that was all…thank God. Nothing to worry about.

Once more, sleep dragged him down into heavy-limbed oblivion, and he began to sink gratefully into its depths. The warmth of the bed. The lead of exhaustion in his bones.

Then came a tiny tap - barely discernible, but definitely there - perhaps simply branches scratching against the bedroom window, though? Yes, that would be it.

He kept his eyes shut, not wanting this, a tiny part of his brain on alert: should he get out of bed? Just to make sure? What if one of the kids was wandering around? If only his dead legs would move. *So tired...*

God, it was unbelievably dark in here. Was it usually like this? Such blackness? Like a porthole ripped into the night - the entry to an eternal abyss - with no air. Sweat clotted on his skin. November. Should be cold, right? Maybe he was ill? Had a temperature?

High on the wall above him, the time glowed in digital green. It was 3 a.m. Precisely.

3am and wide awake. Just like old times - being a junior doctor on call - waiting for news on a post-op patient, the subconscious always on alert for the bleeper - what if you'd overlooked an internal bleed? What if their lungs were filling up with blood as you slept? You never switched that off…

There. It came again. Quite distinctly this time. Three sharp taps on the window pane directly next to his right ear. "Let me in*!*"

Twenty feet above ground?

He tried to sit up. To reach for the lamp.

But nothing happened.

He tried again. This time to lift his own right arm. But his limbs remained as heavy and unresponsive as that of a corpse. Oh God, a stroke? Paraplegic? What the hell was going on? *He couldn't move...* A sharp intake of breath lodged like a nut in his thorax - swelling, choking. His lungs gasped for air as once more he attempted to force himself into a sitting position. Couldn't breathe out and couldn't move. A nightmare. Okay, this was just a nightmare. A bad one.

The digital clock flicked to 03:01 a.m.
A fresh wave of icy sweat surfaced all over his body. Which remained pinned. Firmly. To the bed.
Hannah... Hannah... His wife's name formed on his lips yet no sound came. The words remained in his mind but nothing happened to make them real. Locked-in syndrome? Was that it? Something terribly wrong with his nervous system - or a panic attack? Yes. He'd been working too hard and worrying about that girl on the ward. The one he'd tried to treat this afternoon. Yes - a panic attack. Okay - that's exactly what it was. *So stay calm then. Try to just breathe. In and out. In and out.*
Convincing himself. With a voice as soothing as honey to a sore larynx. As the digital clock clicked to 03:02 a.m. And the vortex of blackness engulfing the bedroom began to work itself into a shape. A shape, which was recognisable and yet not...as some kind of creature...now crawling towards him; pawing at the covers; heaving its slithering form up onto his chest, its breathing wet, rattling, and laboured. Compressing his chest with an iron force.
This wasn't real...it couldn't be...
Foul breath in his face...the creature sniggering delightedly...as it whispered the words, which would be etched onto his brain for the rest of his life, "Good Morning, Jack. Wakey, wakey. It's showtime."

***

Chapter One

Drummersgate Secure Forensic Unit.

October 2015

Drummersgate Hospital sits alone on sodden Derbyshire moor land. Two wings adjoin at right angles - Riber Ward for the medium security patients, and Ash Ward for those under review.

Each client has their own basic facilities - consisting of a sparsely furnished bedroom and an en-suite bathroom. There is a communal art room, a gymnasium, and a large cafeteria with a flat screen TV fixed high on the wall. An office equipped with security staff and cameras, alongside a small reception area for visitors, connects the two units.

The upstairs level of the building houses two staff meeting rooms - one for each ward - and private offices for Dr Hardy and the Medical Director, Dr McGowan. In addition, there is a staff lounge and some overnight accommodation facilities. At the far end of the corridor, above Riber Ward, there is also a solitary confinement bay, and a suite of treatment rooms. Manicured gardens planted with box trees surround the unit, which is reached, by a long, poplar-lined driveway. Around the entire area are high electric fences. And to the rear, mile upon mile of desolate moors topped with flattened tufts of heather.

In winter the sound of whistling wind underneath the doors, through cracks in brickwork and around rattling window panes, overrides the pulsating radiators cranking out heat through ancient pipes. Those inside raise their gazes to the roof whenever another strong gust buffers the slates and grasps the eaves, threatening to lift the roof clean off. God knows what would happen then!

Within each of the ten-bed units, are the female patients. Listless yet restless, dull-eyed and caged, most of them are here for indeterminable years, while society tries to work out what to do with them - with those who have debilitating personality disorders for which there is no cure; the ones who have committed crimes they barely remember let alone admit to or care about; and the seemingly impossible cases. Like Ruby.

***

Riber Ward Staff Room
Case Meeting, October 2015

The psychiatric team had reached an impasse yet again.

Ruby, the girl kept under strict, locked supervision in Room 10, had been at Drummersgate for almost two years without a hint of improvement.

That Friday afternoon the day had set to mizzle - a band of greyness crawling across the moors and plunging them into an early dusk. The fluorescent lights in the meeting room above Riber Ward buzzed and flickered, making the faces below appear peaked and drawn.

Dr. McGowan sighed heavily as he picked up his notebook. He still liked to jot down notes in black and white, never quite trusting today's gadgets - certainly not with the thoughts and suggestions of his trusted colleagues. And definitely not when it came to case histories like Ruby's. But with an ever increasing workload he did need the notes. They really were getting nowhere fast with this young woman. Although many patients took years to recover, and some were never discharged fully, it was unusual for a client to not only show zero improvement on any parameter whatsoever, but to actually deteriorate.

He was, however, not a man to be beaten, and there was possibly one more trick up his sleeve.

The rest of the team knew they'd got to Ruby, the last one on their list, by the way the mood in the room pitted into weariness. The yawn was contagious. What was there left to say? To suggest?

"Let's have some more coffee," Martha said. "I'll pop the kettle on."

"Good idea," Jack agreed, as one by one the others in the team nipped to the toilet or checked their iphones.

He glanced at the clock. Ten minutes and he really needed to be on his way to a court case in Leeds. In his mind he was already half way there - racing against the outpouring traffic. Still, he'd had an idea to put forward and it was doubtful anyone would object. It had to be worth a shot.

A sleety wash of rain spattered across the darkening windows. God, he was tired. Drained, he thought, would be the right word for how he felt right now. Sometimes, he'd just go and park the car at a supermarket somewhere, flick on the central locking and stay there - the only place he could go for some peace - to filter through the escalating chaos of his life, sorting and filing the day away, anticipating problems, pre-empting demands. Eventually, with some semblance of cerebral order, he'd start up the ignition and hope Hannah had cooked something that day, instead of walking in to find a sink piled high with dirty dishes, worktops strewn with discarded fish-finger or pizza boxes, the TV on loudly, and the children fighting.

He smiled as Martha returned with the drinks. Good old Martha, as kindly and maternal as her name - Martha Kind - suggested, handing round a tray of swilling coffee in plastic cups with plastic spoons. 'It isn't good but it's hot,' she liked to say. She'd been their key social worker for nearly twenty years now and heaven only knew what a nightmare it would be if she ever left - threatening to retire to that 'bungalow by the sea.' Whatever would they do without her? She took a quick slurp of her own before shrugging on her bobbly brown coat, and reaching for her walking stick. "I'll leave you to discuss Ruby again, then. Good luck! You'll need it!"

Becky, the ward sister, called after her. "Hey, wait a minute. Need a quick word before you go, Martha. We'll only be a couple of minutes here."

Becky looked at Jack's questioning eyebrow and shrugged. "Well we're onto Ruby again, aren't we? I never thought I'd say this but I honestly think she is the one patient who really does have to be kept isolated and sedated - possibly forever. We can't have her kicking off every five minutes. Not only do we not have the staff - there's only me and Noel on again this afternoon, by the way - but it upsets the others and then we're in lockdown again." She folded her arms and took in a deep breath. "I really am sorry, Jack - but upping the dose of Olanzapine just made her worse."

"Well that's because she doesn't have schizophrenia," Amanda chipped in with that dry, told-you-so voice of hers.

Jack looked hard at Amanda Blue, the hospital Psychologist. "Yes, Amanda. But she does have psychotic symptoms. It was worth trying. Anyway, we'll reduce the dose and increase the haloperidol to calm her down. The thing is, and what I wanted to put to you all, was–"

Beside him, Claire Airy, the new specialist registrar, suddenly interrupted. "Sorry…sorry, but I've been reading a paper by Dr Silver, and she has a patient who sounds very similar to Ruby." She flicked through her electronic notebook. "Apparently, she had a breakthrough with counselling–"

Jack looked at the clock again. "Dr. Airy." He took off his glasses and ran his palms over and over his face, then put the glasses back on again. "Believe me, counselling is never going to cut it. I've had endless discussions with Kristy Silver, who I know very well, by the way. But Ruby is the most disturbed, violent, unpredictable and unresponsive patient we have ever had at Drummersgate. Every DSM classification with a forensic history has surely passed through our doors - but not only is there no diagnosis with Ruby, there is no frame of reference either. Anywhere. Ever. We really have tried everything."

Becky nodded in agreement. Drained her coffee and made to stand up.

Claire Airy's face flushed. She remained seated. "Dr Silver's paper was about someone just like Ruby. It recommended–"

"I read it, Claire," Jack said wearily, reaching for his jacket. "Anyway, I have a proposal–"

"As long as it's more sedation," said Becky.

Amanda shrugged. "And as long as I have full security if I have to take her to the art room again," she added, still raw from the time she asked Ruby to draw pictures of what was on her mind - the team's most recent attempt at trying to get to the root cause of the problem. The incident had crawled under her skin and chilled her to the core. However could that frail, frightened-looking young woman have known such vile words and drawn such shocking images? Ruby had sneered and poked fun at Amanda, positively demonic in her salacious knowledge of every misdemeanour she had ever committed. The horror of it had dirtied her soul and could never be washed away.

There had been one other patient in the art unit that day. An older woman who had been a client at Drummersgate for fifteen years. Who now lay in Doncaster General Hospital with a pencil-shaped wound through her retina.

"I'm actually going to try hypnosis," said Jack.

Silence hung in the air for several moments as the others took in the information.

Claire's eyebrows were nearly in her hairline. "But surely continued therapy will eventually draw out the trauma…I mean–"

"Oh please," said Amanda. "That's what I've been trying to do for months now, only we never get beyond drawing eyes and knives. Every one of us has drawn a blank. And frankly, if anything she's getting more aggressive the more therapy she has."

"Hypnosis, though? Are you serious, Jack?" Claire persisted.

"I'm very loathe to use hypnosis, to be honest with you," he conceded. "In fact I haven't used it on anyone for over six years…but–" He looked steadily at Claire. "Dr Airy, I do know where you're going with what Kristy Silver states in her clinical paper, but Ruby doesn't have the same diagnosis as her client. He has straightforward PTSD from child abuse. With Ruby I can't even get as far as symptom classification - nothing fits."

Claire stared back at him. "Might it not be too dangerous, though?"

But Jack had already stood up and grabbed his jacket. "Gotta dash. Claire - can you go over to Riber and alter Ruby's drug sheet for Becky? Great - much appreciated. I'll be back in first thing tomorrow."

Amanda called after him. "When are you planning to do this hypnosis?"

"Monday - late morning. That okay with you?"

Amanda nodded. "Fine. Have a good weekend, Jack! Doing anything nice?"

Jack picked up his briefcase and smoothed down his unruly greying hair, the bane of his life, and smiled ruefully. "I have five children, Amanda…why do you think I work Saturdays?"

The door shook on its hinges as he left. Receding footsteps echoed through the tile-floored corridor.

After a moment, Becky said, "I've got a bad feeling about this."

***

Chapter Two
Riber Ward

Becky peered through the porthole window at Ruby, who was sitting on the window ledge in her bedroom, knees curled up to her chest. Rocking. Singing quietly to herself. The same lullaby she always hummed, over and over…'Four and twenty blackbirds...'

She tapped on the window before unlocking the door, then softly making her way towards the armchair by the near wall. She didn't speak, but tucked her feet up underneath her, waiting until her presence was felt and accepted. Ruby wouldn't look at her - but she'd know who was there.

"How are you feeling today, Ruby?"

Ruby's singing tailed off as she turned to look at Becky with a puzzled expression. Then abruptly she faced the window again and began to hum - a loud, monotonous, 'mmmmmmmmmm' - which rose in volume and tone, along with an increasingly violent rocking motion, so that her head kept hitting the wall behind with a sickening crack.

Working herself up again, Becky thought. God, what on earth had made this woman this way? Somehow she'd functioned in the outside world for over twenty-five years before she'd put herself on the radar with an attempted murder charge, and made it to the unit. Now twenty-seven, and sometimes as rational as the next person, it was clear she'd been seriously damaged at some point in her life. But who could help her if she wouldn't talk? And with no known relatives and no identity, it was all the more a mystery. Who was she and where had she come from?

But to ask…again…and risk the wrath of the raging monster within? Well not today. And definitely not alone. Best to try and calm her down before she did herself an injury. Becky's hand hovered over the panic alarm she kept on her person at all times: if she touched Ruby in an effort to stop her from harming herself, the situation could escalate in any number of ways and she'd need help.

Outside, the insidious mizzle from the moors had darkened the evening to a foggy gloom, reflecting the women's ghostly faces in the window; an oblong of buttery light bathing the sodden lawn.

Ruby's rocking was escalating, the humming reaching jet-engine proportions.

Becky kept her voice low and even. "Ruby? It's Becky. Would you like some tea? We've got chocolate digestives today! Come on, love, you're hitting your head. There's a good girl."

The humming ceased unexpectedly.

Ruby swung round. The stare blank. Eyes dead.

This was new. Becky waited.

Ruby's stare was so vacant it was as if her very soul had backed down a long corridor and slammed the door shut behind her. The person inside the body had absolutely vanished.

The atmosphere was static. Charged.

Becky forced herself to stay seated; to keep her voice steady. "Ruby?"

Suddenly Ruby's eyes flickered back to life. Someone had stepped up to the plate. Someone other than Ruby, though: gone the appearance of hostility, of wild-eyed mistrust, or sly knowing. Instead the whole face had softened - years falling away - until a dawning expression of untold shock and horror, recognition even, passed over the fragile features, like that of a small child recalling a terrible nightmare. Her bottom lip quivered and then her whole face crumpled like damp tissue paper, and she began to shake violently, tears cascading down her cheeks in an unexpected rush of raindrops.

Becky's instincts broke through. She rushed forwards and took her in her arms. "It's okay, Ruby. It's okay. Whatever it is…whatever it is…it's okay now. You're safe here. You're safe."

Ruby's body seemed to have collapsed in on itself, until she was so tiny there was nothing left, save a few feathery bones.

"I promise it's okay. We're going to help you. There are things we can try. Dr. McGowan has an idea, and we're going to try and unlock whatever it is that's hurting you so much."

Ruby made no sound.

Continuing to murmur softly, Becky pulled herself away a little. It had been a maternal reaction, an uncontrollable rush to hug her charge like this. But she had to step back: Ruby could change in the flick of an eye, as every member of staff knew all too well. She held Ruby at arm's length and looked into her face, expecting to see the tear-stained misery from moments before. Instead she met with glazed, pale blue eyes appraising her as if from very far away, and Becky's heart skipped a beat.

A dreamy voice said, "You're in love, aren't you?"

She smiled slightly. "Oh Ruby - I've been married for years."

Ruby's eyes twinkled with merriment. "I see him. A big man. He's solid and dependable and you can trust him. There is a uniform."

Becky retreated another step.

But the information was coming thick and fast. "You've known each other for ages. He loves you but you don't know if you can leave your husband or what the outcome will be. You're supposed to be together. They're telling me you have to be careful, though. There is a lot you are going to have to deal with, and *they know–* "

Ruby put her head to one side, screwing up her face in concentration. "You'd better watch out because you are in the fray now...Oh and–"

"What?"

"Something really bad is going to happen." She started to shake again. "I can't tell her that. It's the bad man...You have to leave now - all of you–"

Becky held her shoulders and spoke firmly. "It's okay, Ruby. This is all in your head, okay? You can hear voices but we are going to help you, I promise. There is no one here who will hurt you. You're safe."

But the blue eyes had lost their glitter and a vacant expression was back in place - the drugged one most of the patients wore - where no one was home because the resident was living elsewhere these days.

"Ruby? Are you with me?"

A faint rag-doll of a nod.

"I'll get your tea sent down to you, today. Would you like that?"

Ruby shrugged.

"Can you remember what you just told me, Ruby?"

The blue eyes had clouded over, staring at something over her shoulder.

This was a new development: Ruby had classic psychotic symptoms including auditory and visual hallucinations - nothing new there - but that did not explain her knowing about other people's private lives like that, unless she was some kind of clairvoyant - something Becky did not, nor ever would, believe in.

A cold claw clutched at her stomach as the information sunk in. No one knew about Callum, that was the thing. *No one.*

She led Ruby over towards her bed. "Look, most of us have hunches about things, but you mustn't worry too much. Bad things don't always happen. We have choices, and I won't let anything bad happen to you, okay?"

Ruby wobbled a little, and then slumped onto the single bed, curling up in a foetus shape. Oddly, she began to suck her thumb. "I've got a headache."

"I'll send someone down with paracetamol. We'll talk again soon, eh?"

Ruby nodded.

God, she's such a child, Becky thought, reluctant to leave her. But she had to. Late staff would be back from tea-break soon and she was off for the weekend.

"See you on Monday, okay?"

Hurrying down to her office, Becky closed the door shut behind her and sunk onto her desk chair, head in hands. Damn, she hadn't warned Ruby about the hypnosis on Monday morning. Well she could hardly do it now. That psychic thing though…oh my God! The clatter of the tea trolley and distant phones ringing,

faded as her thoughts focused into a nucleus of concentration.
Ruby could not have overheard anything about Callum. *Because
no one knew!*

So was the woman psychic? Clairvoyant or whatever? God,
if she put that forward in a case meeting she'd be laughed out of
the office! No way could Jack or the rest of the medical staff know
about this. Especially from someone deemed not to be in control of
her own mind like Ruby. 'Hearing voices is a symptom of
psychosis,' Jack would say. Well yes of course, except…
hmm…and here was the rub - not even Becky's closest friend
knew about Callum. There would not have been a single whisper
to overhear. No one - absolutely no one - knew. Jesus! She needed
a drink!

Inside her bag she kept a small bottle of brandy - strictly
forbidden, of course, but then everyone had a vice of some kind,
didn't they? And with shaking fingers slugged half of it into a
polystyrene cup. Knocked it back. *Bloody hell, though!*

The phone rang. She ignored it.

It wasn't as if she could even discuss this with anyone.

In all the eighteen years she'd worked here at
Drummersgate and the twenty-three she'd spent in psychiatry,
Ruby was by far the most disturbing and frightening, patient she
had ever come across. Even the other patients, all of whom had
committed serious crimes, wouldn't meet Ruby's eye. For such a
reed-slender girl she certainly emitted a disproportionate amount
of fear wherever she went. It was the unpredictability though, that
total personality change...from incandescent rage…to childlike
rocking and singing…to not being there at all. And now this.

Once the hammering of her heart began to steady, Becky
flicked on the computer and scanned Ruby's case history once
more. At twenty-five, Ruby had been arrested for the attempted
murder of a local middle-aged man - Paul Dean from Woodsend
village on the outskirts of Doncaster. He'd been found in bed with
a knife through his neck by his brother, Rick. Neither of the men
had ever seen the 'crazy bitch' before. A few local people said

they'd seen her wandering around the neighbouring, larger village of Bridesmoor, but couldn't be sure.

On arrest, Ruby had been a wild-eyed, kicking, bucking savage - splattered blood clotting in a parted curtain of dark, oily hair, as she spat murderous obscenities. Wearing little more than denim shorts, thigh high hooker-boots and a vest top, her skin was alabaster white, with wheeled, keratinous scars carved into the insides of both arms, across her stomach, and even between her toes. Although the bones of her clavicle protruded like a wasted cadaver and her chest caved inwards, it had taken four grown men to restrain her.

As for Ruby herself, she had no recollection of the attack. Despite extensive enquiries, it seemed she had no roots, no family, and no formal education. Refusing to talk to anyone and flying into destructive rages, she'd been declared mentally unfit to stand trial. However, during the course of police investigations, it appeared she'd had relationships with various men - rough men who described her in turn as volatile, mad, weird and promiscuous. The only relatively stable point in her life had been when she'd briefly lived at Tanners Dell, south of Bridesmoor village. Prior to that it seemed she had simply not existed.

A comprehensive treatment regime began at Drummersgate Forensic Psychiatry Unit for Women. For several weeks she had been heavily sedated, until finally she agreed not to attack the staff who tried to help her. Endless consultations with both Dr McGowan and his team were recorded. Symptoms discussed. A variety of anti-psychotics, anti-depressants and sedatives had been prescribed, along with psychotherapy and counselling. Yet almost two years on they were no further forward. No conclusive diagnosis. No chance of her leaving Room 10.

Becky ran her fingers through her short, spiky blonde hair and put her feet up on the desk. A peevish rain pelted the windows from out of the squally darkness. On the whole this was an enjoyable job - helping people the rest of the world had forgotten about. That old phrase, 'lock them up and throw away the key,' applied to most of the clients she cared for. Some of those clients eventually moved into supervised housing, had some kind of a life after Drummersgate. But in Ruby's case, she could be one of the few who were here for life. Well, where would she go?

She shut down the computer and stared at the yellow-painted wall in front of her. *Soon home time. What to cook for dinner? Not looking forward to standing out there in the dark and the rain waiting for the bus…*

A thought came riding in - perhaps this business of hypnosis might work? She let Jack's idea settle for a moment, considering it. On the other hand - what if it triggered one of those terrifying, uncontrollable rages again - the kind which resulted in solitary confinement upstairs in the padded room? Ruby. Such a slight figure, so forlorn and tiny with that lank, mousy hair hanging down either side of her ashen face - such fragile bones you'd swear a strong wind would snap them in two - throwing herself around the room in a frenzied tirade for hours on end. She hardly ever ate. Never smiled. What the hell had happened to that girl?

She looked down at her own far too robust thighs encased in black leggings - a black tunic covering up her spare tyre, and grimaced. Too many late nights, hurried take-aways, not looking after herself…Maybe a penchant for grabbing chocolate bars on the way home didn't help, either? *Well some of us eat when we're unhappy…*

Unhappy…was she?

She shook her head as if to clear it of confusion. Sounded like the late shift were coming back from tea break. Good. A whole weekend off. And Callum to look forward to. God, who would have thought she'd ever have a relationship with a copper? She of all people - who'd been such an anarchist in her youth? But it was like - coming back to life!

The disembodied words floated into her thoughts without warning. *You'd better be careful….*

Her smile faded instantly.

Noel, her staff nurse, dashed in for his rucksack and crash helmet. "They're back - we can get off! It's teeming out there. Are you gonna be all right waiting for the bus?"

She nodded.

"You okay, Becks? You look like you've seen a ghost!"

"I've just got this bad feeling."

He raised his eyebrows. "About?"

"Ruby. I feel like something bad is going to happen but I don't know what or why."

He made UFO film noises. "Spooky! Maybe you is psychic and you don't know it, innit?"

She forced herself to smile. "That'll be it. Or it could be they're doing hypnosis with her on Monday and…she's ..well…she's just been a bit odd with me this afternoon. There's something not right but I can't put my finger on it. It's like the more treatment Ruby has the more complex she gets."

Noel nodded. Suddenly grave. "Hypnosis? Are you serious?"

"Jack always said she had PTSD and I think he's right. But she seems to be getting worse not better. So I guess he's thinking if he directly connects with her subconscious, we might be able to circumvent her coping mechanisms and find out what happened to her. Start a more effective treatment?"

Noel narrowed his eyes. "But you're worried unleashing the trauma will damage her even more?"

"Possibly. And she seems to have a premonition of doom. And to throw the proverbial spanner in the works, she's just told me something about myself that she could not possibly have known. It's really weird."

"Oh you mean, *she's* the psychic one?"

Becky grimaced. "Do you believe in all that?"

Noel smiled. "You're talking to someone who believes the daily horoscopes, Sweetie! Anyway, are you seriously telling me that someone who hears voices is erm…hearing voices?"

She laughed. "Fair point! Anyway, Ruby will have to agree to hypnosis first."

He raised an eyebrow. "Jack does it to you without you knowing. I find I tell him all sorts. Usually after a few pints, mind."

"Ruby won't tell him anything. Won't even see him half the time. I'm probably worrying over nothing - it might never happen."

Another belt of sleety rain slashed against the window and Noel drew the blind. "Come on, I'm not letting you wait for the bus up there on your own in this." He handed her a spare helmet. "I'll drop you off in town."

***

<u>Chapter Three</u>

Woodsend, November, 1995

Late afternoon and Celeste was napping.

Rap! Rap! Rap!

She woke with a pounding heart and a surge of annoyance. *If this was local kids again - banging on the door then running away and calling her a witch - well it was beyond a joke and she'd give them what for this time!*

Heaving herself off the sofa, she swished shut the curtains, muttering under her breath as she made her way into the hall. Her steps slowed, however, as she neared the door. A spark of alarm. Through the glass - an outline of a man, dressed all in black.

A nasal voice called out, "Reverend Gordon here! Anyone home?"

He was stamping his feet and rubbing his hands, itching to get in.

Even as she drew back the bolt, her inner self recoiled and a knot formed in her stomach.

Brushing her aside, he swept straight through to the lounge.

"To what do I owe this honour, Reverend?" she said, trailing after him, and regretting not having tidied away her crumpled blanket.

He removed his knitted scarf and tossed it onto a chair. "Just a duty call, my dear."

"Would you like some tea?"

"That would be lovely, thank you."

She bustled around in the small, adjoining kitchen, picturing the man examining her ornaments and books - looking for signs of witchcraft, no doubt! She hurried back with two mugs of tea, sat down and waited.

He slurped. Took his time. Eventually he cleared his throat and said, "You've been having a bit of a rough time from our local scallywags, I hear?"

Celeste watched him closely. For a man of God he had a pretty murky aura. "Yes." She couldn't take her eyes off it. And there was something else too… a dark shadow behind him on the wall.

"Something wrong?" he snapped.

You tell me, Vicar….

"Not at all." Forcing herself to focus on his flinty, almost colourless eyes with their pinpoint pupils, she took a deep breath and tried to calm her racing heartbeat. Should have protected herself. Too late now.

"Look, Reverend - we're not talking about trick or treat, you know? I've got kids daubing 'Witch' across my front door in red paint. Threats to burn me to death on the bonfire on the Common! We've had firecrackers through the letterbox…Quite honestly, I think there's more to it than just naughty kids. Gerry, my husband, is really suffering with the stress and in his condition I dread to think what might happen if this carries on."

"Well it might be best for all then, if you left."

Did he really say that?

The words punched her in the gut. Sending her reeling. "Excuse me?"

Every now and then, doubt crept in concerning her own intuitive powers: that secret, inner knowledge, which warned her where the heart of darkness lay. As if it couldn't reside within a person of the Cloth, or someone smiling right into her eyes. And then that doubt would be shattered with a stark truth, and she was, once again, forced to believe in something very few others could even see, let alone understand.

He took another long slurp of tea. Put the mug down on her coffee table instead of on the coaster. "Well there are people in the village who don't like what you do, Mrs Frost - the tarot readings, for example, and the so-called healing. I can't say the church takes a kindly view of these matters, either."

"I don't believe I'm hearing this. I've had people come to me in bits with grief, and I've helped them more than you ever could. Or would. I've alleviated back aches and gout, migraine and insomnia. I've never done anyone any harm - only good."

"I'm simply pointing out…"

"While those kids run riot. They should be in school or at home under supervision. My husband's not well and we can't afford a house of our own, as you well know. It would take months if not years to get re-housed, and why should we?"

Her eyes narrowed as images formed fast and suddenly in her mind - *some kind of gypsy camp. In the woods. Dirty children running wild… a black stony-eyed stare from a woman hanging washing - who turns to look at her directly - a curse of a look if ever there was one…*

"As I said - I am simply pointing out, if I could be allowed to speak, that the church will not tolerate witchcraft, Mrs Frost. There's no need to take umbrage - I'm only suggesting what might be best for all concerned."

There was a pause, which stretched into uncomfortable silence while Celeste attempted to recover herself. Her gaze, which had been concentrating on an area just above his head, reverted to his face. "Hmm, yes. Oh you are, are you Reverend? Well you can tell people I'm not a witch, I'm a healer. A spiritual healer. And you can also tell them I'm not going to be hounded out of my own home. Not for you, not for them and not for anybody. We've only been here a few months, and it was supposed to be a quiet move to the countryside for Gerry's health and mine!"

Reverend Gordon blanched slightly, then picked up his mug of tea again, revealing a stained ring from where he'd placed it. "It would help you, then, if you didn't run witchcraft classes, would it not? You bring trouble upon yourself, Mrs Frost."

Celeste stood up. "Good day, Reverend. And for the record, yet again, I do not run witchcraft classes. Anyone would think we lived in the dark ages. I run a spiritual development group. In a church. Now if you don't mind…"

Nodding briefly, he took one last greedy gulp before reaching for his scarf and leaving the room. Once in the hall he let himself out, but and before he could turn and speak further, she shut the door firmly behind him and slid the bolts.

Too late, though. Way too late.

She'd felt the warning and still let him in. It was her own fault. A blast of cold, November air swirled around her ankles and she crossed herself. "God protect us this night. Protect us from evil. Please God - protect us this night."

But the damage was done. She already knew. Knew as she bounded up the stairs to their bedroom...

Gerry was a big man. Had worked physically hard - first down the mines, then later in the building trade - wherever he could find some work. Labouring mostly. A few years previously his heart had begun to skitter around in his chest, and his breathing was tight. Angina, the doctors said. Later they diagnosed emphysema too; all due to heavily tarred lungs, carrying extra weight, and now the added stress of little income.

When Celeste walked in, he was on his back, ashen-faced, clutching his arm. "It's crushing me. My chest...I can't..."

She rushed to the phone and dialled for an ambulance.

It would be a while yet before they could leave Woodsend.

***

That night the rain increased in intensity - driving shards into pavements, pummelling roofs, swirling down glugging drains. Celeste sat in the back seat of the taxi, squinting through the car-wash conditions as it slowly took her home again. Gerry was in the operating theatre having an emergency quadruple bypass graft. There was nothing more she could do for him except, as the ward staff suggested, go home and rest, collect his overnight things, and take care of herself so she could take care of him when he came out.

And pray. They didn't mention that bit. No one did these days. No one dared, she thought -and that was part of the problem.

The short dash from the taxi to the front door drenched her - shoes sopping from the puddle-soaked pathway, rivulets streaming down her face and neck, hands shaking as the key went in.

Inside, the house was cold and still. She sat, stunned, at the kitchen table, anorak dripping onto the linoleum, letting the mortis chill permeate right through to her bones, and darkness creep in like a shroud around her shoulders.

Should have known. Didn't listen to her own warning voice. Why had she let him in? Why?

Slowly she became more aware of her situation. Of a silence that ticked. Of black shapes shifting along the walls, and branches scraping at the windows. And of something else…something indefinable…beyond the humming of the fridge. Almost indefinable… but there…*listen, Celeste, listen.. It's a breathing other than your own.*

The sudden recognition of what was about to happen hit her like a hammer in the chest. She scrambled for the crucifix she always wore around her neck. "Dear Lord. Please protect me…Dear Lord, please protect me…"

Along the hallway something was squeaking, making its way along the floorboards towards her. *Gerry's electric wheelchair?*

"*Celeste…Celeste…Celeste…*" came the whispers.

Outside the rain drummed on relentlessly against the windows, the walls, the roof, drowning out her breathing, her heartbeat. She put her hands over her ears and repeated the Lord's Prayer over and over and over.

A door banged shut upstairs.

Don't feed the fear…do not feed the fear…How hard it was to take your own advice, yet imperative. Feel the anger, not the fear…

How dare that man bring bad spirits into her home! Who the hell did he think he was pretending he worked in God's name? That old trick - the cloak of decency! Well it didn't fool her even if it fooled everyone else. And never would. Fury sparked hotly, overriding the fear - just enough to give her courage. Celeste stood up and switched on the lights. "No! You will not frighten me out of my wits and my home. You are nothing. Nothing. Get out of my house and my life. Get out now!"

The kitchen lights flickered.

A surge of strength erupted from somewhere within her, as she hurried from room to room, switching on every light as she went, citing the Lord's Prayer and holding tightly onto her cross. Belief was all she had to protect her as books flew from shelves and curtains opened and closed. But her faith was strong. And her prayers grew louder, until that was all there was: prayers and light, prayers and light.

At 5 a.m. the turmoil ceased, along with the first weak rays of dawn filtering through a biblical sky. Weariness lay heavily in her mind and she fought to stay awake, make coffee, and take a hot shower. The long night was over and Gerry would need her.

At 6 a.m. the call came. He'd made it through surgery and was recovering in Coronary Care. She must take her time bringing in his personal things, the voice on the phone said. Look after herself. No rush.

She sank down onto the double bed they shared, pulled the duvet over her head, and finally gave herself up to exhaustion. The inhuman spirits - because that is what she was dealing with - would wear her down now, draining her resolve, attacking her faith, and her very humanity. It's what they did.

Why ever had she stayed here? When she'd known? Known within hours of arriving.

***

Woodsend was a tiny village on the edge of Bridestone Moors - a forked turnoff from The Old Coach Road between Doncaster and Leeds - and consisted of little more than a collection of residences scattered around a wooded dell. Not one you'd pass through on your way to anywhere, but down a dead-end, dirt road called Ravenshill. A driver who took the track would pass Five Sisters Woods on their left, fronted by a row of council houses; and Drovers Common to the right, which could be walked across to reach the neighbouring, much larger village of Bridesmoor. Dotted around the area were various cottages and a couple of farms. Few made a specific trip to Woodsend unless they were visiting someone, and all essential facilities were over in Bridesmoor.

Drovers Common, sometimes used by travellers and gypsies, was a windswept dumping ground polluted with syringes and the remnants of arson. Green enough from a distance, it provided a rural view for the row of council houses, one of which Celeste and Gerry had moved at the end of September. That view was now blotted with a loaded bonfire that had been piled high with bags of rubbish and scrap, in the name of Guy Fawkes Night, topped with someone's pock-marked old sofa.

No longer able to afford their own home when Gerry's health had deteriorated, Celeste had accepted the offer of the house with gratitude. With Gerry's invalidity benefit and her own meagre earnings from tarot readings and spiritual healing classes, they could just about get by. An offer, in other words, they could see no reason to refuse.

The day they moved in, had been a golden sunny one humming with heavy bees and scented with berries. When evening came, smoky with a welcome nip in the air, Celeste suggested they take a walk. "Not far. Just down to the river and back up through the woods? If you're up to it, that is?"

Gerry, who had been more cheerful that day than he had for years, nodded, "Aye. Good idea."

"Don't forget your GTN."

He tapped his shirt breast pocket. "Come on - let's go before it gets dark."

Five Sisters Wood lay directly behind their house, shimmering in a green and golden haze all the way down to the river. "It'll be nice walking back up through the trees," Gerry said, as they walked hand in hand down Ravenshill. "It's so warm - like it's still summer! I'm surprised there aren't more folk about, to be honest - isn't there a caravan site at the back of those woods?"

Celeste nodded. "Yes. Fairyhill Park. You can just see the caravans from up on the Old Coach Road if you look down. Other side of the woods from us, though. We'll not hear them if there's a party."

She smiled, kicking off her sandals when they reached the river bank, letting her toes sink into the cold, rushing water, recent worries floating away. "It's magical. I can't believe we're here. Or how beautiful it is."

"How lucky are we?" said Gerry, putting his arm round her shoulders. "I love you, Celeste. Always have."

She kissed him on the cheek. "Then I'm the one who's lucky."

They'd sat for a while; tipping back their heads to the deep blue eternity, relishing the silvery, tinkling water washing over their feet. A moment in time. Caught like a feather in the breeze.

Maybe they'd dozed. Looking back, she couldn't remember quite what it was. Except the light had changed. "We'd best start back," she said, suddenly jumping up.

A lone rook cawed as the sun sank rapidly behind the trees, silhouetting the army of trunks against a fireball sky. They began to walk quickly. The shortening days having caught them unaware.

The path by the river had been well-trodden over the years, presumably by local dog-walkers and day trippers. Yet soon they were stumbling over protruding tree roots and ducking from prickly branches.

"I think we've veered off the main path," said Gerry.

"We must've missed the left turn onto Ravenshill Road," Celeste agreed. "Gone too far north."

"Maybe if we carry on we'll find another path off to the left?"

"Well we're bound to, aren't we? I think there are one or two cottages with long drives off Ravenshill into the woods."

For a few more minutes they tramped uphill, Gerry's breath rasping audibly as the path became ever narrower and more overgrown.

"What's that?" he said, stopping abruptly.

"Gerry, take a rest. Stop and rest! Let me have a look."

A cottage squatted in a heavily wooded dell, almost obscured and covered in ivy. She peered through the trees. *Woodpecker Cottage.* "Lovely name! Funny how it's all in darkness, though. I wonder if anyone lives there? Maybe they're still out at work or something? Mind you - it's so neglected."

"I think we should have taken a left by now," said Gerry. "Oh well - let's see what 'appens if we keep going - these folk are bound to 'ave a driveway."

"Are you sure you're okay? Because we've no torches or phones or anything, and I definitely can't carry you."

Gerry smiled. "I'm all right for a bit."

"Do you know though, I can't see a driveway to that cottage? God knows how they get in and out."

A couple of minutes later the path fizzled out entirely.

Celeste whirled round, panting from the uphill exertion. "How odd!"

"Aye! And look at that!" said Gerry, pointing.

Up ahead was a clearing, revealing a ring of luminescent white stones shimmering in the dusk.

Celeste frowned, creeping forwards for a closer look. A violet tinged light hovered above the circle, and the previously still branches began to bob and sway as if a breeze was blowing up. "I don't like it here," she said, turning back to face Gerry.

But the path where he'd been standing was dark and empty.

Panic clutched at her stomach. "Gerry? Where are you? We haven't got a torch - come on we need to go. We have to get out of here!"

But her voice fell deadly onto damp grass, stymied by tree trunks. She swirled around and around, trying to ignore the tinkling whispers in the sylvan canopy.

Overhead the first few stars twinkled amid streaks of mist, and another rook cawed. Closer now. The path, when she looked down again, was now totally dark. "Gerry?"

His voice, when it came, seemed far away. "Hey - come and look at this, Celeste."

She stumbled forwards. "Where are you? I can't see. Gerry!"

Suddenly he was back. Wheezing, he grabbed her hand. "You're right - let's go back the way we came. Now."

There was fear around him. The electric kind you could sense, the smell of it oozing from his pores. "What? What is it?" She panted, almost running to keep up with him as he dragged her downhill.

No answer.

His breathing was tearing out of his lungs. What if something happened to him out here? It was completely black. Roots coiled up from the path, slowing their progress. Branches sprang in their faces. Solid thickets either side.

The smell of wood smoke assailed her nostrils.

"The cottage - that woodpecker place. We must be near it," Gerry said.

"Yes. At least we know it's occupied if they've lit a fire - we could go there if we need to. Are you okay to keep going, though? We really need to get back to the main path."

His grip tightened on hers by way of an answer.

There was nothing now save the sound of their own panicky breaths, and a blackness more intense than either had ever known. Until finally a small light from a window hovered between the trees on their right. Another one next to it.

"Over there," said Celeste. "The houses on Ravenshill. Oh thank God."

And such was their relief, and the hurry to get home safely, that Gerry didn't say what he'd seen. And when he finally did, many years later, it was to recount with the added horror of what may have been prevented, if only he had.

***

Chapter Four

Drummersgate Forensic Unit

October, 2015

Jack McGowan was a busy man. At 6.30 a.m. sharp, he eased out of bed, leaving his wife, Hannah, to sleep on for as long as she could. She'd been up most of the night with their two youngest, but they'd had this out many times - he couldn't be the Medical Director of a top forensic psychiatry hospital, attend court, give lectures, treat patients and write clinical papers if he was up all night with her as well, could he?

She did look exhausted though. And pregnant again. Why oh why had he married a devout Roman Catholic who wouldn't use contraception, even in this day and age?

"For God's sake," he'd said, when she announced their sixth was on the way. "Why would you not let me have a vasectomy? What's so wrong with doing that?"

Glaring through her tears, Hannah shrieked, "Don't you dare bring God into it, Jack McGowan! Don't you dare drop His name to score a point–"

"What? This man in the sky sitting on a throne telling us all we have to live in chaos when we don't have to?"

"Chaos? What chaos? It's the way of the world, Jack. We're supposed to have children."

Not this many…

It hadn't ended well and never did. Perhaps he'd just go and have the vasectomy anyway, damn it, she'd never know! Mentally he made a note to do precisely that. If he'd had his way they'd have stopped at two. Apart from anything else, they didn't have any fun anymore. The kids had a great time, but with both himself and Hannah exhausted, well, no wonder he was prematurely grey. Grey of hair and grey of face, he thought. And her living in a milk stained onesie didn't help, either. Size eighteen at that. Jeez! How had life descended into this deadweight of perfunctory responsibility so fast?

He tip-toed out of the bedroom and checked on the two oldest children - Daisy and Felix - aged five and six respectively. They were wide awake. Of course they were!

He lifted a finger to his lips. "Go back to sleep and stay quiet. Another half hour, do you hear?"

That would give him time to shower and get some coffee filtered before having to switch on CBeebies and referee fights over the Coco-Pops: a few precious minutes to scan the latest British Journal of Psychiatry.

He darted into the bathroom and jumped into the shower. Head under the jet stream of heat. Letting his thoughts flit back to the mention of Kristy Silver's clinical paper yesterday. In all fairness to Claire Airy it was an interesting case, although whether it shed any light on Ruby's, was debatable: Kristy had described a young male patient from Woodsend Village, roughly the same age as Ruby, who had presented with an extreme form of anxiety, aggression and disturbing flashbacks, originally diagnosed as P.T.S.D. - just like Ruby. However, during intensive counselling sessions, he began to switch personalities; and it was during one of these episodes, when Kristy had managed to hold a dialogue with one of the child alters, that sexual abuse had first been described. The account had been related by a six year old child in horrific, graphic and shocking detail. Later, when gently questioned about the revelation though, the patient denied all knowledge of it. No further recollections of who had committed the abuse, or where or what had taken place, had been added to the memory; and there was not enough evidence to pursue a criminal investigation.

According to Claire, who had chatted with Kristy about it over the phone, the patient - Thomas - actually did have family in Woodsend, but they had denied the allegations that he'd been abused. Their son had always had problems 'in the head,' they'd said by way of explanation to the medical team. And no, they had absolutely no idea who could have done it. It was probably 'all in his imagination' and 'total rubbish.'

So was Ruby's traumatic event also a deeply embedded case of child abuse? Yes she was of a similar age, and yes she presented with similar symptoms, but apart from that the only similarity between the two cases, was that Thomas originated from the same village in which Ruby had attempted murder. And that was where a big, fat black line had to be drawn under the comparison, because all knowledge of Ruby's prior existence in the area had been refuted by the family attacked, the neighbours, and everyone in the village who had been questioned. She had not attended Bridesmoor Primary School like Thomas had, and was not on record at the GP surgery. No one knew her. In fact, the attack had been described by the police and in the media as, 'unprovoked and random by a deranged, mental patient.' Despite extensive investigations, nobody seemed to know where Ruby came from or even her full name. And unlike Thomas, she certainly wasn't revealing information or responding through therapy.

Puncturing his thoughts, one of Jack's younger children began to scream louder than a pneumatic drill. Now Hannah was plodding across the landing. He towelled himself off. Perhaps…oh this was no good, he'd lost his thread. Anyway, Claire was flogging the proverbial dead horse with counselling techniques. They'd been there, done that, got the sodding t-shirt. Something far more radical was needed: whatever was locked inside Ruby's head would need to be uncovered soon and dealt with if the girl was ever to recover a fragment of sanity, and have a shot at living some kind of a life. Whatever had happened, there had to be a way of helping her. Anyway, maybe he'd give Kristy a ring if the hypnosis didn't work? Perhaps she'd stumbled on a trigger - a word or phrase - which had sparked the memory in Thomas?

Jack quickly shaved, brushed his teeth, ran fingers through his hair in the absence of a comb, and grabbed his clothes. Then dashed out of the front door amid a cacophony of yelling and screaming from upstairs.

Looked like a doughnut and Red Bull for breakfast in the car-park again, then.

***

"There's a rep to see you, Dr. McGowan," his secretary, Louise, trilled as he dashed into the office two hours later.

Jack called over his shoulder. "Fine, send her in!"

Louise peered over her bifocals. "Are you sure? You've got a very busy day."

"Yes, yes - send her through."

Through the darkened glass to the waiting room, he copped a look at a young woman as she stood up and reached for her briefcase. Jack grinned. Held the door open for her to walk ahead of him in her tight, black skirt suit. Louise was watching him, the interfering old baggage, but so what? What was wrong with starting the day off with a good-looking young woman crossing and uncrossing her legs while she asked him to prescribe her drug? She might even have a tempting invitation in store - a conference abroad and a few days in a 5 star hotel, would be most welcome, for example.

"Don't keep him long, Hayley," Louise called after the girl. "He's got a full schedule."

Hayley sat down opposite him and duly crossed her long, black-stockinged legs. Flicked a strand of blonde hair out of her eyes, then bent down to reach into her briefcase.

Jack's gaze lingered on the small area of creamy flesh where her blouse strained across her chest, letting it travel down to the contours of her outer thighs, which filled her skirt.

When the girl looked up she was flushed. Smiled. "And how are you today, Jack?"

"I'm very well. Yourself?"

Their eyes met and a tacit message of sexual attraction was exchanged.

"Thanks, yes. Actually, I have some good news. You asked if there were any overseas conferences coming up and we have one in March. Vienna. I've got the agenda here if you'd like to look it over?"

I'd like to look you over…

He leaned forwards and took the proffered brochure. "Thanks, I appreciate that… Ah I see Kristy Silver's lecturing. Excellent. Four days too. Can you book me a place?"

She nodded. "Absolutely."

"And will you be going?"

She flushed crimson, the burn spreading like a bush fire up her neck and into her cheeks. "Yes."

Neither said anything while he scanned the conference agenda and handed it back. "Looks good. I'll get Louise to make a note of the days. Just a second…" He buzzed through. "Louise, can you bring in some coffee?" He looked at Hayley. "Milk and sugar?"

Hayley mouthed the words, "Just milk."

"Oh and can you bring in the diary?" He clicked off the intercom and grinned. "She won't like that one bit!"

"Making me coffee?"

He shook his head and laughed.

"Jack - I wanted to ask you if you'd received the paper I had sent over to you on combination therapy. Did you have any success with the patient you were talking about - the violent one with psychotic symptoms who didn't respond to anything?"

He never divulged the names of his patients, but the few reps who came to see him did have an abundance of resources on the pharmaceutical treatment of forensic clients. Those like Hayley specialised in a high level service - organising workshops and conferences, finding particular clinical papers, even experimental anecdotes from other psychiatrists. But they had their limits.

He nodded. Sighed. "Yes. And we tried it."

As the coffee was brought in by Louise, Hayley asked, "I'm presuming it didn't work?"

"Thanks, Louise," said Jack. "By the way, can you put 4th - 9th March in the diary for conference dates? Just block them out for the moment.

"Sorry, Hayley - no it didn't. I've actually decided to try hypnosis. I've taken her off everything except a small dose of haloperidol, so we'll see what happens. I think we're talking Post Traumatic Stress Disorder from a childhood incident, probably abuse, so if I can get to the root cause we can help her better."

Hayley took a sip of coffee. "You know a thought just occurred to me. This is totally off the wall, but one of my customers and I won't say who obviously, but he was telling me about a very disturbed, violent young, male client he'd used hypnosis on. What he did, though, was add in a small dose of LSD - just 0.1mgs. Apparently it worked unbelievably well. I'm not for one minute suggesting it - but anyway, it popped into my head. Sometimes the most bizarre things can get a result." She laughed. "And no - I'm not selling it!"

Jack smiled. "I think you could sell me anything, young lady."

Again she flushed. "Only if it's on the bloody formulary."

He agreed. "Ah yes - you wanted me to write that letter and I completely forgot."

She smiled widely. "I'd really appreciate it. Once it's on the formulary here, I can tell my GP reps it's used at the hospital and the poor things can make a few sales. If you could come and talk to the GPs sometime too - there'll be a good fee and I'll find a posh restaurant."

"No problem. You've got a good product. You know, though–" He did that thing of taking off his glasses and rubbing his face, then putting them on again. "Going back to LSD for a minute: they prescribed it regularly in the 50's and 60's until the hippies started using it to get stoned. But there's plenty of documentation with excellent results for unlocking trauma, so it's not as off the wall as you might think. Just not sure some of the others in the team would agree–"

"Don't tell them?"

He smiled.

"No seriously - do you have to have a team meeting for every little thing you prescribe?"

He looked at her. Puffed his chest up a little. "Of course not."

"Well there you go. Personally it sounds like this person is in a living hell and if you can help her out of it, then why not?"

She delved into her briefcase, providing a view of her white lace bra and the slight swell of a breast. When she stood up, thanking him for his time and apologising for keeping him so long, he found himself holding onto her outstretched hand for just that little bit too long. "How about dinner sometime?" he heard his voice saying. *Was he crazy?*

She smiled. "That would be lovely."

His gaze lingered as she retreated down the corridor to hand in her security card. He watched the shape of her - the small, nipped in waist and rounded curves.

"Jack–"

He'd still got it. Oh, he'd still got it all right! Sly old dog that he was! She'd smiled right into his eyes.

"Jack–"

And such pillow-soft skin. Imagine laying his head in between....

"Jack!"

He spun round to face Louise - his personal secretary of these past fifteen years - glaring at him. "Jack you spent twenty minutes with that rep, and you have a client waiting in the treatment room. Becky's just rung down to see where you are."

Still smiling, Jack bounded up the stairs towards the treatment room with renewed vigour. LSD. Of course. Why hadn't he thought of that himself?

***

<u>Chapter Five</u>

The treatment room had been designed for both relaxation and safety. From the large, double glazed window there was a breathtaking view of wild moor land, painted that day in a glory of purple heather. Clouds scudded across the sky, a weak winter sun chasing shadows over jutting rocks, a kestrel hovering with fluttering, hunched wings.

Jack pulled the blinds, and slats of crystal light filtered onto the walls. Next to his armchair there was a panic button; and high on the walls, tiny blue lights inside cameras, signified he and his client would be observed by security staff.

Overhead, fluorescent tubes fizzed, and bulky radiators thumped out suffocating heat. There were no other sounds, save for the wind buffering the solid walls, occasionally rattling the windows.

A small comfortable sofa had been placed beside the window, and in the far corner of the room there was a desk and another chair. A couple of Monets broke the monotony of magnolia paintwork. And the whole room smelled of floor polish.

Ruby sat curled up on the sofa like a small child with her knees drawn up to her chest, holding tightly onto Becky's hand. Only the slight judder of her legs and the occasional tic in her jaw, gave away the use of anti-psychotic drugs.

Jack sat down. "Are you feeling okay, Ruby?"

Barely perceptibly, she nodded.

He raised an eyebrow. Exchanged a look with Becky. This was not her usual behaviour. Normally Ruby would be eying him suspiciously, recoiling visibly, and kicking out if he got too close.

Today though, apart from the dystonia, she appeared to be almost inhumanly calm, gazing fixedly on the far wall with her pale blue eyes unfocused and glassy. Not really there, Jack thought. Far, far away…

Who knew when the monster would leap out of that tranquility, though? They'd all been caught out before.

"Ruby, you know we want to help you, don't you?"

No response.

"Thing is - I have something new I'd like to try. Is that okay with you?"

No response.

Then faintly, oh so faintly…Jack strained his ears… there came the silvery humming of an old nursery rhyme, as if it had arrived on a mystical breeze from a time long, long ago…'*Four and twenty blackbirds…*'

Fairy-like, he recalled later, a tinkling, ethereal tune, which gradually increased in strength and volume as he explained about the tiny dose of LSD and the gentle hypnosis technique he'd like to try. Anytime she wanted to stop or if she became too distressed, he would bring her out of it. And Becky would be with her the whole time.

The humming became a crescendo. He glanced at Becky. This wasn't going to work, was it? She was blocking him out.

Then suddenly it stopped. Ruby turned and looked at him with a clear, somewhat challenging expression, snatched and swallowed the proffered tablet, then folded her arms across her chest and waited.

A sharp gust of wind shook the window.

"Why don't you lie down and get comfy?" Becky suggested. "I'll fetch a chair over, so if you feel worried about anything you know where I am."

Ruby ignored the advice to lie down, watching Becky go and get the chair.

When Becky returned Jack's voice had softened and blurred, dropping to a velvety monotone with a story about how he used to read alone in his tree house as a child - how the wind whistled through the wooden slats, and he'd thought he was the only boy in the world with a secret hideaway. "Sometimes," he said, "I need to go back to that place in my head. When life's a bit difficult. You know how that is, don't you Ruby? When life's getting tough and you need a place to lie low?"

Later he recalled her total stillness, like a character paused on video mid-movement, eyes half closed even though her body was taut, head at a slight angle. Continuing gently, he asked her to imagine a place of her own: white and clean with the sun shining through every window. Talked her through the view of a sparkling, rippling ocean - the tide washing in and out, in and out; curtains shimmering in the summer breeze, feeling warm and safe, limbs heavier and heavier, dropping into a doze. She could go there any time she wanted. Would she like to go there now?

Encouragingly, she nodded.

"I'm going to count down from twenty...down, down...eighteen....down and down...eleven, ten....three, two. And one."

"Have a look around now, Ruby, and make the room your own."

Twenty minutes passed in this way, until Ruby began to rock back and forth and the humming resumed.

"Stay there as long as you like...you're completely safe...okay? How old are you here, Ruby?"

The humming stopped abruptly. Her head flicked around to face him and a sly mask of pure malice slid across her delicate features, before the face contorted into an all-knowing, mocking leer.

Jack frowned. Had she switched to an alter personality?

He looked over at Becky, who shook her head and shrugged her shoulders.

"Ruby? Who am I talking to? Can I talk to Ruby please?"

In response her entire body began to twitch and then convulse.

This they'd seen many times before - Ruby throwing herself around violently, head twisting from side to side and her eyes rolling back in her head. She fell to the floor, kicking and spitting, pulling at her hair, body writhing and arching in spasms.

Becky grabbed the pillow from the sofa and tried to put it under Ruby's head, then reached for her panic alarm. They'd need back up for their own protection as well as Ruby's.

Jack kept his voice level and calm, never taking his eyes from her. "It's okay, Ruby. You're safe. No one is going to hurt you. Try and relax. Let Becky help you and we'll bring you out of this."

Security arrived. Jack looked over his shoulder and motioned them to hold fire. He needed to bring her round before restraint took place, if possible. "Hold tight. Give me a minute!"

They waited. Everyone watched, transfixed.

Ruby's body had contorted into a grotesque shape. Her fine-boned face was grinning like a medieval gargoyle with its tongue flicking in and out, and her neck jutted out at a painfully dystonic angle. Her glassy blue eyes had darkened to nearly black, the pupils distended and dilated - probably due to the LSD, Jack assumed, as he carefully monitored her reaction. The dose he'd given was 0.1mgs and although she had a slight frame, she should not have had anything like this kind of reaction. His mind was working quick fire along these lines, when suddenly Ruby's body slumped and her head rolled back. Then from between her legs a trickle of urine seeped into a pool on the floor. It looked as though the fitting was over. Jack continued to squat next to her, watching every nuance. A line of blood and spittle around her mouth. A wash of sweat on her skin. She was little more than a rag doll. Dear me, this child was ill.

The following second of time passed as if in slow motion - Becky finally managing to put the pillow firmly under her charge's head, and the security staff beginning to unlock the door. Adrenalin receding like an ebbing tide. Before Jack, wanting to bring her round as gently as he could, said one word, "Ruby."

In less than a heartbeat the room darkened and the temperature plummeted to freezing, along with a long, low whistle like an express train within the room itself.

Someone gasped. Someone's pulse pounding like gunfire - was it his own? Because the desk - the heavy oak one in the corner - appeared to be scraping slowly along the floor towards the door entirely of its own volition. Becky was back in her chair - except, bizarrely - it was at the far end of the room and facing the wall.

And Security seemed unable to enter the room, repeatedly rattling at the door with a key. Jack tried to lever to his feet but remained rooted as if in treacle, at the precise moment the wooden desk shot neatly into place, slamming against the door and effectively locking out the security staff.

Then slowly, oh so slowly, Ruby raised her head and met his shocked stare with an expression of pure triumph. Her eyes were totally black now, with red pinhole pupils. Her smile one of spiteful enjoyment. He reeled backwards like he'd been slapped, as a deep male voice boomed from her mouth.

"Hello, Doctor. Welcome to the Kingdom."

Overhead, the lights flickered on and off. Mostly off. The intercom machine fell to the floor and the blinds whizzed up and down several times.

"We said, 'Good morning,'" said the voice. A hissing followed, which seemed to be coming from within Ruby's throat. "I think we're going to have some fun - what do you say?"

He couldn't move. At all. Nor speak. A look of puzzled horror froze his features, as Ruby's voice began to recount every last detail of his life. Punctuated with obscenities of the type he nor anyone he knew would ever use..."Fancied a fuck with that loose piece of pussy this morning, Mr family man? You filthy low down mother-fucking dog... Planning to fuck, fuck, fuck her in a hotel, you slimy, lying piece of shit! Burn her soles with crosses, Jack my boy! Make her scream!"

It occurred to him with a lurch of panic, that Becky was able to hear this. Becky - her frozen back motionless. His logical mind tried to cut through the panic.

What the hell was this? How come she knew stuff? Why couldn't he, nor anyone else, move? How to stop this? How to stop the toxin coming out of her mouth?

"You fucking two-faced hypocritical cock-sucking twat. Still fucking your wife up the arse, leaving her at home pumping milk into your fat brats while you fan-ta-sise... about a va-sec-tomy...ha ha ha ! You fucked that student, didn't you - oh what was her name, let me see? Ah yes..." Ruby's body sat bolt upright, opened her legs, began to rub herself… "…oh yes… Marie! Marie, Marie….that red-headed cunt medical student you got your cock out for when your wife was pregnant!"

He couldn't close his ears. Or worse - anyone else's. Forced to listen while the filth droned on and on about his mother, teenage humiliations with girls in nightclub toilets, or even once, God forbid, in the hospital morgue after a med-student party. "Oh dear, you just can't keep your cock zipped in can you doctor? Not even when you're on your own in your car? Admit it - what a dirty, evil slime ball bag of shit you really are…Not really fit to be human, ha ha … and now it's all going to get soooo much worse for you…with all your filthy, fanny-licking secrets going to come out! So much salacious gossip - how deli-cious! Unless, unless… ha ha ha …..and here's the deal–"

The pause was filled with hissing and gurgling noises, like slime monsters down a well. His medical reasoning began to lope down the route of Dissociative Identity Disorder. How many alters did she have? Did this evil one become the host at a time of threat? It could have been transposed from her aggressor? Even if that were the case, though, it still didn't explain how she, or the alter, knew so much about him. His colleagues would never look at him the same way again! He ran this place. People looked up to him. This was his whole career. His life. *Oh God it had to stop.*

His brain rampaged through potential exit strategies.
What deal?

"That's better, Doctor Jack. A deal! You see, we are the Kingdom. You recognise us, you know who we are. We are not a medical condition. We know….everything…and we will turn your life to shit. We will expose you for what you are and shatter your precious ego into a million splinters…unless you desist this line of treatment. Desist…" The final word seemed to be a cacophony of voices - a choir of such power it lifted the hair from his scalp and flipped his stomach… "Do not finish this. Stop it Now!"

To bring Ruby out of the hypnosis, he had to start talking to her. Assuming she was the real host, of course. Maybe Ruby didn't actually exist as an entity at all, and was just an alter herself - the most presentable of them? *Hell, what a mind-fuck!*

A gurgling, noxious cackling spewed forth as the creature inside Ruby read his mind. "You can't count to three and snap your fingers, you fucking cretin. This is the Kingdom. You must stop this line of treatment. Altogether. You must agree. You really have no choice."

Dark shapes crept along the walls and with a stab of shock, he realised the sun was going down. They had been in here for *hours*. Soon it would be dark. He became aware of a frantic banging against the door again. Huge, heaving thuds. People trying to get in with no success. But the door was iron-fast shut.

In his mind he rapidly agreed. Okay. No more hypnosis. He would desist immediately. Absolutely.

The spark in Ruby's eyes briefly lit her face before she collapsed.

The heavy desk instantly gave way, and three security men burst in along with two nurses.

Becky had fainted at some point, and lay slumped against the wall. Someone was calling her name.

The next thing Jack registered, as he fell into the armchair, head in hands, was Ruby sucking her thumb, complaining of a headache. Being taken to the padded room again in a straight jacket.

Jesus Christ, he'd aged a hundred years.

***

Chapter Six
Woodsend, December, 1995

The night the call-out to Woodsend Village came, P.C. Callum Ross was working with Sergeant George Mason. They parked the Ford Sierra outside The Highwayman - a wind-blasted stone inn on The Old Coach Road - while George bellowed down the phone.

Outside it was a fresh, blowy night: wisps of cloud dancing across a full moon in a haze of veils. The Old Coach Road was an ancient highway, cutting across the moors past Bridesmoor Colliery on the outskirts of Doncaster. The inn, which had been there almost as long, had a bad reputation, although most nights it played host only to hooded teenagers on slot machines, and grim-faced old men nursing a pint of bitter. From where they sat in the car, the black, skeletal outline of the pithead could be plainly seen, forked against the bruised skyline like a dying tyrannosaurus.

Callum sighed - 9.45 pm - another bloody domestic by the sound of it, just as they were about to clock off. They always took forever to sort out.

"Come on, lad. It's at t' farmhouse over t' road. We'll walk."

The wind soughed in the trees as they tramped along the road towards the driveway.

"Supposed to be 'aunted up 'ere, isn't' it?" said George. "All t' dead miners trapped underground in that accident a few year back? They could never find all t' bodies - buried too deep, and t' roof kept caving in. They say you can still 'ear 'em moaning on nights like this."

Callum looked up at the miles and miles of sodden moor land, echoing with a low, whistling wind. "I wish you 'ad n't said owt."

Sergeant Mason - a man his dad's age - laughed out loud. "Me mother used to say they dug the mine over an old asylum, and you can 'ear mad people shouting when t' full moon's up."

"Right - now I know tha's making it up."

George laughed again. "No honestly - she did used to say that! Any road - you'll be safe wi' me lad. Nothing scares old George! Ah, here we are! 'Highway Farmhouse.'"

The drive down to the farm was long and steep. Either side of them were high poplars to shield the property from the driving cold winds. And soon the surrounding fields gave way to woodland.

"Bit of an odd one this," said George as they neared the house, which was in darkness save for a small light above the door. "Teenager gone mad, can't do a thing with 'er, apparently. They're a rum bunch up 'ere, I'll tell ya. Bloody inbreeds."

"Oh aye? I thought it were a domestic?"

George lowered his voice to a whisper as their footsteps clomped across the concrete yard. "It's these remote villages, Son. Some of 'em still live in t' dark ages." He inclined his head down towards Woodsend village. "We've 'ad a lot of complaints over t' years with some of t' families round 'ere. Ever 'eard o't Deans? Aye, well worse than gypos, lot of 'em. Take back-up if you're ever called out to them lot. "

Horses snorted and kicked in the stalls, and bits of tumbleweed floated around the yard, as George knocked on the kitchen door.

It flew open instantly.

"Oh thank God, you've come," said an elderly lady, bustling them both through to the living room. "Me daughter-in-law's scarpered - that'd be our Kathleen - 'can't take no more on it', she said. And God knows where our Derek's got to. Leaving me 'ere to deal wi' this..."

She opened the living room door - a large room with a brown and red patterned carpet, and pale pink walls. A pile of heavy furniture lay in one corner as if it had been picked up and dumped there from a great height. The television was switched on but not tuned in - the only sound being that of static.

Both officers stared aghast.

A teenaged girl was spinning round and round on her head. Eyes rolling in their sockets. Laughing.

***

Six months later: April 1996

The day was unseasonably warm and Woodsend, Celeste thought, looked idyllic. Through her front room window, the view over the common was one of God-given pastoral beauty, as if centuries of industrialisation had never happened - an expanse of green, late daffodils shivering in the breeze…all as it should be, except that dancing in the corner of her eye was a ghostly ring of girls in white dresses, their voices tinkling in such a high frequency that no one else would hear…'*ring a ring o' roses*…'

Being a spiritual medium wasn't an option and it wasn't ever going to go away. She knew that. Yet still it caught her off guard and made her heart thump. She blinked and looked away. Then back again. This time the ring of girls had gone.

Her attention, however, had now been drawn to the scene before her. A woman, perhaps in her late twenties, very slender - was reading to a child: a blonde girl with a crown of bubble curls. The woman's arm tightly embraced the child's waist, their heads bent over a book; while behind them a few scruffy lads kicked a ball around, their shouts carrying in the wind, which whipped down from the moors.

On a day like this, she thought, a person could almost forget the horrific events over winter. Gerry had been in hospital for many weeks with further complications following his heart attack. Every time it looked as though he'd recovered enough to come home, something else kept him there. It had left her alone and frightened; those endless nights long and dark - often without electricity either, as cables toppled in gale force gusts.

With no television and lit only by candlelight, the wind rattling the panes and shaking the roof, she'd lain in bed for hours, watching shadows form on the walls, trying to keep calm, breathe deeply, and not feed the negative energy assailing her on a nightly basis. The psychic assault had been, no doubt about it, powerful and relentless: images of faces zooming into hers, one after another, every time her weary soul began to sink into sleep - many of them with red eyes or lacerated features. All accusatory, malicious, contorted by hatred, twisted with disease. Sometimes a noise - a heart-stopping bang as if a heavy piece of furniture had fallen over downstairs - would cause her to leap wild-eyed from her bed. Or scratching in the walls, and at the windows. Whispers in corners...*Celeste... Celeste...*Fear bred fear, as well she knew.

Yet the attack continued. Wearing her down. Her strength waned. In desperation she returned to Leeds for a few weeks, staying in her sister's back room over Christmas and New Year, until Gerry was home again. By which time she felt strong enough, and financially desperate enough, to restart her psychic development classes. These were held in Doncaster, and they'd attracted a lot of interest, with some of the attendees showing real mediumistic talent.

But today there was sunshine again and fresh hope. She turned away from the view and smiled at her client. Began to shuffle the tarot cards and fully open up her psychic channels. *Dear Lord, please bless these cards....*The woman in front of her was young - about twenty, maybe a year or two older - and had taken off her baseball cap and sunglasses while Celeste had been looking out of the window. As she turned to face the girl, Celeste realised with a little jolt in her stomach, that she recognised her. Despite a changed name and a slightly altered appearance there was no way she'd forget those ice-blue eyes with their watchful, disdainful stare; and while she shuffled the cards and asked for spiritual guidance, the answer came. Of course. The woman had attended a couple of her classes back in February, then suddenly vanished. Now here she was in Woodsend. The back end of nowhere, as Gerry described it. Coincidence?

There are no coincidences, Celeste...

Uneasiness crept up and down her spine. This girl had said the classes were rubbish and a waste of money, sniggered during meditation, and generally been a bit of a nuisance. It had been a relief to everyone when she left, which had been during the week they were talking about scrying, using a dish of black ink. "Don't do it for too long," Celeste had warned. "Just a couple of minutes at most. You must always close down properly and cleanse afterwards, and always, always, protect yourself."

This girl, having given a different name on the phone - that of Natalie - was now watching her intently.

"Those classes you run are dangerous," she said as Celeste dealt out her cards. "I did that scrying thing and now I'm possessed."

Celeste put down the pack. "Is that why you're really here?"

Natalie smiled. "You should get sued for doing what you do - taking people's money for a load of old rubbish. You're the devil. You never told me how dangerous this was. Now I've got long black shadows following me and I'm hearing voices in my head telling me to do bad things."

The girl's eyes were hard as flint. "My bloke, Rick, says I'm swearing and sweating at night instead of sleeping, and my eyes are rolling back and freaking him out."

"How long did you scry for? I did say to protect yourself and only for a few minutes if you're on your own."

"All day."

"And yet I warned you–"

"I don't want to end up like that mad bitch up at Highway Farmhouse - spinning round on 'er fucking head!"

"Did you seek my classes out in Doncaster?"

Natalie smiled directly into her eyes. "Yes."

"Why? If you don't understand or believe in spiritualism, and you're not going to take my advice and protect yourself?"

"That's bullshit. You're dangerous and someone 'ad to find out what you were doing to try an' stop you. That stupid cow's a loony now and you're causing it all. We didn't 'ave any trouble until you showed up. And now it's 'appening to me an' all. I'm seeing a man in a black suit at night - telling me to top meself..."

Celeste nodded as the woman listed her symptoms. It certainly seemed like she might be under psychic attack and wouldn't know how to deal with it, let alone have the strength of belief essential to ward it off.

Probably best to contact Father Adams then, because if this young woman had been scrying all day, inviting in spirits, which, as with the Ouija board, would attract the lowest astral order - then she may well be under psychic attack. She had explained all this in class, but people's morbid curiosity, lack of spiritual conviction and just plain ignorance of what could happen, often meant they found out way too late.

She could try to exorcise the girl herself, of course, but one of the dangers of exorcism was that, if not done properly, an evil entity could easily climb into the aura of another - putting herself, already in a weakened state, at risk. No, it was best done through the church. She'd ring Father Adams immediately.

Explaining this to Natalie, however, it took a few moments before she realised that Natalie was spluttering with laughter. "A what? Like the fucking Exorcist or summat? Are you 'aving a laugh?"

Celeste took a deep breath and inwardly she prayed for guidance. "You need help, Natalie."

And yet a small voice, part of her, thought something else. It was possible that Natalie, as she called herself, was simply making trouble - if she was really infested with an evil spirit then she would be frightened enough to make that call. If, however, this was just a hoax, then she'd probably done what she came to do: the symptoms she had described were certainly copy book. Anyone could find them on the internet.

Natalie's aura was strange, though, and difficult to read. There was a black, smudged scribble around her - like a child's drawing. Other things too, vague shapes, which implied Natalie had been dabbling in far more than a bit of scrying. Which was when an inner voice replayed Natalie's words, loud and clear - 'We didn't have any trouble til you showed up'

'*We...*'

It clicked into place. The girl was yet again trying to dismantle her business and her credibility. There had never been any intention to sit for a reading.

"Actually I think you should leave now, Natalie. If you are afraid then you must contact the vicar in Bridesmoor, or ask me to phone Father Adams for you."

Natalie threw back her head and laughed raucously.

Celeste stood up and walked towards the door. Held it open.

Outside, in the early Spring sunshine, the woman reading to the little girl looked up and waved as the front door opened and Natalie breezed out. Celeste narrowed her eyes and it occurred to her that the woman was the same one who lived at the end of their row of houses. She'd seen her around a couple of time but never before with a child - in fact, the woman was so very dark and the girl so very fair.

The moment stuck. The little blonde girl rocking to and fro. Chanting. As the dark woman turned to stare over her shoulder. A moment freeze-framed in her mind like a camera still.

And one which would be recalled in every detail twenty years later. *If only, if only...*

A few more seconds passed. Natalie was now out of sight. Neither tramping up Ravenshill, nor down it, nor across the common. Celeste scrutinised the horizon in all directions. Well how odd. Like she'd vanished into the ether.

A dark cloud shifted over the sun, lodging into place and sending a chill into the air. A coiling wind blew around her ankles. Just like the last time the devil had come calling.

They would have to leave. Immediately.

***

Chapter 7
Drummersgate Unit, Riber Ward.
November 2015

Becky looked through the porthole window of Room 10. After the disastrous hypnosis treatment, which had left everyone in the team shocked and unnerved, Ruby's mental health, by contrast, appeared to have improved dramatically.

The first night in the padded room upstairs she'd slept soundly through to the following morning. When she awoke she ate a full breakfast for the first time since being admitted to Drummersgate, and had maintained a calm demeanour ever since. And here was another first, Becky realised as she looked through the window - Ruby was actually making eye contact and, very faintly, smiling.

She rapped on the door and let herself in. Mindful. Hyper-vigilant. And yet…and yet…something fundamental really had changed. Something so insidious as to be almost indefinable.

"Morning, Ruby!"

Ruby looked up from the magazine she'd been flicking through.

"What are you reading?"

Ruby showed her. 'Red.'

"Someone lend it to you?"

She nodded. "Chantal."

"The cleaner? That was nice of her." Becky sat on a chair by the door. "Any good?"

"Yeah. I like the fashion stuff."

Becky's eyebrows shot up. The transformation was nothing short of staggering. This, the girl who would not talk, engage in any kind of communication - refuse to even look at you unless it was a violent rant - was behaving almost like a normal young woman. She'd showered and washed her hair too, which draped damply around her fine-boned, ashen-skinned face. Her bitten nails were no longer bleeding at the quick. Her pale eyes were clear and bright.

'I shouldn't have ever watched 'The Exorcist,' Becky thought, 'or I wouldn't be thinking the rubbish I'm thinking now - like could Ruby have been possessed? And did this now mean she would tell them who she was and where she came from? Had her cure really been so simple, with an exorcism of her demon? Did Jack even know he might have done it?' He'd laugh if he could hear her thoughts, that was for sure.

Well whatever had happened, maybe now Ruby would talk and get well? Then pass her two-year assessment and be discharged into the community again? Strong and able to cope with life. What an achievement. A flicker of excitement fizzed around in her tummy.

"So tell me how you're feeling today, Ruby?"

Ruby turned over another magazine page. "Yeah good."

"Can you remember anything about the other day? In the treatment room with Doctor McGowan?"

Ruby shook her head. "No."

"Can you remember coming here to the unit, or what your life was like before you came here?"

Ruby shrugged, seemingly fascinated with what she was reading. "No."

"But you don't feel angry anymore?"

Ruby's blank stare met her own enquiring one. "Angry? No, not at all. Why?"

"Or sad?"

Again Ruby shook her head. "No."

"Can you remember anything about your family? Where you grew up?"

Ruby pushed the magazine aside. Screwed up her features. "No. Nothing. Just–"

Becky waited.

"…being at the mill. I was with someone. We had to leave - it were a bad place."

"Where was the mill? Do you know?"

"Yes, of course. Tanners Dell in Bridesmoor. Jes left me - we squatted there and it were damp and dark, and bloody haunted as well."

"Who was Jes?"

"Just a guy. Gyppo."

"Where did you meet him, can you remember?"

She shrugged. "No."

"So after he left, where did you go?"

Ruby did not reply but stared into a faraway place.

Had she pushed her too far? It was just exciting - to talk to the woman, discover more of the story...she had to try! Ruby might have family somewhere - any lead would help!

"Okay, well can you remember if you stayed in the mill alone?"

Ruby shook her head.

Becky frowned. Tried a different tack. "What was it like then, Rookery Mill? Why did you say it was haunted? I couldn't have lived anywhere with ghosts - you must have been a brave girl?"

Ruby began to hum.

Becky froze.

"...four and twenty black birds..."

"Ok that's enough for today, Ruby. It's okay. I shouldn't have asked. Ruby...? It's okay. Ruby...?"

Becky stood up, her hand hovering over the panic button on the wall. *Oh God, what was coming?*

Something had been triggered. Ruby was rocking. Consoling herself like she did before the hypnosis treatment. Blocking out the world again. *Oh no, please don't let her have regressed. She was doing so well!*

Ruby's stare had turned completely blank - so blank it was as if she was no longer there at all...The question was - would something or someone else shortly he hopping into the driving seat?

Seconds ticked slowly by.

"Ruby?"

The girl's large blue eyes were widening and then her mouth dropped open in dismay. The face was now, unmistakably, that of a child full of terror, crumpling with misery, tears dripping down her cheeks.

Then holding her throat with both hands, she started to gasp for air. Great, hawking gulps for oxygen, her already blue-veined pallor turning deathly, eyes rolling back in their sockets.

Becky called for backup and within seconds the team had Ruby into a recovery position with an airway in her mouth.

Dr. Claire Airy was on the scene soon after, softly calling her name. "Ruby! Ruby...talk to me, Ruby!"

Eventually, Ruby blinked and gagged on the airway. Sat up. "My throat hurts. My throat was full of something."

Claire and Becky sat on Ruby's bed, each holding a hand. Making soothing noises as if to a frightened child. "Ruby, did you have a flash back, a memory? Can you recall it?"

Ruby was shaking all over. Her bottom lip trembled and tears dripped into her hair.

"Something shoved down my throat," she said. "I couldn't breathe."

Everyone present registered the sickening information.

"I've got a headache. A fucking pole-axe of a headache."

"All right, Ruby," said Becky. "We'll get you something for that. You're safe now, don't worry. We're here for you."

***

It was only four o'clock but the light had faded to a purple dusk. Becky waited at the bus stop. The wind whipped sharply round her legs, cutting into her back through the thin jacket she wore. Behind her, miles of barren moor land. To each side, a grey and empty highway; and in front - the lights of Drummersgate: a galley ship in the rolling fog of a November afternoon. It had been a long and draining day.

The fog was closing in now, quickly enveloping her in its squally mizzle. She stamped her feet, trying hard not to recall the ghost stories they'd all laughed about in the dry, warm safety of the staff room. Circles of ethereal children seen dancing on the highway, faces ravaged with bubonic plague. Tales recounted by workmen laying the new road up to Drummersgate a few years ago - of hearing children's tinkling laughter from somewhere in the fog; of faces oozing with open sores, looming in at the windows of their trucks when they took a nap…

Stop it Becky and stop it now! She told herself. *Think of something else. Ghosts do not exist….* And yet…she had seen those red eyes and heard that guttural, obscenity-ridden voice coming out of Ruby's frail body…*You know now, don't you, Becky? There really is something we can't explain - something not just to be a bit spooked about…but terrified out of your mind…*

Once more her thoughts switched to the hypnosis scene with Ruby and Jack. Replaying it over and over, against her will, as she would do a thousand more times yet - when she woke at 3 a.m. to the sound of a loud bang in the kitchen or a slammed door on a still night. Recalling the heat racking up and up and up in the treatment room, sweat breaking out across her chest, soaking her underarms, trickling down her back… of the inability to move from her position facing the wall. Who had turned her to face it? It had been as if her feet were stuck in sucking mud while the horrific scene unfolded and the men outside the door were helpless to get in - pounding at it with all their collective weight. But most of all she would remember the look of rictus terror on Jack's face. Jack, of all people. Jack McGowan - the medical director they all admired and relied on. The buck stopped with Jack every time - he was the father of the unit, the one they all went to no matter what because he always had the answers.

Yet that slip of a girl had broken him. Physically. Emotionally. Maybe even mentally, with the demonic filth she hadn't been able to block her ears from hearing - powerless as the destructive venom poured out of Ruby and into Jack.

He'd had to be helped from the room like an invalid, and driven home. Took time off and still hadn't returned to work. He'd withered away in front of them, diminished somehow, as though his very spirit had been drained.

Her mind tried to rationalise the event, again and again, ever since and every night, lying awake with her eyes tightly shut. At middle age, suddenly afraid of the dark and what it might be hiding. *How does anyone know anything for sure? If parallel universes co-existed then what if we were actually spirits, with our very beings only a fantasy? And who ruled this kingdom of spiritual realism? What if devils and demons didn't belong to fairytales and old wives talk at all - but were based on a foundation of ancient truth? We like to think we have all the modern-day rational answers - but do we? How arrogant? How bloody, bloody arrogant...and fragile!*

The last vestiges of a bruised sky faded to black, plunging Becky's lone figure into a chill, dark night choked with fog. Dying leaves congealed around her ankles, a faint whiff of wood smoke from a nearby farm.

There was someone behind her... was there, was there...breathing into the nape of her neck? She whirled around nervously. And was that the sound of drumming from somewhere out there in the wilderness? Getting louder? They called this place Drummersgate for a reason, she recalled - the psychiatric hospital had been built on the ruins of an old prison; one in which prisoners, often diseased and half starved, were then hanged to their deaths. People said they were brought out here in wooden crates pulled by horses, accompanied by drummers and dancing children, as they made their final journey at the centre of some macabre carnival....

Becky shivered - how vulnerable she was out here on her own. And not like her to feel fear like this either: a fear she'd never had before while waiting out here in all weathers. Silly really, just silly - a vivid imagination after recent events, that was all. Even so, it was impossible to escape the deduction and she just kept coming back to it - put simply, if Ruby had been possessed, then everything made sense, because the girl was now recovering her personality. But if that *was* the case, then surely it would have taken a man of the cloth to exorcise her not a doctor who didn't even believe in God? So it couldn't have been possession. *Could it?*

She exhaled long and hard. She had to get a grip. This train of thought was way off the scale. No, what must have happened was this -   Jack had brought out Ruby's controlling demon - an alter personality - a result of trauma in childhood. Now that made sense! So much more acceptable. And comforting. Sane. Normal... yet still the words came to her, unbidden on the wind - as objectively and dispassionately as if someone had spoken directly into her ear -*just because you can't see him doesn't mean he isn't there...*

She pushed them back to the recess of her mind. Focused on what looked like the headlights of the bus bobbing solidly towards her through the fog. Whatever had happened in the treatment room that day was all good! Because they could help her now - as soon as Jack felt well enough to come back, that was.

Why was Jack unwell while Ruby was getting better, though? Don't think about it.

The bus was coming - slowing, gears crunching down.

Suddenly a car overtook it and screeched to a halt in front. The passenger door was pushed open and D.I. Callum Ross smiled up at her. "Couldn't get here any faster - stuck behind a bus! Come on - jump in Becks - you must be freezing!"

***

They sped along the highway without talking for several minutes, heater on full blast, Depeche Mode singing, 'All I ever wanted...'

Callum squeezed her hand, not taking his eyes from the road. "What's the matter? Something's on your mind."

She nodded. He knew her. Every nuance. Every flickering thought - something that came from having grown up together. "I'm not sure I can tell you, really. Or what your reaction will be."

"I'm worried. Is it us?"

"Oh no, nothing like that."

"Tell me then."

Neither of them ever mentioned the names of clients they worked with, but sometimes they had to say what was on their mind, and Becky knew Callum would always treat her confidences with the utmost respect. Always had - since they were kids at school together. So over the drone of the engine, she related what had happened the previous week with the hypnosis session, hoping deep down that he'd ridicule the part about Ruby being possessed. It would help if he did, actually. Lighten the mood.

"Somehow he exorcised her demon," she said. "Or at least a dominant alter personality that was protecting the fact she'd been abused. God, I wish the law would introduce castration for those disgusting pigs! That girl will never be well. Not properly. And I'm not sure we'll ever get to know what she really had to endure. That's the rational explanation anyway. It's just - oh I don't know - there's some odd stuff going down as well. She said things she couldn't possibly have known. That's the weird bit. Sorry, I'm not making much sense, am I?"

Callum was quiet as he drove, squinting into the thick greyness and slowing down accordingly. Belts of fog were hitting them like stone walls, and the red rear lights from vehicles in front were suddenly a matter of inches away.

"Sorry," he said. "It's a dangerous night. We'll be in town soon, thank God."

As soon as the road dipped downhill, Callum relaxed, "Did I ever tell you about that night me and George Mason went out to a place called Woodsend, near Bridesmoor? It were years ago now, this - we were called out to a farm just off The Old Coach Road?"

"Really?"

"Well this is my only run-in with owt like that - demon stuff - so here goes! Ah you see - you weren't expecting that, were you? Anyhow, if I 'adn't seen this with me own eyes I wouldn't be taking in what you're saying now. I'll be honest with you - it affected me that much I don't really like talking about it in case.. Well you know, in case I start getting bad dreams again."

"Wow - a big guy like you?"

He laughed. "Aye, well I weren't then - I were about twenty two and skinny as a rake. Not that it made any difference to old George. Anyhow, we got called out because this teenaged girl were going mad apparently. Mother had run off. Father gone out and left his old mother to cope with t' farm and everything else that were going wrong. Well we 'ad to park off t' main road and it were blowing a gale. Dead spooky - full moon - and I dunno - bad atmosphere. Oppressive.

The horses were kicking in t' stalls and everything were in t' dark apart from just one light above the door. Well the old woman let us in, and inside all t' furniture had been moved - and we're talking heavy stuff like a Welsh dresser and oak dining table and stuff - all just heaped into one corner of their front room like some kind of funeral pyre. And in t' middle were this girl spinning round on 'er 'ead."

Becky looked across at him. Solid, early-forties, shaven head and a wide generous smile. She doubted he'd ever lied in his life. He was one of those people who always had your back. A good man.

"Sounds like mania. Pure madness some say - mania! People have blown all their savings, spent tens of thousands on credit cards, cart-wheeled down the street buck-naked and believed they were destined to rule the world! I bet she was high. Or was it drugs that did it? What happened to her?"

He shook his head. "No, it weren't that. Her eyes were like red sparks, Becky. And when we called an ambulance she 'ad this 'orrible deep man's voice and started swearing like nothing I've ever 'eard and definitely not from a lass. Believe me us lot swear like navvies and I'm used to all sorts, but this were really, really bad. It spooked old Mason out. He had a heart attack that night. Died t' following week. It were…well you were telling me about that hypnosis girl…it were like that."

A chill shivered up and down her neck. "Do you believe in the Devil?"

"No," he said. "No - there's stuff we can't explain, that's all."

They drove on for a while until the reassuring lights of town twinkled ahead.

She kept her voice steady. Light. "Fancy stopping off for fish 'n' chips? I'm so tired I won't feel like cooking when I get in. Bet you haven't eaten either, have you?"

"No. Sounds perfect. I was hoping I'd catch you tonight, Becks. It's been ages. Way too long."

"I know. I'm sorry. It won't be forever though, you know that!"

As they sat in the car spearing vinegary chips with plastic white forks, Callum said, "You ever been to Woodsend Village?"

She shook her head. "No."

Callum nodded. "I remember that case - I were on holiday, though. Sounds likely. It's a weird place though, Woodsend. We used to go fishing there in t' summer when I were a kid. We'd wander up and down the river on t' opposite side, trying to find the best spot. There's a caravan site beyond the woods, did you know? Fairyhill? But Woodsend itself - there's nowt there but a row of council houses on t' edge of t' common with the woods behind, and a couple of cottages. It's really overgrown, very dark, heavily forested. Once you paddle over the rocks to that side, I don't know, everything changes - bad atmosphere."

"What happened to the girl who was spinning on her head that night you and George were called out? I mean - where did she end up?"

"I don't know. She were taken away screaming obscenities. Hopefully they cured her schizophrenia or whatever you say it were."

"Mania…just a guess."

"Okay, well whatever it were it were fucking weird. The irises were red, Becky. I'll never forget it. And the voice, like it were out of the gutter - saying something about 'the kingdom.'"

Becky nearly choked. "What?"

"I had these bad dreams for months after. And poor old George. She'd gone for 'im you see - spat in 'is face. He were carrying a bit of extra weight, smoked a lot, and she went at him like an alley cat, seemed to know a lot of secrets he wouldn't 'ave wanted known. I were shocked - it can't be true the stuff she were saying - it were terrible. Anyhow, it killed him, poor old bugger."

***

Chapter 8

Jack woke with a heavy thud of his heart. The small hours. Totally black. Silence except for his wife's steady, rhythmic breathing.

Without needing to look at the neon green reflection on the wall, he knew what the time would be. A surge of anger gripped his stomach. 3 a.m. *Fuck*! *This was the tenth night in a row.*

The air was freezing, a tomb-like waft against his face. Sometimes it would be oven-hot; suffocating and intense, the sweat rising and beading all over his body as mercilessly the temperature climbed steadily higher. This time his features were set to ice, limbs paralysed, spine a frozen shard. His teeth chattered and his skin crawled with goose bumps. Showtime had started, and his whole being ached with fatigue. And fear. Of what was to come - had already come - a monk floating a foot off the ground, its hooded face featureless and blank, the air rank with the smell of decay...Or the stinking creature, which sounded like slime, levering itself onto the bed, pinning him with a ton of weight, so the breath couldn't rise in his chest, and his head pounded like it would explode, eyeballs bulging until they almost popped...Until he couldn't stand it another second. Until he agreed with some internal voice...*agreed to what? To what did he have to agree?*

He waited. Straining into the coalface night. Eyes sore with wretched vigilance.

Bang on cue, a bedside chair began to scrape along the floorboards, inching its way teasingly at first, gradually picking up speed once it had his full attention....before whizzing smartly towards the door and slamming hard against it.

Three taps on the window pane followed. Slow. Distinct. Always three - just to let him know the party had started.

3 a.m.

When he was a child, Jack's biggest fear had been the wardrobe in his bedroom. A cumbersome walnut closet with a vertical mirror on the front, the corner would catch a sliver of moonlight from the gap in the side of the curtains. He'd lie there watching that door - waiting for the skeletal rattle of coat hangers, the rustle of clothing to lift and form into a crawling shape - for it to creak open and reveal whatever monster lurked inside, its red eyes observing him from the black interior. One night he'd been about to drop off to sleep, having temporarily forgotten its undeniable presence, when there had been a groan of wood on hinge, and the door really had swung wide open. He'd screamed. His father had leapt up the stairs two at a time or more. 'What is it, Son? What the hell's the matter?'

With the light on, the wardrobe door was firmly closed for all to see. Jack's dad turned the key in its lock, and shook his head. "You've been watching too many films, Son. It was just a bad dream. All kids have them. Now back to sleep - you've school in the morning."

But the door had opened...

He knew that now.

Beside him, Hannah sighed in her sleep and rolled over.

And Jack kept his eyes on the wardrobes. A row of white painted ones these days. As one, two, three, all four of them, began to creak open....

***

At 6.15 a.m. he finally fell into an exhausted kaleidoscope of dreams. The night had been a journey to hell.

Someone was shaking him. "Jack, Jack. Come on, wake up would you? It's Daisy - she's been sleeping on the kitchen floor all night. I can't move her. She's rigid with cold and heavy as lead."

His eyes blinked open.

"You look like shit," said Hannah.

He ruffled his hair and rubbed his face. "Feel it," and threw back the covers. Looked at the clock as he shoved his feet in to slippers. "What's she doing downstairs?"

"Well I don't know, do I?"

Daisy, a small, fair-haired child, was lying at an awkward angle on the cold tiles of the kitchen floor, her tiny fists balled up and her head jutting back. Dressed only in pale pink pyjamas her body was a block of ice, and as Jack lifted her up he stumbled and his back gave a little with the unexpected weight.

Once they'd wrapped her up under the duvet and started to rub her small body all over to get the circulation going, Daisy's eyelashes began to flicker. She smiled. "The boy came to play again."

"What boy?" Hannah snapped "You should have been sleeping. You've got school today. We found you on the kitchen floor, for goodness sake!"

Daisy pushed out her bottom lip and sucked her thumb. "He said you'd be mean to me so that's why we were quiet."

"What boy, Daisy?"

Daisy continued to suck her thumb. "I'm tired."

"Yes well you would be," said Hannah. "Daisy - what boy are you referring to? Is this the imaginary friend we talked about?"

Jack shot Hannah a pointed look. Why hadn't she mentioned this?

"Who, Daisy?" Hannah insisted.

"The one who always comes," said their daughter. "He's funny! Sometimes he sits on the chair and waits for me to wake up, and sometimes he plays with my dolls to make me laugh."

"You're dreaming, Sweetie. There is no boy - he's not real, you do know that, don't you? It's just a dream and you've been sleep walking again."

Jack backed away. *This was no dream. This was no bad fucking dream. This was fucking real and they'd got to his children. They - yes they!*

Hannah was still questioning Daisy. "All children have imaginary friends, Daisy, and we all have dreams that seem real - but you don't go downstairs in the middle of the night in the dark and the cold, do you hear? Can you wake me up if you have another dream like that? I don't mind–"

Daisy smiled enigmatically, looking at something far, far away over her mother's shoulder.

"Daddy knows what I mean, don't you Daddy?"

Hannah swung round. Then back again. "What do you mean?"

Daisy pointed to the row of dolls on her bookcase. "Milly-Molly does a dance and she talks like grandma. It's really funny."

Hannah looked over at Jack again. "Well you're the psychiatrist!"

"I don't know," he said. "I honestly, truly do not know."

He took a hot shower. Scalding so it burned his skin - anything to make him feel alive and human; brushing his teeth 'til the gums bled; saturating himself in Aramis - whatever it took to force the daylight into his soul. To feel real and normal and in control of his own breath, thoughts, sensations.

The smell of coffee and toast wafted upstairs, and hunger growled in the pit of his stomach, the white-tiled walls closing in on him as his bloodshot reflection stared back through the bathroom mirror. This thing, whatever was happening to him, was grinding him down, annihilating his very humanity, and now it had started on his family - who he had to keep safe. It was his job to keep them safe. His little daughter was being contaminated, it was in her eyes - the laughing, the darkness. If only he knew what to do.

Let me in then, Jack… Let me in…and we'll spare her…

Let who in? And would it matter if he just said 'yes'? Would the nightmare be over if he did, finally, acquiesce?

He stumbled downstairs and grabbed his jacket.

Hannah appeared at the kitchen doorway. "You're going back to work then?"

"Yes. I'm okay. Tired but there's no reason I can't pop in and besides - the work stacks up."

She shook her head. "I still think you should see someone. You're not yourself and you look shocking."

"Yeah right - I should see a shrink, honey!"

Despite her concerns, she smiled. The children were screaming and something was burning on the grill. "Gotta go. Come home if you feel unwell, okay?"

***

Late, very late, after dashing about achieving very little he could remember, Jack walked into the team meeting Becky had organised at Drummersgate, to discuss the latest developments regarding Ruby.

The others looked up as he sat down, shock and discomfiture all too evident on their faces as they registered his dishevelled appearance.

"Sorry, busy morning," he offered by way of explanation.

Claire, Becky, Amanda and Martha - continued to stare at him. Jack's hair, which had been steely grey just days before, was now shock-white; his cheeks caved inwards, and there were saddle-bags of bruises beneath his pin-prick eyes.

"What?" he said, his Irish accent surfacing broadly. "Do you think I've not been busy this morning, is that it?"

His foggy mind groped around for a reason to explain his pre-occupied agenda, but could not recall what he'd done that day. There had been a talk he'd gone to at the university, only to be told, when he arrived, that he had apparently phoned to cancel the previous day. *Had he? Why would he do that?* There'd been a bit of a verbal exchange as he'd tried to explain that he could not have done, but in the end he'd had to concede defeat. And then there had been that bizarre phone call from the other consultant at Drummersgate - a chap he'd known and liked for over a decade - Isaac Hardy. Hardy had been livid - said how dare he call up his wife in the middle of the night with such obscenities.

"I know you've always had a thing for her, Jack, but this is outrageous!"

He'd apologised and begged Isaac to believe he hadn't done it, but the evidence was there on his cell phone. He had made the call. Bemused and horrified, Jack managed to calm Isaac down, said it must have been a hoax or he'd somehow done it in his sleep…but no way was it intentional. Frankly, he couldn't insult the man and say actually, no he didn't have a thing for his dumpy plain wife, but he'd come close - if only to score the point and win his case.

And then came a barrage of faxes and phone calls accusing him of sex abuse, slander, professional misconduct... all from names of people he had never heard of in his life before. Finally, the last one - an irate caller full of indignation - had seemed like a furious human, and yet not one word of the diatribe been intelligible. Rather it had consisted entirely of garbled anger as if from another planet in a language hitherto undiscovered.

He shook his head as if to rid himself of the chaos, before retrieving his notebook in readiness for the meeting. *So this was what it felt like to fall apart and lose your mind. To break down. Jesus. He could barely even function, let alone instruct the team on how to manage poor mad Ruby. That was the problem with being at the top - so alone - not a single person he could tell.*

And if that wasn't bad enough, none of this inner turmoil must show or the others would know and he could lose everything. All that he was. All that he had, and had worked so hard for. They'd recognise the madness, of course they would. They'd see it coming at them like an express train.

He must pretend. Put on a show.

A strong, distinctly male voice cut into his thoughts, speaking clearly into his right ear drum. *That's right, Jack! Put on a show!*

The effect was like being caught in a safety net. He physically jolted upright with surprise. There was someone else here in the black, hollow bowl of his head. Someone to help him. The *only* one who could help him.

Thank you…thank you…thank you…

Well that's my pleasure…I'm the only one you can trust now, Jack! You know that! So happy you decided to see sense, my friend!

He crossed his legs, leaned back in his chair. Smiled to himself. That was all he had to do - let in his friend and it would be okay. Why had he resisted when the solution was so simple? Crazy. It had made him ill.

"It's really great to have you back at work, Jack!" said Becky, from far, far away.

The others were nodding. He'd been off for a week and they were clearly itching to tell him what had been happening.

"You'll be pleased I hope," said Becky.

Jack turned to look at this heavy-set woman with streaked peroxide hair, and frowned.

"We've noticed a marked change in Ruby," Becky continued. "She's communicating really well now, and she's done some quite significant artwork for Amanda. Mostly dragonflies and butterflies, and horses too. She's really good!"

Jack nodded. Trying to recall exactly who Ruby was. What she looked like. "Makes a change from eyes and knives, eh? But the most important change," Becky said "is that since the hypnosis she's been able to bring out the other parts of her personality. Definitely fragmented - I've witnessed several alters, as has Amanda, who's seen and spoken with a child of about ten, called Tara. Tara speaks but the younger baby ones don't - they just crumple and cry, but also gag as if she's been assaulted. Jack - we think we're looking at child sex abuse, and an increasingly likely diagnosis of Dissociative Identity Disorder - very similar to the one Kristy Silver's working with. It's exciting. We really need you back. There may be more alters…Jack–?"

Jack was sniggering uncontrollably. Nastily.

The others stared as he threw his head back and guffawed loudly. "She was fucking possessed, you idiots, and I should fucking know. D.I.D. my arse!"

Becky visibly recoiled.

Claire was ashen.

"Jack. It does look highly probable," Claire began. "The male, dominant alter was totally repressing the other alters with violence, but now–"

Jack smirked, wiping his glasses and then his face again, with a greasy handkerchief. "But now what, Dr Airy? Now the demon is out, eh? Why don't you get some tea, Auntie Martha? And make it fucking hot, and sweet, will you?"

Martha flashed her sharp blue eyes at him. "I don't know what's got into you, Jack–"

At this he seemed to double over with mirth. *She wouldn't be able to guess in her wildest nightmares what had gotten into him! What sat inside him in a smouldering cesspit of inhuman bile. That now it was in him there would be no end to the evil about to be unleashed on the most gullible people on earth and their atheist carers, with no protection from a God they didn't believe in. It was, in short, going to be a walk in the park. Piece. Of. Cake.*

Martha turned to the rest of the team. "Well as we're here to talk about Ruby I'll recap what I've managed to find out, shall I?"

The smell in the room was overpowering - reminiscent of rotting fish guts. Amanda got up to open a window while the others tried hard to focus on Martha. Tried so very hard not to allow their eyes to glance Jack's way, to see the sweat soaking his armpits, or the snickering expression on his cadaverous, bloodless face.

"We know she remembers living in a mill in Bridesmoor - and it does exist. I had a drive over and I've seen it, although it's just a ruin now. The thing is, back in the nineties I was off work for a few years and a colleague who is no longer with us, covered my sick leave. I should be able to locate her notes, but in the meantime what I did find out was that around that time there was a bit of a scandal in the adjoining village - Woodsend. According to the papers, a woman and her husband were hounded out for being witches. She was accused of leading some kind of black witch cult. Anyway, here's the thing - and it's just an idea - but I was wondering if Ruby could have been a child victim? There's a lot of talk about what goes on in the woods behind Woodsend - teenagers mucking about with Ouija boards in the convent ruins and so on. And I'm just wondering - because Ruby would have been about seven years old - if it all ties up in some way?"

"Except we don't know if Ruby comes from there, only that she was residing in the mill in the next village as a twenty year old!" said Becky. "In fact - no one in the village recognised her when she was arrested. That's the thing. She didn't go to school in the area and she wasn't registered with the GP. Ever."

"But if she was there at the same time as this woman, reputedly a black witch performing black arts - what was her name, now - she may have been caught up in it? I'm even wondering if she was from one of the gypsy families who used to camp on the common from time to time? It could have had a seriously detrimental effect on her if she'd been involved," Martha persisted. "You wouldn't believe the number of kids we have to take out of environments like that. Okay, so Ruby may not have lived there as a bona fide resident, but we've a case up in Leeds of a child who did! Same village. Similar symptoms. Similar age. There's something in it."

Jack's giggling caused her to glare at him again. "Oooh," said Jack, "witchcraft and demons, Martha. Whatever next? Surely you don't believe in all that pagan shite?"

Martha, whose cheeks had flushed crimson, said, "Jack, I don't think you're at all well yet. You're not yourself. Perhaps Claire should see Ruby today instead–"

Jack jumped back in his chair like he'd taken a punch. "That will not be necessary. I can handle Ruby. In fact," he looked at his watch. "I'll go and talk to her right now - or whoever she thinks she is this time, eh? Won't be the first time we've had a multiple personality in here, eh? Love a good multiple–"

He rushed from the room, leaving a sour stench of garlic and stale urine, instead of his usual soap and aftershave.

Amanda collected her bag and belongings. "I need some air. I feel sick. Is he having some kind of breakdown, do you think? And who do we contact in a case like this?"

Becky, Martha and Amanda all looked at Claire.

"Isaac, I suppose," she said. "But I'd like to speak to Kristy Silver too. Is that okay with everyone?"

Martha nodded. "See if you can find out more from her about the other child too, will you? Let's see if we can piece this thing together."

"Yes, and can you do it quickly?" said Becky, her hand on the door. "Find out how Kristy's feeling after talking with his alter - was it as nasty and did she have any after-effects? Something's seriously wrong with Jack and I've got to stop him going to see Ruby. I can't let him anywhere near her while he's like this. She'll freak."

As she hurriedly left the room, someone, who she could never say - except that it was a large person wearing a black hood - bumped into her. The charged collision catapulted her forwards, throwing her weight against the crash trolley parked against the corridor wall.

Her head smashed hard onto the iron defibrillator, blacking her out instantly.

***

Chapter Nine
Tanners Dell, Bridesmoor
Summer 2008

I don't like it inside the mill. There's something weird about it here. Spooky. Still, it's a roof over my head, I suppose. Like Jes says - beggars can't be choosers and we're definitely beggars.

I'm lying in bed, if you can call it a bed - a few blankets piled on top of an old mattress we uploaded from the tip. My breath condenses on the air, and in the background there's the sound of running water - fresh and fast and cold, the brook racing down to the river. We're in a dell - overgrown with trees and grass and wild flowers - so crisp and natural it makes you feel clean all over, just to wander through the fields and feel the breath of spring water on your skin.

I'd stay outside all night if I could, just watching the violet and crystal light on the water. Tons of it - rushing over the rocks, gurgling with fairy chatter as it hurtles down from the moors. Those wild, sprawling moors that tower over us, howling and moaning in winter like a thousand trapped souls; I can hear them.

As kids we used to play Tag up on the rocks, hiding in and out of the wind-worn caves, me and…me and…who? I've lived here all my life and yet I can't remember being me. If I try then I hit a wall. Like when you try to think what's beyond the universe - okay so it's infinite - but what's outside of that? Where does it end? You hit a wall - no answers, right? Just a massive mind-fuck. So imagine that's your history - your life - and you can't see it? That's me. Sometimes, there's a fragment so fleeting, like a butterfly's wing…I try to catch the memory in a net but then it's gone, fluttering on the periphery of my mind. Just out of reach.

I'm living with this guy, Jes, at the moment. A Romany gypsy. 'Don't ask questions' would kind of sum him up - stashing bags of cash from the jobs he does. He calls me a whore and a tart and a piece of scum and he's probably right. I was up to my thighs in the ice-cold river when he dragged me out - a bag of smack in my sodden jeans, my tooth-pick limbs covered in sores and needle lines. Said he'd dry me out and 'fucking well make you remember who y'are you fucking druggie.'

So how long have I been here? There are birds pecking on the roof. Branches heavy with leaves, swaying against the windows. He's out on some kind of job. I'm thinking it must be lunch time.

"Ruby! Ruby! Shhh....Ruuuuuuby...."

No, no, no, I'm not listening. To the whispering from empty rooms shrouded in gloom. It's just the busy brook, the rustling of the trees, the fog of drug inducement lifting off my brain like mist from a murky swamp. He said I'd go half crazy when I came off the drugs. Why did I take them? I don't know. I have no idea how I even got here.

"Ruby...Ruuuuuuby.... We see you..."

I am not listening. Not.

The bathroom, and this is kind of ironic, has no running water! He's left some in a bowl for me to wash in. The mirror above it is cracked and rust-spotted with age. My face is slashed in two separate halves. Limp, light brown, wavy hair. A distorted image of a tiny person with pale blue eyes and jagged features in a dim room that squeaks with rats and scratching noises.

"Ruby..."

That's not me, though really, is it? The face looking back? Is it? She looks different from what I expected, with that knowing look in her eyes and a sneer. A teenaged slut from the streets...someone I don't know at all.

My head hurts - one pole-axe of a headache - and there's this feeling that someone's watching me. I keep winging round - a breath in my neck, a hiss of words over my shoulder...I mean, he said there'd be rats in my head and faces looming out of the walls like monsters; and my stomach would crush inwards and the pain, the nausea, would cripple me. He warned me and I know it's just that. This fear can be bottled and put in a compartment. I have to be over the worst soon.

Who the hell am I, anyway? And does it matter? I deserve it.

Downstairs the windows are smashed and a waft of cool air ruffles my hair on the last rung of the staircase. A light bulb fizzes on and off. Jes managed to spark up the old generator but it's hit and miss. Mostly we light a fire and have toast or boil up soup. I wonder why he's left his family, to come here and look after me? But of course I know the answer to that one. Anything recent and I know. Not always at the time but certainly later because the pain between my legs is pulsing and sore. My feet are covered in dried mud and there are bruises on my wrists and the tops of my arms.

But it's not that bothering me - I imagine I'm somewhere else I think - when it's happening. What am I good for anyway? I must have been on the streets doing it, but smothering the shame with drugs. Is that what I did? Somewhere along the line I shot my brain in two and this is just the shell that's left.

No, what really bothers me is other stuff. The faceless forms hovering about three feet above the ground - like monks only with no features - sort of drifting down corridors or in the corner of the bedroom. It's usually when I'm half asleep I see them, and when I least expect the onslaught to start. One after the other then. Hundreds. Bad people, I can tell. Really bad - as malicious and cold as hell. Over and over and over.

Then sometimes, like now, a bottle top suddenly flies across the room or an empty lager can scuttles across the kitchen surface before dropping onto the floor.

Wait. Here it comes again: stomping boots upstairs in the room I've just been sleeping in. Clomp, Clomp. Clomp. Heavy boots. Workman's boots. Clomp. Clomp. Now clomping downstairs. Following me.

Without warning the temperature plummets and the kitchen freezes. Outside I know the birds are singing; the brook continues to tumble merrily to the river, and sunshine glints through broken glass… and yet the room is darkening by degrees, shadows creeping along the walls. "*Ruby, Ruby, Ruuuuuuuubyyyyyy….*"

It is the drug withdrawal, isn't it?

The kettle starts to boil but I hadn't switched it on. Or had I? Light bulbs flicker …swinging gauntly from cables clinging to crumbling plaster. But it's the feeling more than anything. Oppressive like someone's at your back. Like when all your hair stands on end and you have to run and run like you've never run before.

Out into the sunlight. Into a lush, overgrown, dappled summer woodland. My heart hammering hard. It's just the drug withdrawal. That's all.

Over my shoulder, the old stone mill stands as it has for centuries, its windows like hollowed-out eyes, walls smothered in ivy.

I lift up my head. There, look - peering from the bedroom - a blurred, pale face looks directly at me. Someone who wanted me out of there.

***

Cloudside Village

I'm telling her, "It's been going on for months."

Her name is Celeste and she's a spiritual medium who runs classes at her home in Cloudside near Doncaster. It's a neat bungalow and her husband is an invalid in one of the bedrooms. The whole place is fitted out with handrails and wheelchair access.

She's an older lady - plump with dyed red hair the colour of Jessica Rabbit's. And around her there's a halo of white flecked with gold. She's got warm, brown eyes buried in a cushion of powdered wrinkles; and I feel like she's so much older than she is - older than time even - and I can talk to her like no one else about this. I'm glad Jes mentioned her: said his own mother (a pickled walnut of a woman who's spent her life swaying in the doorway of a painted wagon), swore she was the real deal - that she'd tell me for sure if the mill was haunted or not.

"It's like, I don't know–" Oh God, how to explain it without sounding like a mad woman. "It's like things explode when I touch them. It doesn't happen when Jes is around - only when I'm there on my own - like someone's watching - that sounds bonkers, doesn't it? To be honest I don't like being inside the mill at all - I think it's haunted, I really do."

Her eyes bore into mine and somehow I know she's been there - knows what's coming. "Tell me what happens, Ruby."

"Well if I get up in the night they're in the corridors."

"Who?"

"Like, sort of monks in long, black cloaks floating off the ground. Hooded. Hissing they're going to kill me. And they know my name too. It's like running the gauntlet - you look down the long, narrow passageway and they're all there, waiting with long fingers to touch me and pull at my hair. The atmosphere as well - it's so menacing - I could wet myself I'm that scared. And then when I'm in bed just dropping off to sleep, or trying to…well it's really dark down there in the woods with no streetlights or anything, so how come I see all these faces zooming into mine? And I mean right into mine - just centimetres off - some are covered in sores or they've got features missing; like they're diseased or they've been shot through the head, or hanged so their eyeballs are bulging, and it goes on and on - hundreds of them. And then other times I hear my name being called and the sound of footsteps pacing up and down outside the door in heavy boots. Jes doesn't wake up, so I keep thinking it's just me and my imagination and the fact I'm coming off drugs. But–"

"You believe it's real?"

"Yes, because I've been clean for a few weeks now. There's other stuff too - sometimes what wakes me is a kind of frantic chattering, like excited children are on the bed. But when I open my eyes there's no one there and it all stops. And here's the really weird thing - when I look over at Jes his face seems to have changed and I don't recognise him. I sit up staring at him trying to work out who the hell he is."

"Have you ever experienced anything like this before?"

"I don't think so but then I've wrecked my head with drugs, haven't I? So now I can't remember anything."

"What would you like me to do?"

"Tell me I'm not going mad, I suppose."

She reaches over and squeezes my hand. "It's a tough call, Ruby, what you're going through, but I think you have the gift of second sight - that in itself can take some getting your head around - it's frightening and I should know. Look, I can do a reading for you if you like? If you think it would help? Or you could join my classes to develop as a spiritual medium yourself? It helps enormously to understand it all and be able to control it - to protect yourself. Have a think about it."

The information sinks in. I don't know. "A medium? Like, talk to dead people and stuff?" This isn't what I expected. Not at all.

Celeste is watching me carefully.

The decision pops out of my mouth. "I think a reading. I'd really like to know who I am - what happened to me and where I came from. If you can tell me, then maybe I can go home again - to wherever it is I belong - and forget all about the mill completely?"

Celeste continues to watch me. Frowns suddenly. There's something behind her eyes - a knowledge - I can't say what. Then she starts to shuffle the tarot cards. "I'll try but there's a block for some reason." Eventually she asks me to cut the deck. Swiftly she spreads out a selection of cards before one by one, turning them over.

She doesn't look up. Just stares for ages and ages.

She doesn't want to tell me what's there, does she? My heart pumps heavily. "What? What is it?"

When she finally lifts her gaze to mine there are tears streaming down her pillow cheeks. "I can't tell you, Ruby. I simply can't find the words…"

***

Chapter 10

After Ruby had gone, Celeste sank onto the sofa. Unfocused, with heavy limbs, she sat as if in a trance. In all her years as a spiritual medium - most of her life, once she'd accepted that's what it was and she was stuck with it - she'd never had an experience like it.

The encounter had left her utterly drained.

While the girl - what was she? Eighteen? Twenty? - had related her story of amnesia and how she had found herself living in a mill, which seemed to be haunted - her face and voice had kept changing. One minute Celeste had thought she'd been talking to a young woman asking for help, the next a cocky teenager had been sneering at her, only to be swiftly replaced by a fading expression, as if the girl was falling backwards inside her head - before another personality came into being. That she was damaged mentally was undeniable. The whole thing was extraordinary.

And that was just the visible stuff. The spirits who had come forward for Ruby, on the other hand - Celeste's spirit guides - had shown her something else on top of that. All the time she'd been shuffling the cards, asking for guidance and protection, there had been a clear voice telling her this girl was special and very important. There would come a time when Celeste would need courage because this girl was here to teach the world a lesson.

What lesson?

A lesson, Celeste. A lesson.

That she herself would be part of that lesson was obvious, alas, the 'how' was shrouded in obscurity. Celeste screwed up her face in concentration. Perhaps her job was to help Ruby develop as a medium? The girl had described an explosive energy around her. Of kettles boiling up at rapid speed before fusing. Of light bulbs popping. Radios turning themselves on. Objects whizzing around the room. Was it the haunted mill, Ruby wanted to know, or was it to do with herself?

Celeste had heard similar stories many times. But whatever negative energy was trapped inside the mill, it was nothing compared to the energy Ruby herself emitted. What she'd seen when she looked at Ruby were crowds of ghost children, lurking in gloomy corridors. Small faces peeping out from behind barred windows. And the whispers - an omnipresent chattering. Almost like, she thought, a kind of children's prison inside the soul.

Ruby had slunk forwards with her head in her hands, as she recounted the faces looming into hers when she tried to sleep. Of voices in her right ear, shouting out her name until she woke. Of a an elderly lady she knew to be her late grandmother, standing in the bedroom about three feet off the ground - the overpowering aroma of her lavender scent dizzying her senses. Of opening the wardrobe to find a bruised and battered woman in an apron looking straight at her - like someone caught hiding, blood dripping from a ravaged cheekbone. And so it went on. Just that morning, Ruby had been looking into a cracked mirror when it fell to the floor with her face still in it...

"I think you have a special gift, my dear," she'd said, after looking at the spread of cards and realising she couldn't do a reading for the girl. "Like me - you're undoubtedly a medium."

"So how does that work for you, then? I mean, things aren't blowing up in your house, are they?"

"They used to. Especially when I was a teenager and I was scared. My radio would come on in the middle of the night and my mother'd be shouting through the walls to turn it off. The television blew up in the middle of a film. All sorts - hairdryers, bedside lamps... And I'd come home from school to find my bedroom in a blitz. I always got the blame: me and my mother had terrible rows. I tried telling my parents but I had to stop doing that - they were one step away from having me sectioned! So I kept it all to myself until one day I met someone who helped me. I'd gone to a spiritualist church and immediately I was told! It was a huge relief in some ways, and in others it felt like a lifelong burden - I knew life was going to be hard."

"Weren't you terrified though? I mean - I jump out of my skin when I walk into a room and someone's sitting on my bed staring at me, and they're like - white faced and really, really still, and the room's so cold!"

"Very. And the more scared I was the worse it got. I was told that bad spirits are attracted to it. Like attracts like. So the more fear you emit - the worse it's going to get! "

"That's cruel. I can't take much anymore - my heart's going to give out."

"Well you're attracting the worst sort at the moment. You can control that and I think that's what we need to teach you right away. Today. You need to know how to shut it down - right now you're like a beacon of light saying 'yes please - come into my world.' Ideally, I'd like you to come to my classes if you can, but let me explain it to you here and now just in case I never see you again.

"You are attracting the lowest of the astral planes. It's what happens when people do Ouija boards or hold séances and stupid things like that. They don't know who they are inviting into their lives. Ouija means 'Yes' and 'Yes' basically - in French and German. You wouldn't just invite anyone into your home no matter if they were thieves, murderers or just downright nasty, would you? So why invite in all and sundry because they're spirits? They can do you harm! Real harm! And many are used by the inhuman - the demonic - they can destroy your soul. It really is dangerous."

Ruby shook her head, listening like a fascinated child to a bedtime story.

"These spirits can attach themselves to you, Ruby. Most people don't believe in any of this until it's too late. But you've seen it - you know it all exists. So you need to learn how to close down and you need to do it now!

"You have seven major energy points called chakras. Energy is channelling through you because yours are wide open and shining brightly - spirits are manifesting. Believe me, it can and will, wear you down and leave you open to all kinds of nasty things. You are already carrying some of these negative spirits with you - I've told them to go but they'll be back as soon as you go home again. So imagine a brilliant, white light like a tube running up from your solar plexus to the top of your head…."

The lesson had lasted an hour and during that time she'd tutored Ruby on how to close off her energy channels so she could get some peace; enlightened her as to the difference between ghosts and the inhuman; and shown how to psychically cleanse herself.

"Are you religious?" she asked.

Ruby shrugged.

"Were you ever baptised?"

Ruby frowned and shook her head. "I don't think so."

"My classes are held in church and this is the address. You really need to come - it's every first Tuesday of the month. I'll write my number down too - in case you need me urgently."

Ruby took the card and for a moment their fingers touched.

The spark travelled all the way up Celeste's wrist and seemed to wrap around her heart. "Take care dearest child. Your journey is going to be a difficult one. But you are very important - you have a job to do and you will be rewarded by 'them up there' - they have great plans for you. Just believe me for now." She smiled and imagined a powerful white light encapsulating the young woman in a bubble. It would keep her safe for a little while.

Ruby turned to go, looking over her shoulder as she reached the door. "And if I tell the bad stuff to go - it will, yes?"

"Believe it. Be strong!"

She never did get to tell her what she'd been shown when she dealt her cards. And frankly, it would be best if Ruby never got to find out, because there are some things a person should never know. Including herself, because what she'd seen would leave its mark.

Hopefully no well-meaning medical professional further down the line, would ever attempt to unearth it for the poor child, either.

***

Chapter 11
Leeds, November 2015

Kristy Silver took the call as she hurried down the hospital corridor to her next lecture. She stopped and leaned against the wall, straining to hear, to understand. Jack McGowan's garbled message - part English, part gobble-de-gook - left her open mouthed. He was cancelling again. Or at least that was what she *thought* he said. Not only that, but he sounded absolutely furious. How odd!

She'd particularly wanted to meet up because of what she now knew about the striking similarities between her client, Tommy Blackmore, and via Claire Airy - Ruby. It seemed increasingly likely there could be a history of child abuse in one of the outlying mining villages near Doncaster - a place called Woodsend. The police and social services would need to get involved quickly if her suspicions were correct. They were onto something and she knew it.

Listening to Jack's message she had to hold the mobile away from her ear, trying to fathom the high-pitched angry words. This didn't sound like the Jack she knew and admired: the medical director and consultant in forensic psychiatry who had mentored her as a specialist registrar and taught her so much - the grey-haired father figure who seemed to have all the answers, and if he didn't then he'd sure as hell find out!

She'd even had dinner with him and Hannah one evening at their home - a large Victorian stone house set back from the main road out of Leeds. It was one of those old houses that swallowed up a fortune to modernise and furnish - unremarkable from the outside, with its swaying poplars and modest lawns, yet stunning inside. There were black granite work surfaces in the kitchen, complete with wall-to-wall glossy, white cupboards, an island, a double Belfast sink, and of course the ubiquitous age; upstairs was a sumptuous black and white tiled bathroom complete with a huge gilt edged mirror, elegant slipper bath and luxury walk-in shower; there were long sash windows in every room with silk curtains looped into swags. Gorgeous, opulent, warm and homely. A home that oozed with taste and money. In the bedrooms lots of noisy kids rampaged around; and there was Hannah rosily pregnant again, her face glowing contentedly as she served up warm mulled wine by the fire. If ever there had been a picture of a perfect Dickensian style family - it was the McGowans.

She stuck a finger in her ear and shouted into the phone, over the noise of passing medics. "Are you all right, Jack?"

A screeching noise came over the air waves like a microphone fault, before the line cut dead.

She speed-dialled straight back but there was no reply.

She rang Claire.

"Yes," said Claire. "There is something wrong - he's behaving really oddly. It's bizarre."

"In what way?"

Claire hesitated. "Oh God, Kristy, I don't know if I should say."

"Claire - he's just been talking to me in gobble-de-gook. What's going on - is he ill?"

Claire's answer flew at her in a panic. "I don't know. I honestly don't. All I know is he's rushing about giggling to himself. Swearing. Stuff like that."

"Sounds like he needs time off. He's not seeing patients, is he?"

"Well he went off sick after treating Ruby a couple of weeks ago - he did some hypnosis on her and Ruby had a bad reaction - it really drained him. Anyway, we thought he was better, but yesterday when he came into the team meeting he clearly wasn't well - he was acting strangely and really rude to Martha. No one thought it was a good idea but he went off to talk to Ruby. Becky tried to stop him but she had an accident - tripped - and because we all rushed to help her we couldn't stop him in time. We didn't realise."

"What happened?"

"Noah caught him putting Ruby into a trance. He didn't think he'd got very far with it, but Ruby was completely unresponsive for hours, and she hasn't properly come round again since. It's like she's not really with us - just staring into the distance. And he disappeared afterwards without a word. I hate to say this but he's really scaring us. With Becky still in hospital–"

"What? Becky's in hospital? I thought you said she just tripped - I was picturing a sprained ankle or something."

"No - she fell against the crash trolley and hit her head - it's suspected concussion and they're keeping her in for a second night. Kristy, I think Jack's having some kind of breakdown. And now he's–"

"Have you spoken to Hannah?"

"Yes. I was really uncomfortable about it but she jumped at me down the phone - pouring it all out - his insomnia, outbursts, foul language - moving furniture in the middle of the night, smirking to himself - oh all sorts of stuff. She's got one of the children sleep walking and another saying one of her dolls is talking to her during the night. She sounded at the end of her rope, to be honest."

Kristy listened to the static coming down the phone for a moment, while her thoughts processed. First they had to get Jack away from the patients. She'd need to speak to Isaac Hardy as soon as possible. No one needed a consultant psychiatrist with a mental breakdown treating forensic patients. Jack needed help and he needed it immediately.

Next she had to see Ruby: there was a connection between her and Tommy for sure, and Jack McGowan going off the rails was not going to stop her helping her clients. Finally, the whole thing was vital to her research project: Dissociative Identity Disorder was political, and she was going to back its existence and pioneer its treatment if it was the very last thing she did.

"Claire. First things first. What's been done about Jack? He can't be allowed to treat patients the way he is."

"Yes well we've tried to talk to him but as I was about to say, he's barricaded himself into his office. Someone's coming from the crisis team as soon as possible, and yesterday Isaac informed the Board of Directors, so he's technically suspended."

"I beg your pardon? Boarded himself in? I'm so glad I rang you - I had no idea. Oh poor Jack. Poor Hannah! Oh my God."

"You know, what happened with Ruby was really traumatic, but I never thought Jack would crack under the strain. Never. I always thought he'd be the very last psychiatrist on earth to let it get to him."

"Me too. It's come at the worst possible time too because you've had a breakthrough with Ruby and I've had a breakthrough here - we're onto something! There's a connection, I'm sure of it. So with or without Jack, our work has to go on - I need to see Ruby. Well actually I'd like to oversee her care altogether - something I was going to talk to Jack about. Would tomorrow afternoon be all right if I come over?"

"Yes - tomorrow's fine. Ruby's stable, although not talking. Jack wasn't with her long."

***

Kristy's lecture was delivered on auto-pilot, her thoughts elsewhere - Woodsend village: Tommy Blackmore had grown up there. Admitted a couple of years ago as a young adult with chronic depression and symptoms of P.T.S.D. he'd been slow to respond to therapy, but once he'd been on the ward for a while, the staff noticed he lost hours of time in trance like states - often lying on the floor sucking his thumb with no recollection afterwards of having done so. A diagnosis of D.I.D was eventually made after episodes of switching personalities had been observed. With 90% of these cases originating from child abuse, Kristy had started to ask his alters, when they presented, more searching questions about his life growing up in Woodsend.

Then on hearing about Ruby she began to wonder. Could it be that both patients had been victims of child abuse in that particular village?

There was more evidence to substantiate the theory. After a few hours Googling, 'Woodsend', she'd stumbled on the witch hunt articles from 1996: a lady called Celeste Frost had been hounded from her home by villagers who claimed she was a black witch. All sorts of 'goings-on' had been cited, from black cats appearing at their windows, to sudden childhood illnesses, to chanting distinctly heard through the thin walls of her council house. Then a young girl found spinning on her head had been taken from her farmhouse home by police after her grandmother claimed the girl had been a victim of witchcraft.

1996 - so both Ruby and Tommy would have been around eight years old. What was going on there? Anything, or a series of coincidences? Certainly there was no denying both Tommy and Ruby had similar symptoms. That kind of serious mental illness didn't happen for no reason. Had that woman gathered together some kind of satanic cult involving children? And what had Jack found out during the hypnosis session, which had left him seriously disturbed? It would have been good to talk to Becky, who had witnessed it, but, and there was another coincidence - Becky was also off work.

Well, with the pressure having got to Jack, she'd have to get to the bottom of this alone. Maybe start with a drive out to Woodsend when she'd finished up here? Just to get the feel of the place. See it for herself.

***

At just before 4 p.m. Kristy jumped into her white Audi A4 and backed out of the cramped, hospital staff car-park. The plan was to make a quick detour to Woodsend and then back to her city flat.

It would be nicer, far nicer though, to go straight home. Home as it now was for a divorced consultant psychiatrist - comfortable, spacious, elegant and all white. White walls punctuated with shockingly bright paintings. White rugs on polished floorboards. White bedclothes. Lots of sparkling crystal. Shards of light. A kind of heavenly, high-rise duplex, a cocoon in the sky - from where, depending on which direction you looked, you could see the neon city lights reflected from rooftops, or fleeting clouds scudding over the moors on a blue-sky day. Most of all - it was a retreat. For God only knew, a psychiatrist needed to re-centre themselves after a day with the most disturbed and disturbing people on earth.

All a far cry, and sometimes the sadness welled up inside, from the life originally envisaged in what now seemed another lifetime. But life moved on like the rushing of a river downstream, to the inevitable. So here she was. Craving solitude. Searching for the meaning inside her.

Alone and without distractions, her sharp, incisive mind focused on the mission - to lead the way in the treatment of patients with identity disorders. Without doubt her obsessive dedication had taken its toll. Relationships, friendships, a social life - all had fallen away to the edges of her consciousness, with the red-blooded woman in her swallowed by the machine she had become. Her whole being now concentrated on breaking through to the cause, treatment and future for these damaged people.

A migraine sparked suddenly in the trigeminal nerve above her right eye, as her thoughts deepened, tunnelling through the doorways of her mind as each fresh seam of ideas opened up. The sickly cramp escalated rapidly, forcing her to pull over and take an habitual supply of Sumatriptan and Migraleve with a few gulps of bottled water. She'd be okay for a while, but the fatigue would hit soon. Probably an hour. She pushed aside the annoyance, firing up the ignition again - the curse of the forty-something peri-menopausal woman. So much easier to have been a man. She allowed herself a smile. Put her foot down. Not as much fun though.

Right, where was she? Okay, on The Old Coach Road heading out towards Bridesmoor. On the left, sprawling for bog-ridden miles, was Bridestone Moors; ahead - the blackened corpse-wheel of Bridesmoor Pithead. There'd been riots up here in the eighties when closures were announced. And before that, many a mining accident. As a medical student she'd witnessed a few stretchered cases rushed into A&E - blackened with soot and gasping for air - and her young mind had fallen prey in the early hours, to rumours about the miners who were never found - the ones who still lay trapped hundreds of feet underground. If you went hiking out on the moors, people said, you could still hear their moaning cries carrying on the wind.

She kept her eyes fixed on the long, straight road ahead. So many spooky tales about this area…The Old Coach Road having been a favourite haunt for highway men; or horse-drawn carriages racing in the dead of night with gruesome cargoes of disinterred dead bodies for sale. On their way to Leeds or Sheffield.

A belt of November fog was rolling in, and night fell as abruptly as a theatre curtain. An instant wall of grey. Visibility nil.

She hit the brakes in surprise, reaching for the Audi's fog lights, at the same moment the signpost to Bridesmoor Village flashed into view. A steep lane veered downwards, and a church spire pierced the smoky dusk from somewhere in a hollow of trees.

Woodsend should be next on the right, then. From looking at the map, there was only an area of common land separating the two, so any second now...

Spectres of mist crawled across the road in shifting shapes, making it difficult to see. Then suddenly a right fork appeared, so she took it. Foxley Lane. Not the main road down to Woodsend, which was Ravenshill, but probably a cut across the common. So straight ahead should be…ah yes… a row of council houses, which backed onto the woods. No facilities here, apparently. Just the row of houses, the farmhouse off the main road at the top, a couple of cottages - including the one her patient, Tommy Blackmore, had grown up in - and a caravan site down by the river, apparently. *Goodness, what on earth was she hoping to achieve by this?*

At the end of Foxley Lane, she turned right and drove carefully downhill. Abruptly the fog cleared to reveal a charcoal sky streaked with fuchsia, and plumes of wood smoke coiling up from various chimneys. Sodden leaves plastered the lane, and ahead lay the gurgling freshness of a swelling river.

She parked and got out.

To her right the River Whisper. To her left, a public footpath trailed into woodland. She grabbed a torch from the glove compartment, locked the car and headed left. Half an hour at the most before the light would be lost completely, she estimated. It was just to see. To satisfy a curiosity, and be able to relate better to her patients - to understand the geography and picture what they were remembering. That was all.

The peacefulness was silvery in its beauty as she strode away from the river and up the well-worn path towards the back of the council houses. Presumably local dog walkers and maybe, because there was a caravan park on the opposite side of the woods, holiday makers used it too. An owl hooted and she smiled. How magical. Like a fairy tale.

The path began to arch to the left, and it looked like it would come out just below the council houses. A perfect triangle for a little dog walk. So if she carried on climbing then she would surely come to more tracks for the cottages, which would have drives connected to Ravenshill. It would be possible to double back at any time. Any time at all.

From the back of the houses, lights spread buttery oblongs onto gloomy lawns, plunging the adjacent woods into blackness…*it was okay - yes really - she could quit at any time. No need for the disquiet at her back. No need...* An ancient fear, she told herself, a woman alone in the darkening woods - it was natural - and besides she could take that straight path she'd just passed - turn and quicken her pace at any time! Tell that to herself enough times and she'd believe it.

After a while there came only the sound of her own breathing, heavier now as the hill steepened and the muscles in her hamstrings began to ache. Here the path was much narrower and more overgrown, branches swiping at her face with scratchy fingers.

Darkness descended in an instant.

One moment the forest had been shaded grey. The next it was utterly black. The beam from her torch mingled with wisps of mist as she climbed. *Actually, this was stupid. To have put herself in this position. She ought to turn around and go home right now: it didn't feel safe. What if there was something going on here for real and...*

Kristy stopped dead in her tracks.

In front lay a clearing, and in the centre was what appeared to be a dilapidated cottage. Covered in ivy, shrouded with evergreens, it sat in darkness, save for a single lamp on in an upstairs window.

She looked from left to right. There didn't appear to be a driveway, a path, or a car. How did the occupant get in or out? She switched off the torch to disguise her presence, and picked her way through the undergrowth, as far as a rickety, heavily rusted gate which sagged from its hinges. 'Woodpecker Cottage,' had once been painted in fine italics on a crumbling wooden plaque, which hung crookedly from one side.

So this was where Tommy Blackmore grew up. A flicker of a chill chased up her spine. Like someone was behind her. Pure imagination, of course, but even so…

She backed up, branches snapping in her face, snagging in her hair. Time to retrace her steps towards the safety of the car immediately. But…Kristy looked ahead into the fog-cloaked woods. Her eyes had adjusted to the gloom now and she must be near the top, so it may be as well to keep going - do a big loop and then walk back down Ravenshill? Seeing as she was here? It could only be a few more minutes.

Honestly, she was such a scaredy cat!

After all, if Tommy had been a victim of abuse it wasn't the village ghosts, was it? No, she'd spooked herself with it being dark, that was all.

***

Chapter 12
One hour later

The journey home was a blur of shock. Kristy gripped the steering wheel with ice-numb fingers. Her heart pulsed through her body in thick, sickly waves. Everything was so much worse than she'd feared. The whole visit had been on a whim, a hunch, curiosity…call it what you will, but now…now it was like having walked through the back of a wardrobe into a fairytale horror and not being able to get home again. *Something was very, very wrong in Woodsend.*

She turned up the heater and flicked on all the lights because at this speed no one would see her coming. The Audi powered at 80 mph through thick, grey fog, driven by a woman with the devil on her back.

On either side of her, the waterlogged moors seeped darkly. As if in wait for that second's loss of concentration, a swerving of the wheel, a screech of tyres, and the sucking of metal drowning in the bog.

Squinting into the mist, her eyes flicked to the lit dashboard - how odd - the temperature was dropping rapidly. *Why? The car had just been serviced.* Her breath steamed on the air. Muscles rigid. She wriggled her toes - no, nothing - no warmth from the engine at all. There should have been heat surging through by now. Instead it was getting colder than it was outside. Freezing, in fact.

A creeping awareness was how it started, she recalled later - as she lay awake night after night trying to understand, to rationalise what happened next - a musty smell like unwashed clothes on an unwashed body; a sigh of sour breath on the side of her face; a feeling that someone or something, was on the passenger seat beside her, waiting for her to take her eyes off the road and look round. No, not waiting - *willing* her to…

A shape. Growing. The sound of salivating, raspy breathing. Like a very old man smacking his gums, drawing air from diseased lungs.

Kristy concentrated hard on the road ahead. This was just fear talking. It had a hold on her mind. *Focus on the job in hand - on driving safely home - reduce speed and don't take your eyes off the road for a moment...* The car's headlights reflected their own swirling white light. A fragment of memory - being in a plane - engines humming in a blanket of grey over the North Sea - the unrelenting aborted landings, one after the other, and being unable to see a damn thing. Then suddenly the tarmac and a crack, a bounce, and the relief of touching ground. Soon the lights of town would be ahead and the fog would lift.

But someone really was in the passenger seat.

The strength of presence grew, along with the irresistible desire to turn and see who it was.

A smell - putrid now, decaying, salty blood and sulphur - permeated the air.

Keep looking ahead at the road - each millisecond more is another moment of life....don't look around...don't look...

The presence was squelching - shape-shifting - into a recognisable form. Kristy's side vision deciphered an old hag with ancient, tissue-thin skin and heavy, gnarled features. She knew the look in the woman's eyes would be older than time itself, and if she met that look the car would go off the road in a heartbeat.

This was a journey she could never relate to another living soul. No one would believe her. Imagine trying to describe it at a dinner party - a few shudders, some more wine-pouring, meaningful glances exchanged - another psychiatrist having a breakdown...Especially since most of her friends were doctors. Well, all of them. How terrible to be thought mad when you were supposed to be saner than sane. To experience what seems real but cannot be. To have to lock all this inside because you can never tell.

Lock what inside? What was this?

The temptation to look at her passenger grew stronger with every passing second, the pull like a magnet.

Don't look round - whatever you do, Kristy - do not look...

That voice - it was her late father's...

And then the sharp descent began. The Audi's headlights picked out the rear-lights of a truck. The belt of fog broke, and ahead lay the metropolis - a basin lit with yellow lights.

The temperature shot up. And the presence evaporated.

***

Real fear. Well if that's what she'd gone to find, that's what she'd got.

She parked, locked up and then quickly ran up the steps to her apartment block, not daring to look over her shoulder. On entering, she walked briskly from room to room switching on all the lights, then poured herself a double scotch from the bottle kept only for Christmas.

And then another.

Only a scalding bath and turning up the heating full pelt, managed to thaw the chill, which had permeated through her to her bones. Afterwards, she curled up on the sofa in a fleece dressing gown, hugging herself and knocking back another glass of whisky. If she had been terrified out of her wits at Woodsend - a grown woman with a rational mind and no religious beliefs - then imagine growing up there! Imagine being a small child.

In an effort to rationalise her fears, she finally gave in and let her mind rake over what had happened. Maybe fear had bred fear and there was really nothing to justify suspicions of any mal-practice? Intuition and facts must be distinguished from one another.

Beyond 'Woodpecker Cottage, the path had twisted and turned so there was no chance of knowing which direction you faced. Some of the old tree trunks had peculiar markings on them and she'd taken a few snaps on her phone. It would be best to come back in daylight but hopefully the flash had caught the impressions. Then a little way ahead were lights from another cottage. She decided to walk towards it, thinking it likely there'd be a driveway out to the main road.

Indeed there had been a driveway - a muddy track rutted by 4x4 wheels by the look of it, and who could blame them needing a truck - it probably got so boggy out here. But not knowing whether to turn left or right she'd punted on a right. By then the fog was as thick as a blanket and progress was halting. So into the rutted track she plodded, cringing as her boots splattered with mud. She'd soon be on the road, though, and mud would brush off when it dried. *How stupid she'd been to come out here - honestly, really!*

The torchlight bobbed up and down, not illuminating much, and it soon became apparent the forest was growing ever quieter, closing around her in a hooded cloak. Not even a hoot from the owl. A velvet-muffled night without a sign of life. After a few more minutes though, came a stab of realisation: she was heading the wrong way! After all, if this track was leading to Ravenshill then it should have been possible to hear the main road traffic by now.

She stopped, about to do a U-turn, but the torch had picked something out. Ahead were white, wrought-iron railings, which appeared to enclose a patch of ground. She walked up to the periphery and peered through, mildly surprised to see a tiny graveyard. Ancient, moss-covered Celtic crosses, some of them leaning at an angle, others having crumbled many years before, marked each burial plot. It must have been used for the Woodsend villagers many years ago, she assumed. It definitely didn't look as though the place was visited anymore, though.

Whatever, it was one hell of an eerie place. Really creepy. About to back track once and for all however, something else caught in the hazy beam of the torch: on the other side of the little cemetery was what looked like a set of ruins.

Fascination taking over, Kristy picked her way over through the thicket and noted with astonishment and not a little glee, what appeared to be the ruins of an abbey. Well, well - the little place had real history! Just wait til she shared this back at work!

Maybe they could come out here in the summer for a team picnic? Find out a bit more? God, how enchanting! So who…

"Looking for something, dear?"

The nasally, sharp male voice came from over her shoulder.

She swung round, torchlight shining into another's.

She shielded her eyes. "Oh hello, sorry, no - I um–"

"Only this is private property, duck!"

"Is it? What - the ruins? I didn't realise."

"Not wise for a young lady to be out here in the dark on her own like this. You are alone, aren't you?"

"Pardon?"

It was then the disembodied voice revealed its owner as he stepped forwards a matter of inches from her face. Way too close. The permeation of cheap aftershave, oddly familiar, and strong garlic breath, caused her to stumble backwards as mesmerised, she'd found herself looking into the coldest blue eyes imaginable. On a sub-conscious level she took in the details, while recalling with a degree of panic, that she hadn't told anyone where she was going.

No one knows where you are…

He had white hair and a distinctive widow's peak. Late fifties/early sixties at a guess. Slight build but wiry. Lizard skin. The eyes held her stunned gaze. Enjoyment, she realised with a jack hammer to the heart: the man was enjoying her fear.

His cold eyes began to sparkle in direct contrast to her own depletion of energy. Such power - feeding off her fear like a vampire drawing blood.

In an instant she'd become a child again. A child caught doing something naughty. Who would be punished and deservedly so. She scrambled around for the vestiges of her adulthood, her status…"Look, I..I…I'm so sorry–"

Behind her, in the density of the woods, a humming noise - or was it drumming? A feeling that someone else was coming. Or had been summoned? Which? Should she call out?

She dared not take her eyes from the man in front of her. *What to do? Decide, Kristy, you have a second at best…*

His glance flicked to a place over her shoulder - so there *was* someone about to join them - it wasn't her imagination!

Something else - her glance noted something in his right hand - he was holding something. *OhmyGod!*

Too late - he'd seen her reaction. The glacial blue expression hardened to flint as recognition passed between them. And in that fractured second she took off and ran for all she was worth.

Keeping to the tyre-rutted track, she reasoned in her adrenalin-saturated state that if she'd taken the wrong direction first time then this must, had to be, the right one. Would she ever get out of here? Every breath sliced hard into her lungs, leg muscles screaming.

Were there footsteps behind?

Just keep running. Faster and faster and faster…

To her right now, lights - a cottage - lots of lights - maybe caravans? The drive opened out like an estuary and a wider, flattened track, dimly lit from the camp, for that's what it seemed like, some kind of camp….lay straight ahead.

The pain seared like a knife through her chest as she gasped and lunged for each gulp of oxygen. Then ahead, thank God, lay the glistening tarmac of a road. She risked a look over her shoulder.

No one.

At the end of the track she doubled over, stitch in her side, gasping for breath.

Don't look back.

She had to keep going. Anyone of them, because he was undoubtedly not alone, could still waylay her. So wheezing painfully, leg muscles weak beneath her, she stumbled into the middle of the glistening lane, hopefully Ravenshill - footsteps echoing deadly, as shrouded in fog, she hurried as best she could to the car.

It stood as a white charger next to the black, gurgling river

Almost there. Almost safe.

Almost.

Inside. Central locking on. Ignition fired. And then came the blinding, horrible connection of subconscious to conscious -

the realisation of what he'd been holding. That man had been holding a black cross.

***

Chapter 13
Doncaster Royal Infirmary

Later that same evening, Becky opened her eyes and stared at the small guy sitting on the plastic visitor's chair next to her hospital bed.

Small was an understatement. He was minute. His legs swung to and fro about six inches from the floor, and the top of his bowler hat only just levelled with the back of the chair. Without him speaking she knew his name was Chester. Perhaps she'd heard that while unconscious? They said your hearing was the last thing to go and the first to come back in these situations.

Chester had his head cocked to one side in an enquiring tilt. An old guy with deeply wrinkled skin tinged with jaundice. "Good morning, Becky. How are ya?"

She stared.

Chester examined his finger nails. "You had a good night? That's good - excellent. Feeling better, huh? More like talking, huh?"

Becky blinked and blinked again. Okay, so she'd taken a bump on the head, passed out, and been prescribed heavy duty painkillers. But this was no dream. *She could freaking see him!*

Long ago, a student friend had taken some dodgy E's after a few too many pints of snakebite. On the way home he'd been jumping out of his skin - screaming as imaginary pythons slithered up from the drains, and grizzly bears leapt out from lamp posts. Those hallucinations, he'd said later, were so *real!* He'd known they weren't but they'd still scared him half to death.

She thought about that: surely you were only psychotic if you actually believed the hallucinations were real and not simply images your brain was conjuring up for entertainment? And only bona fide crackers, out of your tree, and in deep shit - to use a technical term - if you answered them back? So, then - all she had to do was accept little Chester was a hallucination and not respond? And she would be fine.

"Ah, that's what you're thinking is it?" said Chester, springing off the orange, plastic chair and onto her bed as adeptly as a tree monkey.

He crawled on all fours up the bedclothes until he was sitting within arm's reach. He smelled overpoweringly of urine and sulphur.

Becky's brain chipped in with the added possibility of an olfactory hallucination, along with auditory. She really ought to see a doctor about this. Smiled at her own joke. An Alice in Wonderland experience after a head injury - maybe she should sit back and enjoy it?

"Best thing, Lady," Chester agreed. "Enjoy the ride! Hey - that nurse, whassername - Kelly? Hey, she's sure got a fat arse!" He cackled as the staff nurse, Kelly, entered the side ward to check Becky's observation chart. Craned his neck to give her the once over. "She sure got to the pork pies first!"

Despite herself, Becky snickered.

"Hey," said Chester. "Her arse is so big it follows her round like a separate person! She keeps whipping round to see whose followin' her! Ha ha!"

Becky said, "Shh….stop it!"

Kelly looked up. "Ooh, sorry Becky. I didn't realise you were awake. How are you feeling today?"

"I'm fine," said Becky, trying not to giggle as Chester did a cheap imitation of Kelly waddling over to peer into her face. Behind the nurse he wiggled his butt and the more he messed around the more Becky struggled to control her laughter.

Once Kelly had left the room, the pair of them doubled over in hysterics. "Hey - you and me - we have some fun, don't we? Hey, you and me, Becky?"

She nodded and wiped the tears from her eyes. Maybe this head injury business wasn't so bad, after all?

"And hey," Chester added. "You make out you've gone a bit…" and here he did what she'd normally hate, pointing his finger to his temple and rotating it… "ya know…loopy-loo…you can get loads of time off work! You don't have to wait at that bus stop in the dark no more, or get up at five in the morning. Hey - we can have some fun, Becky. Whadya say?"

"Yeah," she said. "Let's make the most of it Chester."

She'd worked hard all her life. Why not?

***

The following day Noel arrived; as daylight faded and the new moon cut a scythe in a granite sky streaked with ice blue.

Becky woke with a jump.

He seemed to fill the room with his broad shoulders and biker leathers. He ruffled his dark hair into a rooster look and pulled up the orange chair.

"How you doing, Becks?"

She smiled sleepily. "Good. Brilliant technicolored dreams with surround sound and 3D effects. Better than the cinema. I think it must be the analgesics."

He frowned. "You're only on a bit of codeine."

"Feels like I'm on diamorph."

"That good, eh? Anyway, here's the news - I had a chat with Kelly and she says they couldn't find any problems on the scan, and your neuro-tests are fine too. You're a bit sleepy but that's to be expected. You should be going home tomorrow."

A flash of annoyance shot through her. "You'd think she'd discuss it with me, first."

Again Noel frowned. "She said she did and you agreed - you even said you'd arranged a lift home."

"I did?"

Shit! Can't remember that!

He nodded. "I'm pleased for you. Relieved too. To be honest I'll be glad to have you back at work because it's all going tits up without you."

From somewhere inside her head came a mocking, whingy voice, 'Oh poor me, I can't cope…ooh dear….boo hoo…diddums…'

"In what way?"

"Well Jack locked himself in his office, for one thing. He's completely lost it, Becks. Just the most bizarre behaviour. Anyway, after he barricaded himself in his office, Isaac and Claire called in the crisis team, and the board suspended him. They're saying it's a breakdown. It's awful - it's really shaken everyone up. Obviously he can't go near the patients until he's better.

"Anyway, he was sectioned but discharged shortly after, and now he's at his holiday home in Hathersage. He probably just needs a few weeks off, poor sod. That session with Ruby must have seriously taken it out of him. I hope he's going to be okay, I really do. "

"That's terrible."

"I know. I wish you could remember what happened when he did the hypnosis because it does all seem to stem from that."

She shook her head. "I just can't. Only what I said before about having lost all sense of time and being unable to move. I came to the conclusion he must have hypnotised me too!"

Noel nodded. "That would make sense. But it still doesn't explain what happened to Jack."

"Well hopefully he won't be off work too long. I suppose Claire will manage in the meantime. I'll be back in a few days as well."

"Hope so. Oh - Kristy Silver apparently wants to take over Ruby's management as soon as possible and I think Isaac's in agreement – probably just as well with a work load like his and Claire out of her depth. Personally I think Kristy's out to make her own name - put herself centre stage!"

Chester was sitting in the sink in the corner of the room, shaking his head sorrowfully. "That bitch is trouble, Becky - you godda put a stop to this! You need to get out of here!"

"Kristy Silver? Taking over Ruby?"

He nodded." Mmm. Claire phoned her. Something to do with a similar case that turned out to be D.I.D. Her client came from the same village where Ruby tried to murder that poor sod with a kitchen knife– "

Becky threw back the covers. "I'm not having this. That woman's stirring up all sorts of trouble just so she can write more articles for the press. That's all Ruby is to her, you know - an interesting case! She could really traumatise Ruby if she brings out all those alters: kids protect themselves like that for a reason - if whatever happened to her as a child is revealed to her she won't be able to handle it. They should leave well alone."

"I thought you wanted the trauma to be unlocked and treated? What's changed?"

"I think Ruby is doing fine, getting better at her own pace. I've had time to think that's all - sometimes certain things are simply best forgotten. There's loads of evidence now to support not uncovering lost memories, you know? It can do more harm than good."

"Not if those stored memories are damaging the person - taking up space in the form of multiple alters so the individual doesn't know who they are, so they can't function or cope with life."

Noel put his hand on her forearm but Becky threw it off, reaching for her jeans at the exact moment Kelly came in. "What's going on?"

Noel shook his head. "I'm not sure. Becky seems a bit confused."

"I am not confused. I just want to get out of here - I have to stop Kristy from hurting Ruby."

Kelly bustled in and took the jeans off her. "Becky, you can go home tomorrow. Right now it's getting late and you're still on strong painkillers. Try and relax."

Reluctantly, Becky acquiesced while Kelly tucked her in, peering into her face with concern.

Suddenly a voice shouted nastily, "What are you looking at, Fat Arse?"

Kelly's jaw dropped and Becky realised she'd been the one to speak. Her stomach clutched inwardly in shock.

Had she really said that out loud?

It must have been Chester. It couldn't have been herself. No way!

She looked over at the sink but Chester wasn't there. Nausea rose in her throat.

And from far, far away, the nurse and her friend whispered together. Something about not being ready for home yet, odd behaviour, totally out of character.

"And there's another thing," Noel was saying.

Becky strained to listen as the whispering continued.

"We've now got the CCTV coverage of when she fell. She said there was someone rushing up the corridor who she bumped into. But there's nothing there, Kelly. Absolutely nothing. She just fell forwards and knocked her head onto the crash trolley - almost as if an invisible hand pushed her. Are you sure they didn't find anything on the scan? I'm really worried there might be a–"

As the door shut softly behind the pair, the light in the side ward faded to grey. Becky, left in silence, looked over to the plastic chair for her cheery companion to reappear, but there was no one there. She was all alone then. Alone in the dark bowl of her own madness.

Funny. She kind of missed him.

***

Chapter 14
Woodsend Village
1995: Age 7, I think.

I'm lying in bed, watching the clock on the bedside table tick through each minute. Another hour has passed. No sounds now except the drone of canned laughter on the television downstairs. Probably Mum's asleep on the sofa waiting for *him* to get home. He can't be back yet. It could still happen tonight, then.

I hug the blue bunny with floppy ears Nana Cora bought for me. She said I was a special child, but it made my sister mad I got the bunny and we fell out again - I hate it when we fall out. Nana bought me some clothes too but I hid them. It makes me wonder if Nana Cora knows?

He says it's a secret and if I tell my sister he'll kill her - not me - her! And if I tell anyone else he'll have us both put into care and we'll be separated. But Nana Cora doesn't buy stuff for my sister - just me - and it makes me wonder why, and why she says I'm special like *he* says I'm special? She knows - she must do - but I can't tell her or we'll go into care. But if she knows why doesn't she help me?

My sister lies next to me and I can hear her rhythmic breathing. Fast asleep in rosy dreams. I hope it always stays that way for her.

How many times have I lain here? Wanting someone, anyone, to catch the tears and hold me, to say it will be all right? That nothing bad will happen.

I sat in the forest last night, watching the sun go down behind the trees. I was in my favourite place down by the river. The pink light of home and love was painted in the sky. I could see that love and feel it, but it couldn't make me whole. I'm trying so hard to remember what it felt like to absorb that love, hugging my pillow so tight to stop the fear from rising in my tummy, and if I try hard enough I can be back there again.

Then it happens…gone the pink sky.

And I'm staring into his ice-blue eyes. Reading the mood. Measuring the anger and how bad I am, reflected in them. Watching as the hand comes down and roughly grabs my hair.

He yanks me out of the warm bed. My sister murmurs in her sleep and turns over into the warm dip I've left. While he reaches above the door and gets the stick. It's a good place to keep a stick - you've got to run underneath to get out. I wonder if he realises how clever that is? Funny the stick is so perfectly rounded and smooth. So pleasing to touch. Until, it's brought down hard across your legs.

Keep quiet. On the cold landing floor while the house sleeps. Don't make a sound. Take it, just take it.

After the first swipe and the praying, it will be done quickly.

Nana Cora says we must go to church and pray. I sit next to her on Sundays with my hands clasped tightly. Eyes shut fast even through the sermons. Over and over I pray. Please God, please help me. And he does - you see I'm no longer in my own head but floating high into a princess sky of meringue castles with drawbridges and moats. And my body is not mine anymore - no longer a bony sparrow-child in pink pyjamas - but weightless and free. There is burning on my thrashed legs now, and searing pain scoring up the buckling skeleton of my body; sick lodged in my throat, which I'm desperately trying to swallow down; and stinging tears in the ghost child's eyes - the one crumpling onto the floor.

But I am not there.

He shouts and spits in the ghost child's face about how bad she is. Not me. Another child - a really bad one.

Don't breathe in or you'll vomit. Don't cry or you'll be hit again. Don't hold your legs or he'll sneer at you and hit you harder. Don't look. Don't hear. And most of all don't think about what's coming next...When his rage is spent...

***

Chapter 15
Drummersgate Forensic Unit
December 2015

Kristy found Ruby in the art room with Amanda Blue - someone she had worked with many times - and found highly competent and open minded. A little brusque at times perhaps; but with Amanda there was none of the sceptical, academic pontificating Kristy found so negative and depressing in many of her colleagues: Amanda simply had a no nonsense - 'let's do everything, try everything, listen to everyone,' approach, which was refreshing, and in this case a huge relief, because frankly, Ruby was going to need the strongest and most open of personalities to cope with what was coming.

After several sessions of intensive art work with Amanda, it had become clear Ruby's personality was highly fragmented - way more than any other patient either had worked with before. Kristy realised Ruby had a rare case of poly-fragmented DID, which involved not dozens of alter personalities, but possibly hundreds. A major breakthrough would be for Ruby, in time, to recognise that, and become the host of the system, which controlled her, rather than its victim - because the victim lost time - hours, days even - which would explain the fact she had no recollection of her frenzied attack in Woodsend.

Whatever worked, in terms of helping Ruby come to terms with who she was and to function in a reasonably self-reliant manner - well that, they decided over the phone, would be their aim.

Amanda looked up as Kristy sat down, her tentative smile indicating satisfactory progress had been made today. Yes it could take years, but there was hope now - right in front of their eyes.

Ruby's tongue was sticking out slightly as she drew with crayons in the exact same way a child of around five would. The house she'd drawn had a one dimensional aspect - a box with four windows and a doorway in the middle. The sun was a yellow ball in the top right hand corner and there were stick figures with scratchy black hair and triangular bodies, standing on a patch of spiky, green lawn.

To the side of the picture, stood a tree. In the tree was a cat. Underneath the tree were grave stones, and on the trunk - a red mark.

As Ruby drew, humming to herself, 'Four and twenty blackbirds...baked in a pie...' Amanda silently passed previous drawings to Kristy. Eyes. Lots and lots of eyes. Crosses. And a church with a spire. All as seen and depicted by an infant-aged child. In addition to these were castles with moats, princesses looking out of windows, and a fairytale, turreted palace balancing precariously on a high rock, surrounded by clouds and angels. Fairies and elves and lots and lots of daisies, and yet more trees. Trees with cats in them. Trees with engravings on the trunk, and pictures of the moon.

With a flourish, Ruby finished her drawing of the house, dropped her crayon, and sat back. Done.

"These are really good, Ruby," said Amanda. "Is this where you used to live, then?"

A slight frown creased Ruby's brow. Her voice was breathy and childish. The image she projected was of being extremely small, her body folding in on itself as she looked up from under a floppy curtain of hair. "Mmm."

Amanda began to gather up the materials, chatting brightly. "We've had a lovely afternoon, haven't we, Ruby? Do you want to tell Kristy what you told me about being a beautiful princess in a castle? That was when you were very little, wasn't it?"

The tiny girl inside Ruby, appeared to diminish further, as if she was disappearing altogether now the painting was over, and attention had focused on herself again. Over her head, Amanda mouthed a word to Kristy, 'Tara.'

Kristy nodded. Okay so she was dealing with Tara today. Amanda had explained that Tara was the child who presented herself during art lessons. Sometimes a babyish persona would appear, who didn't speak but snuffled with misery. Another time there would be a bolshy teenager who called himself Dylan; or a girl who appeared to be almost indecipherable from Ruby, but whose eyes were more unfocused. This girl had a bit of a temper - like a teen who'd been told she couldn't go out that night. This was fifteen year old Eve.

But today it was Tara. Possibly five years old - maybe six - Tara did not seem to be educated, or able to read and write.

"Who am I speaking to? Am I talking to Tara?" Kristy asked the child-woman kicking her heels against the chair.

A faint nod and shy smile.

"Do you think you could go and get Ruby for me? I'd really like to speak to Ruby today. Tell her it's Kristy."

No answer.

"Please tell Ruby it's safe. It's Kristy, her doctor."

Kristy kept her voice steady and reassuring, softly requesting Ruby to come to the fore and take control.

The switch, when it came though, was shocking. The light in Ruby's pale blue eyes faded rapidly, registering Tara's surprise at falling backwards down an internal corridor - followed by a trance-like stare. For several minutes of unblinking nothingness, there was no personality in there - no conscious mind in the driving seat. It was like, Kristy thought, looking at a shell, a human body devoid of any spiritual presence.

She waited, repeatedly saying, "Ruby, it's okay. Ruby, come back. Ruby, you're safe—"

A flicker of an eyelash. The slotting in of a person behind the eyes. Confusion as the face adjusted to its new owner. A flash of fear and then finally, recognition. Ruby blinked and swallowed.

"Hi there, Ruby. It's me - Kristy - your doctor. Would you like some tea with sugar?"

Ruby nodded. A brief flicker of a smile - maybe relief.

"How are you feeling?"

"Have I been in 'ere long? Only I—" She looked around at the art work spread all over the table. At the child's drawings. "Were that me?"

Kristy handed her a cup of sweet tea and nodded. "I take it you don't remember?"

"No."

"Nothing?"

Ruby shook her head and looked away.

"Are you aware you lose time? That when you came into the art room it was lunchtime, and now it's going dark?"

"Yes."

"But you don't recall what happened while you were here?"

"No."

"Okay, I know that happens a lot, but there's good news! I can help you. On a practical level, your main problem is you're timing out and losing control of your own body. We need to keep you conscious and in control, but to do that we have a lot of work to do."

Ruby nodded.

"Are you good so far?"

"Yeah."

"I need you to work with me. It's going to be very difficult and it may take years, but I have a lot of experience in this field and believe me you are not alone. What you're suffering from Ruby, is something called Dissociative Identity Disorder. This means it's highly likely something very traumatic happened to you as a child - maybe repeatedly - and as a child you protected yourself by pretending it wasn't happening at all, at least not to you! This was where you were very clever indeed, because many people can't do this: in order to keep yourself safe, you made up other personalities and pretended it was happening to them while you yourself went somewhere else in your head. Somewhere nicer. We call these made-up personalities 'alters', and it seems you've got quite a few of these alters. You had an amazing imagination! But because you were growing up and your mind was still developing, these alters became part of your own personality, do you see? They and you are one and the same thing! And what that means is - when they are in control, you are not - and so you don't remember anything. It can be very distressing because you lose time–"

"I'm there sometimes."

Kristy stopped short. "As in co-conscious?"

"Whatever - kind of like I'm in the back seat but someone else is driving. Sometimes it feels like I'm falling back and someone else is doing the talking, but I can't stop them saying whatever they want. But I can like, hear it. That'll be Eve usually. Yeah it's Eve who does a lot of talking. Eve talks to Becky."

Kristy took in the information, sitting in silence for a moment. So Ruby knew all along that she had other characters acting out for her!

Ruby smiled faintly. "It doesn't always happen - she just sort of shoves me aside and I can't stop her."

"She's a tough cookie, is she, Eve?"

"Yeah. Sometimes, though, I kind of like Eve taking over cos I've like, had enough."

After a while, Kristy said, "It's good actually. It's good that you know when it's happening and who some of your alters are. That will help us piece it all together bit by bit, and put you more in control. What do you think?"

Ruby sipped her tea for a while. "Bit of a mind fuck, innit? Bit much to get my head round thinking there's like a whole bunch of us in here? Like - it could be mad Dylan who attacked that bloke they said I tried to murder? Do you think he did it?"

"We'll come to that," said Kristy. "But not until you're ready. Like I said it could take time."

Interesting! Tommy Blackmore had revealed several alters once the aggressive male who dominated him, had been persuaded to take a back seat - the 'Gatekeeper' as Tommy called him. Perhaps Dylan was the dark entity Jack had encountered when he hypnotised Ruby?

Question was - would it ever be possible to cohese all of Ruby's hundreds of alters into one dominant personality - Ruby herself? Assuming Ruby was the host, of course? With Ruby not knowing who she herself was - well, what if the Ruby character was an alter too? Who on earth was this girl?

As Kristy's train of thoughts tunnelled along, another idea occurred - what if the events this girl suffered were too horrific to ever be safely retrieved? Maybe if they were revealed to Ruby it would destroy her, and all the complex mechanisms her child self had put in place would have been for nothing? Could the woman, realistically, ever be made whole again?

"Anyway, we'll leave it there for today," said Kristy. "We don't want to rush you. And you've made huge strides already. Huge. Really well done. You're a brave girl."

A cloud passed behind Ruby's eyes.

Kristy, who had been about to turn and get her bag, caught the look and frowned. *What? What had she said?*

Ruby's face had darkened in an instant, her eyes dead.

She'd switched again.

Ruby had gone. And someone else was coming.

Who? Who would it be? Kristy's hand hovered over her panic alarm.

It took around forty seconds of ticking silence for the new alter to appear. Kristy's heart pounded hard against her ribs.

A new person had arrived: a smiling, secretive teenager. A challenging smirk. Different voice - higher and breathier - as Ruby swept her hair over to one side and examined her finger nails.

"Who am I speaking to?" said Kristy.

"Who wants to know?"

"Kristy. I'm your doctor. Who am I speaking to?"

"Eve."

Eve rolled her eyes and slumped back into her chair. Affecting the sullen, bored, I-am-so-embarrassed stance of a typical teenaged girl. Kristy narrowed her eyes - there was still something of Ruby there -the girl was not wholly in character and didn't seem to be dismayed by the shapeless sweater and jeans she was wearing.

"Is Ruby there, Eve? Can you go and get her back please? We were talking."

Eve shook her head. "I'm in charge now. She's upset. Can't cope and so you've got me."

"I see. How old are you, Eve?"

"Fifteen, nearly sixteen. Why?"

Kristy took a deep breath. "Are you aware of a fragmented personality? That you and Ruby share thoughts and feelings?"

"God, like, only for ages. Years. There are lots of us."

"And how long has Ruby known?"

"Yeah - ages. But she didn't want to admit it 'til *he* left. She thought it was too dangerous for *us* to come out. He kept us locked in. It's fantastic since he pissed off. Poor doc, though, eh?"

"Since who left? Who kept you locked in?"

Eve looked away.

"Was it Dylan who terrified you all?"

Eve snorted. "That jumped-up little twat? Don't make me laugh."

Okay, so not Dylan then.

"Eve, how many of there are you, do you know?"

Eve shrugged and then began to count on one hand. Then two. "There's Ruby, me, Dylan, and Tara. Then there are the little ones but you're not speaking to them. And Minnie. And there's our manager who decides who's gonna speak to who. And then you've got Lucy and Emma but they keep all the bad stuff. And...do you want me to draw it for you?"

Kristy nodded and passed her a sheet of paper.

Then sat back in astonishment as Eve drew a map of what she called, 'The System' living inside Ruby's mind - of tunnels and compartments and secret lock-down places, safe rooms and quiet rooms, communal rooms and a vault. In all, there appeared to be over one hundred different alters in addition to corridors roaming with ghost children who had no names.

"Do you speak to each other?"

"I speak to the little ones sometimes. And Dylan - I tell him where to get off, the bastard. He doesn't want me to tell you about anything that happened. He's bad. He doesn't want me to tell you about the baby either."

"What baby?"

"The one we had."

"We? When?"

Silence.

"Eve - are you saying that you, that Ruby, had a baby?"

A faraway look passed over the young woman's face.

"Eve - what do you mean? What do you know about a baby?"

Eve's look became sly, her glance flicking to one side, head tilted. After a moment she shook her head. "I'm not allowed to tell you that."

"Does Ruby know?"

"We all know."

"I see. But you don't know when this happened, or what became of this baby?"

A Mona Lisa smile flirted briefly with Eve's lips. "No."

"I see. Well we've probably done enough for now, anyway. Can you get Ruby to come back and talk to me?"

Eve nodded but seemed vague.

"Ruby, can you hear me? Ruby - we need to talk!"

Ruby nodded. But she'd dipped her head. Her lower lip trembled and an age old weariness passed over her face.

Kristy reached over and squeezed her hand. "It's going to be okay. I'm here now and I'm going to help you if it's the very last thing I do."

"I'm so tired. And I've got a headache - a really bad one."

"All right, I'll get someone to bring something for that. I know this is all very frightening and exhausting. Let's get you back to your room now, okay?"

***

Outside, the car park glistened with evening drizzle, and Kristy hurried to the Audi. For a moment she sat in the driver's seat gazing at raindrops scurrying diagonally across the windscreen.

There was a lot of Ruby's life missing - somewhere between being an abused child and appearing as an adult living at the old mill in Bridesmoor. This woman had been living somewhere with someone. Someone who must have noticed her switching personalities. Not to mention the fact she may have given birth. Did she go to hospital? Was there a record of this? And where on earth was that child now? Who with?

The more the mystery was mined, the more tunnels appeared.

After a few minutes she pulled out her ipad and typed in some notes. Then paused. Of course, the trigger had been, 'You're a brave girl!" Quickly she added the revelation and underscored it in red. Anyone working with Ruby was going to have to tread extremely carefully if the origins of this case were ever to be unravelled without excessive trauma to the host.

She fired the ignition. Maybe she'd go and see Jack before her next session with Ruby. Find out a little more about this alter Eve said had kept the rest of them locked in. If this alter had now vacated, then Jack could be the only one who'd met him.

Poor doc, though, eh?

What had Eve meant by that? Hmm… yes, it would be good to see Jack tomorrow.

***

Chapter 16
Hathersage, Derbyshire

"I don't think you should come in," said Hannah.
The following morning, Kristy stood on the doorstep of the
McGowan's holiday cottage in Hathersage. The December North
wind blew sleet around her ankles and she hugged her body to
keep warm.

Saturday morning. How much nicer to have stayed in bed
under the soft, down duvet and slumbered on, icy rain lashing the
solid stone walls of her apartment block instead of herself. Yet,
here she was - tired and travel weary as the wind swept off the
Pennines straight through to her spine.

"I've come a long way, Hannah. Please - just a few minutes
- I really need to discuss a client's case…she's very sick and I hear
Jack's going to be off for a while?"

The thought crossed her mind - it was a minor miracle
more of her colleagues didn't suffer from mental collapse really:
the deciphering of what was sane and what was not, being so often
blurred with rationale, political correctness and the current
psychological zeitgeist. Interminable questioning, ongoing
research and moral relaxation, had on occasion left her reeling for
her own sanity. What was right and what was wrong? Was
anything real anyway? Who was to say? Who decided? Because
ultimately all we have is a set of criteria for reasonable behaviour
within the confines of modern society. And of course, every
culture is different. Really, all any of us have, she thought,
standing on Jack and Hannah's doorstep, was a tenuous grasp on
the here and now.

All of which meant it was so important to take those
holidays, ground yourself in family and friends… and be in
life…just do the daily job. Yet here she was, going out on a limb
to help a girl who had traumatised her doctor so badly he'd had to
be suspended from duty and have the crisis team called in. They'd
had to break down the door. Heavily sedate him. This man she had

learned so much from, who had mentored and inspired her - a bastion of family life, of all that was good and honest and admirable.

His wife stood looking at her, ashen and aged before her time. No make-up. Hair greying at the roots, roughly scraped back in a band, her glance darting nervously towards the staircase.

Kristy took a deep breath, quashing the disquiet in her gut, willing herself not to look at the gloomy staircase behind Hannah, or be cowed by the banging noise from upstairs - like someone was lugging heavy furniture across a room. "Hannah, I'm sorry. I truly am. How's he bearing up?"

Tears welled in Hannah's eyes. She squeezed them shut and blinked rapidly. Pushed the door a little further closed. "I can't…"

"Hannah - what is it? Can I help? Oh my God!"

Hannah hesitated for a moment, came to a snap decision, then reached for her coat. Quickly she stepped outside and shut the door behind her. "Let's walk."

The icy wind cut into their faces as both women dipped their heads. The cottage sat squatly in the centre of a few acres; the hardened ground coated in sparkly frost, trees cadaverous against a stormy sky. On reaching the path, which led a slippery route down to the swirling, lapping Derwent, Hannah said, "The youngest are with my mother; and the older two are with a neighbour so school isn't affected. I honestly don't know what we'll do at Christmas."

Kristy frowned. "Things must be pretty bad if you've had to leave the kids?"

Hannah picked up pace and Kristy hurried to keep up.

"Who's his doctor?"

"That's just it. No one. He was sectioned for less than a day: Isaac discharged him here, as long as I looked after him. I was a psyche nurse, you see? And Jack was completely acquiescent at that point - agreed to everything. Like everyone else, I thought it was depression, overload, a breakdown… and he just needed a rest."

"Is Isaac still responsible for his care?"

She nodded. "It's what Jack wanted. What he agreed to. But he was lying to everyone. Playing the game so he could get out of there. He reverted to his bizarre behaviour the second we got in the car."

"How do you mean?"

"Being disgustingly nasty about 'the morons' who'd treated him. Saying stuff - horrible stuff laced with blasphemy - about me, and oh honestly, Kristy, I can't repeat it. He kept snickering to himself - I'd catch him looking at me like he thought it was all a huge joke."

Kristy frowned, deep in thought. "Is he not improving as the days go on? What's he on? Anti-depressants? Sedatives?"

Hannah pulled her coat around tighter, avoiding eye contact. "Well yes - both. He was lucid, you see - totally articulate and reasonable - so I can understand why Isaac thought it would be safe for him to come home. But now, when I think back, I saw the glitter in his eyes when he suddenly decided to change tack during the assessment - you know - what he had to do and say to get out?"

"I don't follow."

"No, well you wouldn't. And neither did I. God, this is so hard because you're going to think I'm bonkers...so I'll just blurt it all out so as you know as much as I do. And because I need help and I don't know where to turn. Okay, here goes..."

Hannah stopped abruptly, and the two women locked expressions.

Kristy steeled herself. *Something bad was coming.*

"Where's Becky?" said Hannah. "Do you know?"

Thrown a little, Kristy said, "Um...I think she was discharged from the D.R.I. a few days ago."

"You need to go see her as soon as you can. Look, something happened after Jack hypnotised that girl. I'm deadly serious. He couldn't sleep. Said he kept seeing things in the dark like hooded monks with no faces, ink-black shapes crawling over the walls, pin-prick red eyes staring at him from the corner of the bedroom–"

"All symptoms of psychosis secondary to depression–"

"Well yes, but he was wrecked, Kristy - drained of everything that was him! It's hard to explain. His whole personality changed. He wasn't washing himself but still he went out to work - unshaven, stinking of sweat, with his hair all greasy. He's normally so fastidious about hygiene. And he'd laugh at things that weren't funny like a bad news report; and every other word was 'fuck.' Or worse! I've never heard him use language like that - ever - and certainly not in front of the kids."

"And it started the same day he treated Ruby? Are you sure?"

"Yes. A hundred percent. He came home and said he felt terrible, and frankly, after he described what happened that day I could understand why. The next day, when I woke up, he looked like shit. Said he'd had a sleepless night, But then it got worse and worse and worse, and I don't think he's slept since! I honestly thought it was the pressure, that he needed a holiday, maybe some anti-depressants, but then things started happening with Daisy, and Jack seemed to–"

"With Daisy? Like what?"

"Well I'd find her unconscious on the kitchen floor in the early hours, stone cold. She said one of her dolls - Milly-Molly - had told her to go down there; and here's the funny thing - she kept saying, 'Daddy knows what I mean'. I'd have put it down to this imaginary friend she says she's got if it wasn't for that…that *look* they exchanged! And the smile."

"It can still be explained."

"I wish with all my heart you were right. But I promise you this isn't anything you can explain, Kristy. This isn't anything you can diagnose, treat with drugs, or improve with therapy sessions. I'm afraid it's far, far worse than anything you could possibly imagine, and I'm not sure I can keep a lid on it for much longer. I think when you actually see him you'll understand"

Kristy reached out to touch Hannah's arm. "I'm so sorry, Hannah. This has been a huge strain for you - I can see how it's worn you down - but you mustn't give up hope."

Hannah stared into the dark, swirling waters of the river as they neared the edge. "Sometimes I stand here, and I can see myself floating away...face down–"

Kristy folded Hannah into her arms and hugged her. "I think I should see him now. Let's sort this out - it's way too much for you! Jack needs admitting, and you need to get back to your children."

Hannah's weight sank against her.

"Come on. Before we lose our nerve."

Suddenly Hannah drew back, searching her face, trying, it seemed, to gauge how she'd react. "Kristy, do you believe in God?"

Kristy didn't even blink. "No, of course not. I'm a humanist. Why?"

Hannah pulled a tiny silver cross out from beneath her sweater. "He's okay til he sees this, that's all."

"Well you two did always argue about religion! I remember having dinner with you a few years ago and he was really cross about it."

"Oh it's more than being really cross, believe me!"

They turned to walk back to the house. "I did have an odd experience recently, though," Kristy said. "I've a client who grew up in a remote village - Woodsend, near Doncaster - the same village where Jack's hypnosis client was arrested for attempted murder. Well they have uncannily similar symptoms and so I acted on a hunch - took a drive out there, just to get a feel for the place. I thought I could see a possible pattern - a link. Anyway, this is going to sound daft - but on the drive home I felt a presence in the car with me. An old woman. And I felt she wanted me to look at her so the car would go off the road in the fog. Fear...it was like a steel band round my stomach and I thought I was going to be sick. Then the fog cleared as I headed downhill and she vanished."

Hannah walked on in silence.

"I knew it sounded silly. Well anyway, I put it down to some kind of physical manifestation of evil - I do believe in negative energies being very powerful and we certainly don't understand everything - I mean you've only to look at quantum physics...anyway, I'd run into a pretty hostile looking man in the village - in the woods to be precise. There was a cemetery there and some old ruins...I got badly scared, so I can imagine - you know, if you're depressed and things are getting on top of you, and frankly, with the things we have to hear and know...Look, all I'm saying is I am sure we can help Jack out of this. If his client grew up there like mine did - well she may well have revealed some pretty black stuff."

The cottage was back in view.

With linked arms they made their way up the garden path, heads bowed.

"Kristy, I wish you believed in God," Hannah said quietly. "If Jack had believed, I swear he'd have been protected from that girl. I think that whatever evil spirit resides in that village - it got into her and now it's attached to Jack."

Kristy smiled sadly. "It's only the fear within us, Hannah. Fear of the unknown. There is nothing else."

***

Inside the cosy kitchen with its chugging aga, a sheet of rain spattered the window, and a row of droplets shivered their way across the glass. The two women sipped hot tea in silence. Upstairs all was quiet. Nothing but the rattling of the keys in the front door as another gust whipped the cottage walls.

"Are you staying the nights here too?"

Hannah nodded, ran her hand over her bump. "I sleep in the spare room - on and off."

"Have you contacted anyone else, other than Isaac, for support? I know you're a devout Catholic - have you told the local priest? It might help you."

"I phoned a couple of days ago, once I'd plucked up the courage, but all the stupid man said was that my husband was in need of a rest and was I sure I wasn't over-exaggerating things? That hormones did funny things to pregnant women, and all that baloney. I asked if he'd come and see Jack, because it's not me who needed a priest, but my husband! And he said he would, but so far he hasn't. I think he thinks I'm crazy. Well - if the Church doesn't believe in possession then how will anyone else? Only in horror movies, right?"

"Possession? Oh Hannah! No! Honestly, that really doesn't exist, it's just superstitious religious nonsense and–"

Hannah's eyes filled with despair and Kristy stopped herself from going on.

Hannah almost laughed. "We nearly divorced over religion, Kristy. Jack only converted so we could marry in church and all the family - my side, that is - were happy. Then afterwards he told me he'd just said the words to keep the peace. It was all a sham."

"I thought he was brought up a Catholic?"

"Oh no. His father's side are all Irish Catholics but his mother's aren't; and his father's a GP who doesn't practice religion at all. No, we argued about it big time and he'd always laugh at me and shout me down - theorising about Darwin and evolution. Yet now - well if you could see his face when he sees my cross, you'd doubt everything you ever believed, I swear to God. We humans think we have all the answers and the buck stops with us, but you know we don't really know anything. That's what makes it all so scary - we don't know what we're dealing with and if we can't even acknowledge the enemy exists, then how do we fight it?"

Kristy frowned. "So you really think he's possessed? With the devil or something?"

"I don't think it - I know it. And it's going to take more than the local priest to sort it out. He's too busy with coffee mornings and fund raising events. I'll tell you though - I'm not letting the devil take his soul. He's a good man and I'll go to the Vatican if I have to!"

A blast of cold air plunged the kitchen into a freezer-like chill and both women gasped, their breath suddenly steaming on the air. The lights flickered on and off.

"He knows what I'm saying," said Hannah. "It was like this when I phoned the priest."

Overhead the heavy kitchen light fitting began to sway, and an acrid smell permeated the room like rancid drains.

Kristy drained her mug and stood up. "This storm is creating havoc. I'll just pop to the loo and then go and take a look at Jack. I'll tell him I'm taking over Ruby's case so he can take as long as he needs to get better. Then I'll let Isaac know the situation and have him re-admitted as soon as possible: he'll get treatment and you can have some much needed rest. Let's get you back to those children of yours. Christmas coming up too soon–"

At that moment a loud bang, like that of a wardrobe toppling over, crashed so heavily into the floor above, the walls shook.

Both women ran upstairs.

***

Chapter 17

It had got to her. That same evening Kristy lay in bed with every single light on in the flat. Trying not to think about what she'd seen. Seen more than heard, which was bad enough - but those images of Jack would now be hard-wired into her brain, seared to memory, and left to haunt her dreams. Whatever had any of them done to deserve this?

After leaving the cottage she'd immediately called the crisis team. With the benefit of hindsight, that may have been a bad move, but it had been an instinctive one - to help a person in need - to do what was logical and reasonable, and in line with everything she'd been taught. And Hannah desperately needed a break: the poor woman was six months pregnant, with small children who needed her.

Most of all, Jack had to be moved into a safe environment. But was it the right one - amid some of the most psychically vulnerable people on earth - those who had little enough control of their conscious minds as it was? Had she now put other poor souls at risk? Oh God...what else could she have done, though?

Once the team were on their way, she'd put her foot down hard in the opposite direction, passing The Foxhouse Inn before pulling over and vomiting repeatedly, dry-retching until the acid burned her throat. And then wept. For her colleague. For herself. For Hannah. For mankind in all its fragile ignorance. Because her life and how she saw it, would never be the same again. Rather like believing you're looking at a picture of a princess in a long, flowing dress - only to suddenly see it differently and realise you're actually looking at the profile of a wicked witch's long, hooked nose instead.

The turnaround had come after she's bounded up the stairs on Hannah's heels, only to find absolutely nothing to account for the almighty, foundation-juddering bang they'd both heard less than a second before. Nothing had fallen over. Nothing had been moved.

Hannah walked into Jack's room first.

Everything was calm.

He'd been sitting at the window, looking out at the rolling moor land.

The room smelled bad - like stagnant sewage - and damp seeped up the pretty, flock wallpaper leaving tide marks. The pine dresser and wardrobe, along with a chest of drawers and a chair, were all piled up in one corner as if ready for removal day. And Jack's shoulders were shaking so hard, like he was having the best laugh.

Hannah froze, staying by the door.

Kristy breezed in, affecting a confident, professional approach. "Hello Jack! I thought I'd come visit, cheer you up!"

He turned. Slowly. And Kristy's heart slammed against her ribcage. *Dear God!*

Jack's white hair looked like he'd been pulling at it, so clumps stuck up in patches, leaving parts of the skull exposed and pink. He'd lost at least half his body weight - taking him from being a big man to a gaunt, scarecrow figure with skin that hung from his bones. And his lips, always ready with a gentle smile, were twisted into razor wire. But mostly it had been his eyes, and she wished with all her heart and soul she'd never looked into them. Bulbous, pale, no longer laughing with kindness, but glinting with hateful cruelty. And the pupils had been red. As scarlet as freshly drawn blood.

Her hand flew to her mouth. "Oh my God!"

A deep, vibrating guffaw erupted from deep inside him. Not one voice, but many - like an evil choir - and she backed away - footstep by footstep - as he turned, his skull creaking round on its stem, to face her.

Feeling for the door handle, Kristy retreated through the doorway after Hannah, just as a wooden chair hurtled on its own accord from the pile of furniture in the corner, and hit the wall beside her head.

She yanked the door shut behind her.

The breath wouldn't come from her lungs. She forced the oxygen in, gasping painfully. The landing was unlit, the staircase in the far, far distance…such a long way off. She tried to get to it, every limb a dead weight, running but not moving. Nasty laughter reverberating through the house. The staircase still unreachable…lungs heavy…lunging for the banister, pulling herself forwards until from there, like in some kind of underwater nightmare where everything was murky and oh so slow, she'd managed to propel herself down towards the front door, and finally, out into the icy December day.

OhmyGod. OhmyGod. OhmyGod…

How long she'd sat there in the car, stunned, unable to think, she had no idea. Probably only a few minutes. But when a rap came on the window, it made her physically jump. She buzzed it down.

Hannah leaned in. "Now do you see?"

Kristy's throat dried to crust as she tried to form words. "I'm calling the crisis team. He needs to be taken in because you can't do this, and frankly, neither can I."

"I can tell you now there isn't a psychiatrist in the world who can cure him, Kristy. Surely you can see that? He needs a priest. And one who knows what he's doing too."

"I think," said Kristy, firing up the ignition, "that you may well be right, but I'll arrange for his care anyway. This can't go on for another day. You get onto the church. I'll make sure your priest gets in to see him."

"Well I guess we don't have much choice. One more thing though," said Hannah. "And I'm serious - watch out for odd things on the road - I mean you personally. You're involved now. I'm talking about things like a car coming straight for you at speed. Don't swerve, keep your nerve, be vigilant. They will want you dead."

"Who? Who will? Why?"

"You still don't get it, do you? Look - I had a couple of incidents recently. A black sports car tailing me. When it overtook I couldn't see a driver. Then I'd turn the bend and it would be

facing me in the middle of the road. No driver! I swear.
Fortunately my brakes worked and there was no one behind me.
Take care, Kristy. Go slow. That's all I'm saying - I'd never
forgive myself if I didn't warn you - even if it does make me
sound insane."

Even then, there had still been a tiny percentage of her,
which remained sceptical. There were explanations…had to
be…anything other than the most frightening one imaginable - that
negative energy could possibly live and breathe as an intelligent
life force.

Until, accelerating down from the Sheffield moors, she'd
turned a corner, and come to point blank range with a dead-eyed
child standing in the middle of the road. The reaction to break hard
was automatic, and the Audi span round several times, eventually
reversing up a grassy bank before grinding to a clunking halt.

She looked back at the road. No child. Walked back to
survey the scene. Nothing. Not so much as a footprint on the sleet-
covered tarmac.

Now do you believe?

She pulled the blankets up higher, trying to get warm,
praying the lights wouldn't start flickering or the temperature
dropping like they had in the cottage kitchen that morning.

Fear. That was all it was. Her own fear. Get a grip.

More important was the question of whether or not she'd
done the right thing in admitting Jack to a mental health unit?
What about the other patients? And had all of this really come
from one hypnosis session with Ruby? How come? And if Ruby's
evil alter had somehow attached itself to Jack, then why hadn't
Ruby been affected in the same way?

It was like she'd been a carrier only…but for how long?
Where had she been during her life and why had this demon only
been inflicted on Jack?

Questions rained on her mind. Eyes wide, staring at the
ceiling into the blinding lights. Every noise screamed in the empty
apartment. Every sensation prickled the nerve endings on her skin.

What was there?

Who was here?

***

Chapter 18
Woodsend. Aged 11, 1999

The minute I get up, my mother says Nana Cora wants to see me. She lives in a bungalow in the next village to ours - Bridesmoor - which has shops, a church and a school. She'll want me to go for a reason - usually to buy me something or ask about stuff. I don't mind going as long as Uncle Rick's not there.

My stomach's churning with hunger but I daren't ask for owt.

Outside, my mother's pegging out washing in a light, spitting rain. Rooks are cawing in the trees like grumpy old men in black rags, watching her, as she hums with pegs in her mouth, 'Four and twenty blackbirds baked in a pie...'

Suddenly she stops pegging, and turns to glare at me.

"You still 'ere? Piss off! Go on - just piss off! Oh and don't speak to anyone on t' road o'er, or you know what'll 'appen!"

I start to run down to the river because it's always best to run. On past Tommy's place, always making sure to keep out of sight.

Once down to The Whisper it's flat, and the tow path leads straight to the bottom of Bridesmoor, coming out at Tanners Dell. Just the sound of my own breathing and the rushing river now. Stitch in my side but I keep running.

There's an old man lives at the mill. It's falling down round his ears. Sometimes he cooks his food outside in the yard and shakes his fist if he catches sight of you. Mad as a March hare, my mother says. I don't like him, he gives me a bad feeling. Best to keep a watch out - skirting on the edge of the trees in the shadows in case he's out shooting rabbits or fishing. He could be anywhere. Sometimes he just steps out into the path. He's right in front of you and it makes your heart stop. Pale eyes. Pale as glass.

The river's dark today, swirling and gurgling in a myriad of plug holes. In places it's really deep and I know because I've been in there. Uncle Rick chucked me in after the last time...but I don't want to think about that. Crawling home with wet clothes stuck to my skin, shivering so hard my teeth chattered and my legs turned blotchy and blue; my mother slapping me round the head for 'falling in', and Uncle Rick standing on the doorstep having a laugh with my dad.

It's Uncle Rick I've got to be on guard against now I'm older. Dad takes the stick to me and Marie, but it's Uncle Rick who watches me, follows me, brings other men with him.

I start to run faster, keeping up speed until the houses where Nana lives come into view.

She's waiting on the doorstep, and turns to lock the door as soon as she sees me.

"Get to the bus stop and flag it down!" she shouts.

Once in town we get off at the market. She buys me pink vests, knickers and socks, and two dresses. We have chips in a steamy café, and I have a milkshake as well. If we see anyone she calls me Marie - my sister's name - and I'm not to say owt different. The thing is - our Marie goes to school, but because I'm a special child I have to stay at home. If I tell anyone about it I'll be taken away by The Social, so it's really important not to. If ever we bump into a friend of Nana Cora's, she calls me Marie.

After, when we get back, she puts me in the bath and gives me a scrubbing down with a hard brush. "Is he still at you?"

I don't say anything. Not a word. If I do he said he'd kill Marie. If we say owt about the beatings we'll get put into care and we'll get it a lot worse there because we're bad children. Really bad. Born bad. He said my mother cried for weeks after I was born. She had to go into hospital because of it. So it's like his job to punish me every day. A cross he has to bear. Our mother didn't want girls, he said. Especially a backward one like me. A retard. A stupid bitch. Marie never got it as bad. And she won't get it much at all, he says, if I keep my gob shut.

"Aye, well you're not too bad. Not as bad as last time, any road," says Nana Cora.

Mum stayed here with me and Marie a few years ago. There were suitcases in the hall and talk of moving away; but then they had this massive argument and Nana made her go home again. 'You've made your bed and you'll 'ave to lie on it!' We had to carry all the bags back again across the common. Me and Marie - we kept asking why we couldn't stay with Nana, but Mum said our place was at home and Nana was right. Only it wasn't Mum getting the stick, was it?

Thing is - Social Services is a really bad place to go, and this is what happens - it's where you're sent if you don't do as you're told. My dad says you live in a poorhouse. You get locked in a room and someone comes to get you in the middle of the night, and they put you in a cellar with no clothes and starve you. Worse - you never, ever see your sister or brothers again. I could never leave my little sister. My sister is my world.

Anyway, it's not so bad at home now if we avoid him. He's out long distance lorry driving, but if he comes back when we're on the sofa watching television he'll get the stick from over the door and start on us straight away. So we know to watch the time. Make sure we're gone.

Marie tells me stories about what goes on at school when we're under the bedclothes at night. If he doesn't come for me that is, which he doesn't much anymore. Not like when I was younger. We'd both pretend to be asleep but he only ever took me. She doesn't know where he took me and I never told her. Never told anyone.

One time, he came for us both and we had to go through the woods to this place - it was a long walk and pitch dark. Marie started to cry out loud - she's a lot noisier, and although she's younger she's bigger than me - and he strapped her right there on the path - and then we were in this caravan and he told her to shut up and stay there until we came back. As we left I could hear her whimpering and trying to control her sobbing. I thought if I let him take me then she would be safe. I said that to her - 'don't worry, Marie - just stay here and you'll be okay. Don't make a sound. Keep quiet.'

I can't remember anything else except just this vague thing - going upstairs in a house, into a back room, which had candles lit everywhere, and a purple cloth and there were men there. A loud humming noise - a kind of chant. I can't remember anything else because I was that scared and I think I fainted or something. Marie remembers the caravan because she was there all night and next day she couldn't go to school because she had a cold. She said there were screeching noises in the forest and she could see torches but she didn't dare come out. She crept under the table and curled into a ball until he brought me back. She said I was asleep and he was cursing because he had to carry us both home.

When Nana finishes scrubbing me she rubs lotion into my back and then we have tea. Quickly. Without speaking. Because it's getting dark and I have to leave before the pit closes and Uncle Rick gets back. Like I said, it's Uncle Rick I have to worry about now.

Once he came home early. Nana had been on the phone and he caught us. His face was covered in coal grime and his eyes looked red and sore. The stink of sweat and pee was overpowering. And then he smiled and I knew I was done for. I shot out of the house and got as far as the woods, but he caught me up and…I can't think about that. That was the worst time. Afterwards, he opened up his zip and peed all over me, in the face. And laughed. He walked away laughing.

One time I was playing at making camps in the woods with my sister and her friends when he cornered me and told the others to shove off; and they did, and I wanted to shout after them not to leave me because I knew what he'd do. They didn't know any better - it wasn't their fault.

Now, as I hurry down the road in the fading light, swinging my carrier bags, I can feel his presence. A quick glance over my shoulder. No, no one.

Fear. It's a tingling sensation starting deep inside my stomach, spreading alarm like a bush fire, to every nerve ending. I pick up speed.

Down at the river the water is chill against my face. Fresh and clear and cold. Washing away all the dirt and sins. It washes away my evil and my filthy blood. All that I deserve. That's what he said.

Uncle Rick. I can hear him on the forest path. Catching up. Already smell the sour ale on his breath. In my face. Getting my spine rammed hard into the trunk of a tree. Fore-warned. Somehow.

Start running.

Along the riverside path my own rapid footsteps pound through my body. Level with the forest now. *Keep running. Faster. Faster.* I can see the white of the caravans up ahead and cut a hard left up the path into the woods. *Please, let there be someone walking their dog or something.* But as dusk drops and lights snap on inside nearby houses - there is no one. I'm totally alone out here.

My heart thumps like a drum against my chest wall. The carrier bags are slowing me down but they're mine and my hands grip them tightly. Nails digging into my palms. Breath hurting. He knows I have to run from village to village and I've no other way of getting back. If I go across the common someone will see me and Social Services will get me and I'd never see my sister again.

Huge hands lunge for my shoulders, and shove me hard into the thicket.

"Now then, you little tease," he says, unzipping his trousers. "Tha can't run faster than me."

I'm up again, scrambling to my feet, but he swiftly wraps rope round my wrist and ties me to one of the branches in the tree. Slams me hard against the bark so my head cracks against it. Sometimes there is another man who watches and smokes; and sometimes he cuts or gags me. I don't bother screaming anymore, there's no point. The other man shoved things into me and then urinated on me as well. I had to go into the river to get it off or my mother would thrash me for being a 'dirty little bitch.' I don't want to go in the river again or get a beating so I lie still.

For a while he talks about a special girl. A good girl.

And I float away. Looking up at the light through the trees…the fading pinks or purity and watch the broken doll on the forest floor - the stupid, dirty, evil girl - as I float higher and higher into castles of cloud.

***

Chapter 19
Tanners Dell, Bridesmoor
Summer 2008

Celeste stood outside Tanners Dell Mill on the overgrown path leading up to the front door, and squinted up at the windows - hollowed-out eye sockets in a wall of solid stone.

After their first meeting, when Ruby had phoned to arrange attendance at one of her spiritual classes, she'd thought the girl was all right. Had been pleased, even. But two days had passed since she had failed to show, and there'd been no answer on her mobile phone either. Ruby had meant to come, she was sure of it.

Something was wrong.

Celeste walked around the outside of the building. On the far side, fresh water rushed down from the moors to the deep river in the dell. The air was sweet and chill, the whole place lush and sylvan, chattering waterfalls cascading over shiny rocks; wagtails and dippers busying themselves on and around the water.

Eyes on her back.

She swung round.

Facing her, legs apart, hands tucked into the belt of his ripped jeans, was a dark-eyed swarthy man in his late twenties, perhaps early thirties. Rough skinned, hard mouth. "Can I help you?"

His voice wasn't local - slightly foreign. Was this Jes - Ruby's gypsy boyfriend?

"I was looking for Ruby. She had an appointment with me but didn't show up and I was worried about her. She said she lived here." She held out her hand. "Celeste Frost."

He shrugged. "I was just packing up the van. *She's* stopping, though." He indicated towards the mill with his head.

"On her own?"

He eyed her for a minute, then shrugged again and began to move off. "Damn right. Got to earn a living. Besides, she's as mad as a shithouse rat, Missus. Don't say you haven't been warned. Take care, now!"

A few minutes later the sound of the van's engine died in the distance. Despite the warmth of the day, the dell was cold and Celeste pulled her cardigan closely around her, before knocking on the door.

The sharp rap echoed inside.

No reply.

She knocked louder, stinging her knuckles.

Still no answer.

Go in…

Obeying her inner voice, Celeste pushed open the door and stood in the hallway. Dust motes hovered in a square of sunlight. "Hello? Anyone home? Ruby - it's Celeste!"

Go upstairs… Celeste…Celeste…

Some of the steps on the stairs were missing, and being of substantial weight, she trod carefully, cringing with each groan of wood as she climbed. Damp permeated the atmosphere, and the thick stone walls glistened.

Halfway up, Celeste stopped and listened. There was a strong, negative energy in here. Children whispering, giggling in the shadows, *shhh*... A feeling of being watched...God, what a place for a young girl on her own! Automatically she crossed herself before proceeding.

A faint sound came from one of the front rooms, at a guess a bedroom. It wasn't easy to distinguish one room from another since much of the main roof was missing, and doorways lay open to the breezy corridors. Once on the first landing, Celeste moved from room to room, peeping nervously into each one. Darkness. Emptiness. Peeling wallpaper in one of them. At the end of the corridor she pushed open the door to a makeshift bathroom, taking in a cracked mirror on the floor, the stained linoleum, a rusty sink...Before her gaze rested on the bath, and revulsion came like a punch to the gut.

Oh my God.

She flung herself against the wall outside the door, breathing deeply. In and out. In and out.

Oh God. Oh dear God.

The scene replayed before her eyes - a mottled body lying bloodless in the bath. *Going to be sick, going to be sick.* Something awful had happened here. A suicide? A murder?

No wonder Ruby had sought her help. Imagine living here! Bad enough for anyone, but if the girl was a medium who couldn't control it, then this would drive her insane.

Celeste...Celeste...

She took a deep breath. What was in the bath was only a vision. Not real. What was real, however, was the fact that a young girl had been left here on her own and she needed help. One more room lay ahead- the largest at the front of the building. She walked into the gloom.

Ruby lay on a stained mattress, facing the window in a slice of sunlight.

"Ruby? Are you okay? It's Celeste."

Ruby didn't move. Was she breathing? Had the man killed her? She took another step towards the inert body just as Ruby turned over onto her back and snapped open her eyes.

Celeste recoiled.

The girl's eyes were sunken in her skull, underscored with deep purple bruises. Her alabaster skin shone with perspiration, and her hands were folded across her chest in the shape of a cross.

The whole room stank of fear, sweat and filth.

Help me God, please help me God.

Celeste crossed herself before moving closer.

The girl's lips were moving slightly: she appeared to be chanting.

Celeste stooped to hear. "When the pie was opened, the birds began to sing...wasn't that a dainty dish..."

And then recognition hit her full in the stomach: the girl was trying to protect herself. Against what? Possession? How in God's name did anyone protect themselves from possession?

There was no time to lose.

A dark shadow loomed on the wall behind, as Celeste took out her mobile phone. No signal.

Hurriedly but carefully, she picked her way back down the rickety stairs, as one by one the wood splintered and broke behind her. This was seriously dangerous now - she must keep her wits about her - who, or whatever, wanted Ruby, was not going to let her escape easily.

Letting herself out into the sunlight, she walked smartly down the pathway to her car. *Please God help me. Please God help me save this girl.*

Overhead, a leaf-laden branch cracked loudly, landing heavily inches from her head.

Celeste crossed herself again and recited the Lord's Prayer, all the time checking her mobile for a signal. *Come on! Come on*! Magically a single bar appeared on the phone, and seconds later she was through to a good friend, Father Adams - a priest she knew well. He'd helped her hugely after the trauma in Woodsend and it was only to be hoped he'd help her again

Thankfully he took the call straight away, promising to be with them by late afternoon.

"She might simply be mentally unwell," Celeste explained. "But there's something very negative in the house - there are no facilities and she's so alone. She desperately needs our help."

"Don't go back in there on your own," he advised. "Pray for her and I'll ask my colleagues to do the same. I'll be there as soon as I can. Oh - and I suggest you call the local doctor."

The medical receptionist informed her that a doctor would not be available until early evening, but that someone would come. Meanwhile, as the hours passed and the afternoon grew heavy, the thought came to her that her phone would ring, and she would be informed that Father Adams would not be coming.

So when she answered and a distraught female voice informed her that Father Adam's car had gone off the road south of Dewsbury - straight underneath an articulated lorry, it came as little surprise.

141

With a heavy heart as old as time, Celeste called an ambulance instead.

Alas, when it arrived, Ruby had vanished.

***

Chapter 20
Doncaster, December 2015

Becky stared at her mobile phone for several minutes after taking Kristy's call. It had been an odd conversation and one she never thought she'd have: Jack had been sectioned again, and admitted to a secure unit miles away, up in North Yorkshire.

Kristy had glossed over the details, telling her only that his confusion had increased and his symptoms had generally worsened, so it had been best for all, particularly Hannah, if he was re-admitted. Without preamble, she then wanted to know if she, Becky, felt okay - bombarding her with questions like if she'd had any odd experiences since coming out of hospital; how she'd come to collapse in the first place; and if she'd fill her in about the day Jack had hypnotised Ruby. Oh, and when did she intend returning to work? How did she feel about that?

Why would Kristy Silver - a specialist from Leeds - be interested in herself?

Becky's conscious mind sat in a pudding of fog. Caught on the hop, she told Kristy she'd just tripped on coming out of the meeting room - that she'd been sure someone had been about to bump into her, but no, she couldn't describe the person. It had all happened in a blur.

The day of the hypnosis? No, she couldn't remember a thing. That would be the concussion, though, wouldn't it, doctor?

Since being out of hospital? Yes, she'd had odd experiences, but that was probably down to the painkillers she was taking, wasn't it?

As for going back to work - yes, she felt fine about it. Thank you for caring. How odd. How bloody, bloody odd, for Kristy Silver to ring her at home. Kristy Silver who usually walked past her in a huff of perfume.

Well, no way was she telling that self-serving madam a damn thing. The woman spent her time swanning round the world, staying in luxury hotels making a name for herself - using the mad, the bad, and the pitiful - to power forth her career. Did she actually cure the poor souls back home? Did she hell?

The bitch got rich!

She sure does, Becky, she sure does...

Becky reached for her box of pills. She was swallowing shed loads. It was a laugh, frankly, when the girl at the chemist asked if she'd taken codeine before and advised her not to take it for more than three days. She had to stop herself from smirking. Right now she was taking 60 mgs four times a day, plus ibuprofen, paracetamol, anti-histamines and Tramadol. The cocktail knocked her out for six hours at a time. Good.

Although she still saw Chester.

Not that she was going to tell a shrink about that. Not bloody likely. Psychotic? Tick. Career down the drain? Tick.

She put her feet up on the sofa and tried to force her mind to function. If only fatigue didn't keep washing over her in waves. It was like fighting anaesthesia.

Mark was out at work. Mark her safe and reliable plumber husband, who would understand nothing. He stood in the doorway looking at her like she was an alien species. "You're all right though, aren't you? You'll still make it to t' pub for a drink, eh?"

God, her husband was thick. However had she come to marry him? Suppose he'd been good-looking once; that it was uncomplicated and sexy. Imagined a future in the little terrace with washing blowing in the back garden, a glass of wine on the patio in summer...bought into a dream...and then woken up. Quite quickly.

And Callum had gone by then, of course. The door closed firmly shut in that direction.

Callum. Her tummy did that fluttering thing. Kristy said he was the one picking her up tonight, that she'd requested his presence at the meeting...*why*? The main reason for her call had been to round up the team. They needed an urgent review of recent events, and it would be very helpful if Becky could make it.

Of course she could make it. Why wouldn't she be able to make it?

Becky stared at Callum's name on her phone screen. She couldn't tell him anything. If he thought for one minute she was nuts she'd lose him. Again. For the first time the full impact of what was happening, hit her head on - just how all-out terrifying was it to lose your own mind? To no longer be 'you'?

Upstairs in the chilly front bedroom, she pulled on a pair of jeans she hadn't been able to get in to for nearly a decade, followed by a bright pink sweater to brighten her mood. Then brushed and backcombed her lengthening hair, sighing at the dark roots as she applied lip gloss and a few sweeps of mascara. She forgot to eat properly these days, went on long walks - usually at night - and rarely slept. It paid to be vigilant when you were psychotic, in case some of it was real. Not that it ever could be. Of course it bloody wasn't. That would make her a lunatic. *Wouldn't it?*

"Oh it sure does, Sweet Cheeks," said an all too familiar voice from a chair in the corner.

Chester was getting cocky now. Less flirtatious and more insistent. *Let me in... Let me in...* Like a lover who no longer bought flowers and dinner out, but idled in front of the television all day instead, demanding attention and carping about every little thing.

It helped to be outside - walking along a towpath or pacing across the fields kept him out of sight and out of mind. At least for a while. But not here in the house. And even in sleep there was no escape. She'd open her eyes. 3 a.m. Always 3 a.m. And there he would be - sitting on the edge of the bed, swinging his little legs to and fro - tip his bowler hat and smile.

"Well hiya, Becky! You know a guy can get awful bored waiting around like this. You gotta keep me occupied or I tell you - I'm gonna make trouble. Really I am. Like you wouldn't believe."

That evening Chester sat on the backseat of Callum's car as they wound their way through the late night traffic towards Drummersgate.

Becky pulled down her passenger mirror, pretending to fuss with her hair, while eyeing the little fella in the back. He was looking out of the window at the shops bedecked with Christmas lights, at the heavily laden shoppers tramping along glossy, wet pavements, and the town's twinkling decorations swinging overhead in the drizzle.

She turned to Callum. "Can you see anything on the back seat?"

He glanced briefly into the rear-view mirror, shaking his head before breaking suddenly as a gaggle of drunken teenagers stumbled out of a pub and straight into the road. "No, Why?"

"No reason."

Shit! This really was in her own head then. It really was. Psychosis pure and simple. Psychosis secondary to depression? Could she dare say anything to the GP, who'd taken over her care? A chirpy woman from Surrey called Penelope who worked part time, in-between baking cupcakes with her privately educated, rosy-cheeked children? *Thanks for the painkillers. Oh and by the way there's a little guy in a black hat sitting on your consulting couch. What should I take for that Penelope?*

Oh God, to be alone with this….Would it be safe to ask Kristy, after all? At least she would understand the condition, and it might be better to have treatment, because it was getting worse and …

"You're definitely not yourself," said Callum.

"What? What do you mean?"

"Since your accident. You seem jumpy, nervous. Is it me? I mean - do you think Mark knows?"

She relaxed a little. Oh so he thought it was just that - something normal. Relief! Sometimes she found herself snapping at Chester in public, and one or two people had looked at her a bit funny. How difficult it was to cover your own madness!

"No. I doubt Mark would notice if I danced round the garden naked."

In the back, Chester sniggered. "Now that would be worth seeing, Sweet Cheeks."

Callum shook his head. "That bad?"

Becky shrugged. "It's okay. I know we've reached the end of our road and so does he, I suspect. But it's finding the right time to discuss it all, and the thing is - I don't want to be on my own at the moment…"

"You wouldn't be," said Callum. For a moment it looked like he was going to say more, except he didn't. .

Becky looked out of the window; the bright shop windows had given way to sprawling estates and windswept car parks. This, she thought, was like not having a safety net, when beneath your tightrope there swirled an endless abyss. No one to help. No one. Not a soul.

In the back, Chester tut-tutted, raised his sunken gaze to the car roof and held up his hands. "What can I say, Becky? Things are gonna deteriorate just like I told ya! Ya know that!" Then his voice changed to a whine, "Oh why won't you let me in? All ya gotta do is say, 'YES!' That's all ya gotta do…the boss ain't pleased right now, and Lady - you gonna feel the pain when my boss gets angry. Know what I'm saying?"

Becky eyed him through the mirror. His boss? Chester was like some kind of little gangster from Chicago, circa 1930's, in his little pinstripe suit and bowler hat. Talking about his boss like he was some kind of mafia godfather. Except for the rancid smell enveloping him, and other things - like the phone calls she answered to furious rants of utter gobble-de-gook; and appointments she'd made, just for her hair or the dentist, only to find when she turned up, that someone had cancelled them for her and the receptionists had all said it had been herself. And the way everyone seemed a long way off. Even now, Callum's voice seemed to come from the end of a long tunnel. Yet Chester's was loud and clear. More real than real.

"Oh just go away!" she snapped.

Callum swivelled round to look at her and the car veered across two lanes of the carriageway.

"Don't!" she yelled, grabbing the wheel.

"What have I done?" he yelled back.

"Nothing. Sorry. I was talking to myself, that's all."

"Yeah," he said. "You've been doing that lately."

***

Drummersgate was lit up like a galleon on the high seas.

The hospital's Christmas tree stood swaying slightly in the mizzle outside the main entrance as they drew up.

"You get out here and I'll go and park," he said.

With a quick glance at the back seat, which was now empty, Becky did as he suggested, wrapping her long woollen coat around her as the wind whipped sharply off the moors. What was real and what was not? Tears sprung into her eyes as she thought of all the patients she'd nursed over the years - the tortured souls who dipped in and out of sanity. And now it was happening to herself. When would the mocking voice resound inside her head again? When did the little chap in the bowler hat re-appear?

"All right, love?" said the security guard as he buzzed her in.

The look in his eyes told her what she needed to know. She was haggard and nervy looking, wasn't she? Aged ten years almost overnight. The peace in her soul destroyed. Once you crossed a certain line, people knew. They could tell with one glance.

She smiled. "Yes thanks, Pete. Really good. I'll be back to work soon - we're just having a meeting."

He nodded. Eyes knowing as he buzzed her through.

People could tell... it was just as Chester said - things would get worse and worse until she did what he wanted...would it be so bad?

"Becky!"

She swung round and it took a minute to recognise him. "Noel! Hi! Oh it's great to see you!"

He gave her one of his massive bear hugs and for just a minute there was safety. Normality. She was back.

Then he held her at arm's length. "You look like fuck!"

"Charming."

"No. I mean - you've lost masses of weight - what? A couple of stone in just a few weeks? That's not normal, Becks. Are you eating properly?"

She frowned. "Yes of course. It was just the hospital food and then Mark hadn't got anything in and I kind of lost my appetite. Not like me, eh?"

"You aren't sleeping either."

"Well, that's probably with not working, and keeping odd hours. I'm all out of sync. Honestly, I'll be fine once I get back to work."

"Are you sure you're ready?"

"Yes. I want to. I suppose a bump on the head can affect you in a lot of ways, can't it? I think I'd be best coming back, though. Getting back to normal and everything."

"You've heard about Jack, then?"

"Kristy said he was really ill - that she'd been to see him and he'd deteriorated again. That's all I know. What's going on, Noel?"

"Thought you'd know, of all people? I mean - you were the only other one there at the hypnosis, and it all seems to originate from that."

She shook her head. God, the nausea. It was so hot in here. Radiators blasting out full heat. She took off her coat as heat flushed into her head and neck.

"Are you okay? Shall we go up to the staff room and let you sit down for a bit?"

He took the stairs two at a time and she lumbered after him feeling like lead weights were attached to the soles of her feet. There was a sensation of wading through water - not getting anywhere - each step a gigantic effort, the temperature racking up until sweat surfaced all over her body.

"God, I feel like I've got the flu or something. The heat in here!"

Noel waited at the top. "You're not at all well, are you?"

"No."

Let me in...Let me in...

"No!"

Noel eyebrows shot up. "Pardon?"

"Nothing. I just need to sit down. I thought you said something."

Behind her, Callum's footsteps raced up the stairs. The two men exchanged a worried look over the top of her head.

"She's not well," Noel said.

"I know. Talking to herself an' all…I reckon she must 'ave picked up a bug in t'hospital. It's a fever. Becks - come on, I'll take you 'ome. No matter what Kristy said - you're not up to a meeting."

Callum's voice was faint, miles away. What had he said?

Let me in… Let me in…

"No! I said no! I meant no."

She heaved herself on to the top step just as a door opened ahead. Kristy Silver stood silhouetted against the light. A tall, elegant blonde in her uniform of a black pencil skirt and crisp, white shirt belted today with red patent. Immaculately made up with cat flick black eyeliner and soft pink lipstick, her brow creased intently.

"I'm really glad you came, Becky, and I've got a feeling it might be in the nick of time. The rest of us have got a few bits of the jigsaw to put together but we'll have to act fast."

Don't go in ..oh please don't make me… don't …no…..

Chester's whiny voice turned in to a childish tantrum.

"Oh yes you are," she said, quelling the sickness in her throat. "You most definitely are going in, and I will make you if I have to!"

***

Chapter 21

Inside the meeting room, all appeared normal. Except it was night.

Sweeping across the moors, a low, moaning North wind occasionally buffeted the walls and shook the windows. While inside, under the fluorescent glare, each looked quizzically at the other.

Kristy sat where Jack normally would - at the head of the table. Isaac Hayes sat next to her, then, around the circle - Claire Airy, Callum Ross (at Kristy's request), Noel, Becky, Martha, and Amanda.

"Thank you all for coming at such short notice," Kristy said. "Particularly Becky, when you're still on sick leave - we all really appreciate it. But this is a crisis, frankly like I've never known, and we really do need every single one of us on the case before it blows up into something none of us can handle."

"Is it about Jack?" Noel asked.

"And the rest," said Kristy. "But yes - Jack is the main reason why we're here." She sighed, keeping her eyes down for a moment. Eventually she seemed to pick up courage and took a deep breath. Eyed them all in turn. "This is going to sound way off beam, and I'm sorry for that, but everything and anything we say in this room tonight has to be totally confidential, okay? I wouldn't normally say anything at all, but we need to be up to speed on recent developments because seriously - if you don't know what's going on, then you may inadvertently put yourself and others in danger. Oh - and every single one of us, myself included, needs to keep an open mind."

She took a sip of coffee, appearing to steel herself. "I think we're all aware that Jack recently treated Ruby with hypnosis? Except something happened during that hypnosis session, which we, as yet, don't understand."

She nodded towards Becky. "Becky, who was present, is unable to remember precisely what took place, which again, is strange. In her own words, she felt, 'numb - as if time stood still.' She recalls time having passed - hours - but not what happened."

She looked at Becky for confirmation and Becky nodded.

"Then shortly afterwards, Jack's behaviour changed dramatically - something everyone remarked on - appointments cancelled, smirking to himself, swearing in front of patients and colleagues. Not to mention his hair turning snow white! And all this while Ruby herself exhibited a quite remarkable and rapid recovery.

No longer aggressive or abusive, she began to make direct eye contact, communicate coherently and take care of her own hygiene. And both Becky and Amanda noted her switching personalities. Amanda and I have spent a considerable amount of time with Ruby since then and she's even drawn us a mind-map - exhibiting probably hundreds of alters, all of which you are aware of. What's odd though, and possibly what you don't know, is that her most aggressive alter seems to have vanished, a fact which appears to have set her free in terms of the others coming forward.

"There are more oddities yet - Ruby's case presentation, along with the location in which she committed her attempted murder, rang alarm bells with me because at around the same time, I was treating another client with a very similar history - and even more astonishing was that he came from the same village. So I took a wander."

"Where?" Noel asked.

"Woodsend."

"Why?" He shook his head as if bemused.

"A whim, I suppose. And this is why I wanted D.I. Ross to be here. Thing is - my client revealed some rather disturbing facts during his counselling sessions - he also has Dissociative Identity Disorder, by the way, although nowhere near as fragmented as Ruby's. Coincidence?"

Kristy took another gulp of coffee and tried to squash the residual feelings of terror as she recalled her trip. "That village - Woodsend - well I can tell you it's a highly unusual place just past Bridesmoor Colliery. Well anyway, it was going dark and stupidly

I took myself off for a look around all on my own. Like the victim in a horror movie, eh?"

A couple of the team laughed.

"Why is it highly unusual?" said Becky.

"Well, nothing apparent at first except it's a bit spooky being in the woods. Anyway, I parked down by the river, which is lovely - enchanting even - and set off walking up the forest path. I honestly thought I'd do a round walk and come home again. But Becky - here's where it got unusual - the path sort of fizzled out and then as the light went, I can only describe what happened as having a nasty encounter: I kept walking up the track, against my instinct to tell you the truth, and there were strange marks on some of the trees, which I took photos of. Then at the top I took a wrong turn and discovered an old cemetery and the ruins of a church or an abbey."

"Five Sisters Abbey," said Martha.

"Oh right - you know of it? Well, yes, anyway, I realised I'd gone too far in the opposite direction but you know how it is - you've stumbled on something interesting so you linger? And then suddenly there was a really hostile man blocking my way. There was a bad atmosphere. ...and I found him very threatening."

A wintry gust rattled at the windows.

"I ran. I know it sounds silly but there was someone else coming and I just ran like a terrified kid. And I kept on running, through the fog and the dark, until I finally got to the main road. And then on the journey home, I felt I took something bad away with me." She glanced at Isaac, who was shaking his head as if he thought she'd lost the plot. " I know - I'm not making sense - but then nothing is making sense, is it? I suppose what I'm saying is that the terror followed me home and I can't get rid of it."

"Terror of what?" Isaac asked, in a slightly mocking tone. "You were a woman alone in dark woods, and you met a man who unnerved you. I'd say that was reasonable. But terror? Really?"

"I can't explain it any better than this, Isaac - but in the car on the way home - something happened - it was like a voice telling me to drive off the road, and no I'm not ready for anti-psychotics, thanks. I mean it - the compulsion to drive off the road was extremely powerful. And back in the woods there were those marks on the trees - like etched codes, just as my client described them. And the man - he was holding a cross. It was very very spooky, I'm telling you. And of course everything can be rationalised at this point - well, if it wasn't for two childhood traumas…"

"One. We don't know about Ruby," Isaac corrected her. "She attacked a man there but didn't necessarily grow up there. There are no records to connect her."

Kristy sat back. "I know. I just have a feeling this is all interconnected. And then there's Jack - because you see, I went to visit him and I have never in all my life seen anything quite like it. And we have to accept that what happened to Jack happened immediately after that hypnosis with Ruby. Okay, are you ready for this?"

The others waited. What on earth was this woman on about? It was written all over their expressions.

"Look - this is the God's honest truth. When I got there, Hannah was in a terrible state. Physically sick with exhaustion and what can only be described as hyper-vigilance. And Jack was unrecognisable."

Kristy described what she had seen and how a chair had hurtled across the room aimed straight at her head. Without him touching it. And laughing like a demon. She related some of the conversation the two women had had, and the mention of a priest being allowed to help him.

"He's now in a secure unit - in isolation. But there won't be a psychiatrist who can treat him - sedation is the only temporary solution we can offer. Hannah has insisted he see a priest. She believes, and after what I've seen I'm not in a position to argue, that Jack is possessed."

A cry of disbelief broke out.

Except for Becky. "Jesus Christ! So that's what it is!"

She covered her face with her hands and started to sob, rocking herself back and forth, back and forth. "Something did happen. It did. I couldn't say in case you all thought I was mad. It's day and night - wearing me down–"

Martha hurried to her side and put an arm round her. "What is? You can tell us - you're quite safe - what is it, Becky? We really do need to know."

"He's always there - a man speaking to me - every time I wake up he's there. It started in the hospital, but I thought it was a knock to my head or being depressed. Thing is, though - he's not going away. He's everywhere and getting more and more insistent." Her voice trailed away. "He's saying, 'Let me in, let me in.'"

Martha and Kristy exchanged a puzzled look.

"Can you remember anything else from the day of the hypnosis," Kristy asked.

"Just sitting down at the far side of the room after Ruby settled down. Then it's all a bit vague - a rapid darkening of the day, and then an odd feeling of detachment like I was at the bottom of the ocean and all the voices were muffled and far away. Almost like coming round from a general anaesthetic when you don't quite know where you are for a minute, and you don't know what happened while you were out. Like that. A sickly wooziness."

"Like you were hypnotised too?" Kristy said.

"Yes. Except…I woke up facing the wall. I hadn't put myself there. The chair must have turned around. I felt dazed for a few days afterwards too, a bit kind of drugged. Then when Jack came in for the meeting and was behaving oddly - cruel and mocking - I had an almost overwhelming feeling of terror. I knew I had to stop him seeing Ruby and so I followed him out of the room, and that's when I must have tripped. You know the rest, except I didn't tell anyone about Chester in case–"

Kristy interrupted. "Chester?"

Becky hung her head. "I've been in mental health too long - I thought if I said I was seeing a small guy in a black suit and hat on the edge of my bed, then hearing him speak to me - even making me laugh - that I'd have my card marked. I thought…I thought…that it was a temporary hallucination and it would wear off. Now though, I'm not so sure. Maybe something did happen that day with Ruby - and maybe Jack and I were attacked by some kind of evil spirit."

"This is patently ridiculous," said Dr Hardy, standing up.

"I would have said that too," Kristy agreed. "I really would - before I visited Jack. And Woodsend. I really do think something is very, very wrong here. We can't pretend any of this is normal, and right now I believe we have to recognise it and pool our resources in an honest and professional manner. No one round this table is a fool and no one is making anything up. This is real terror talking."

"If this stems from whatever happened to those kids in Woodsend, are you saying there's a paedophile ring there, do you think?" Callum asked.

Martha nodded. "It's not unheard of for people to affect each other in a negative way, you've only got to research mass hysteria: if Ruby's experiences were so dark she suppressed them, it is perfectly possible that some material representation of that affected our colleagues to the detriment."

Kristy nodded. "Yes, well put, Martha. Yes, I think that's highly credible. In which case D.I. Ross - yes I do think Woodsend should be investigated."

"On what grounds, though?" he said. "I need a bit more than a few ruins and a creepy forest."

"On the grounds that 90% of Dissociative Identity Disorder cases arise from child sex abuse, and we have two patients presenting with this at the typical age of twenty-five to twenty seven - one from the village in question and the other of no known abode but who attempted murder in the same location. The two men she attacked are from the Dean family are they not? Paul and Derek Dean? Well I've matched the newspaper photograph of Paul Dean and he's the same man who creeped me out in Woodsend: same distinctive white widow's peak. Prominent pale blue eyes. Medium height but wiry looking. It's beginning to tie up."

"Where do we come in?" Amanda asked.

"Talk to Ruby as much as you can - find out what she can remember and what her triggers are."

"She's got a few - someone coming up behind her or breathing into the back of her neck," said Amanda. "Also the smell of Brut aftershave, semen, urine, and wood smoke. Also people in black hoods, people lurking in corridors or doorways."

Kristy nodded. "Yes, and she'll switch to a small child, a stroppy teen or an angry boy, sometimes with no control and sometimes with partial control. Slowly she's coming to realise that she's the host and this system was a genius way of saving herself from the horrors she's endured. I think, believe, that we've only scraped the surface of what has been going on, and Ruby may never be believed or able to live a normal life. We don't even have a birth certificate or a single relative who will vouch for her existence. But she is the key. What is unfathomable to us as mental health workers, is the other matter - this matter of an evil spirit - that's what we can't come to terms with and want to dismiss. None of us are religious. None of us believe in God and none of us believe in the devil. And yet...and yet...if you saw Jack - a man we have all worked with and respected for longer than some of us have even been qualified. Well - we have to do something for him if nothing else–"

"Jack's a huge atheist," said Isaac. "We had a night drinking Bourbon once, discussing religion. Boy is he an atheist!"

"I believe in God," said Martha. "And I don't know about anyone else but I've known Jack since he was a medical student and I'll do whatever it takes to help him. Look, I'm ready for retirement and, frankly, I'm not afraid of anyone in authority, so I'll do some digging on the Dean family - let's see if we can get to the root cause! I've never been out to Woodsend because, as I said before, I was off sick in the mid-nineties and it was my colleague, Linda Hedges, who was working the area during the time when there was all that hoo-ha about a black witch. Then Linda died suddenly." Her hand flew to her face. "Oh my goodness - another coincidence? I went to her funeral, you know - her husband said she'd been fit and healthy. He was heart-broken. 1998 - both Ruby and Thomas would have been junior school age…! Do you think we're talking about black magic or something like that? It does still go on, even in this day and age?"

Callum sat up straight. "Bloody hell! Martha, I think you've just hit on something - this is beginning to fall into place. You won't believe this but one night after I'd just joined the force - about eighteen months or so before your colleague's funeral, Martha - we 'ad this call out, me and my sergeant, George Mason - we went out to this farm on t' top road and there were this teenage girl spinning round on her 'ead. God, it were 'orrible. George died of a heart attack soon after. But it were at the same time! I remember noticing in the local paper about the witch woman and thinking it were odd."

Isaac shook his head. "Religion and pagan superstition by the sound of it. All in an isolated village: poor education, bit of the black arts going on. No wonder a couple of kids got damaged."

"I'm going to look into it anyway," Martha insisted. "There may be nothing in it, of course, but let me investigate. I know Linda left some notes and I've never talked with her husband, so…well, I might start there."

"I think we should meet once a week from now on," said Kristy. "Pool our knowledge - because separately it might seem like nothing - just a series of explicable coincidences - but together there's a picture forming, and we may be able to help our clients, and Jack too. But only if we know what we are dealing with. We've got to be brave and share this now we see it in a different light. And above all we must keep an open mind. Strange things are happening to all of us individually and we have to talk about them, okay?"

Isaac pulled his jacket on. "Dr Silver - I am more than happy for you to take over the care of Ruby. I am more than happy for you to correlate notes on both clients and work closely with Claire and Amanda. And of course," he indicated Callum, "if there is anything untoward in Woodsend then a child abuse case is a distinct possibility and will receive our full and active cooperation. However, what I cannot condone is this talk of evil spirits. I shall go and see my old friend, although I can tell you now that he is not the first and will not be the last, to suffer a breakdown–"

"I bet he'll be the first who can telepathically throw a chair across the room, though," said Kristy, unable to help herself. "And I bet he'll be the first to be able to tell you every last detail about every single transgression you have ever made since childhood!"

Isaac bundled his notes together. "If you'll excuse me I must get back to my wife and family." He nodded at the group. "Good night."

After he'd pulled the door firmly behind him, silence descended on the group.

Amanda reached for her jacket, touched Kristy on the shoulder and said she'd be working with Ruby again tomorrow. "I'll report back," she said, rooting for her car keys. "See you all soon. Next Wednesday's team meeting?"

Becky reached for Noel's hand as he stood up. "Noel - please," she whispered. "I don't want to go home. I can't face another night of it."

"Another night of what?"

She shook her head.

"What do you want to do? Where do you want to go?"

"Church."

He looked askance. "Why?"

She looked away. "I don't know."

He sat down again, keeping his voice low as the others continued to pack up. "Becks, I've never seen you like this. You of all people. God knows what happened in that hypnosis session with you and Jack…but you can and will get through this, okay?"

She looked into his eyes. "I've never been so scared in all my life. It's like everything I thought existed doesn't, and things I thought couldn't hurt us - actually can. I'm sick, Noel. And the reason I want to go into a church is because I'll be safe. Do you understand?"

He shook his head and smiled softly. "Yes, okay, if that's what you want I'll take you - you all right on the bike?"

Becky looked over at Callum, who was earnestly chatting to Martha. No way could he know how bad things were. Her heart swelled into tears. "Yeah, yeah - let's go. Let's go now."

He reached for his crash helmet. "Do you know what I'm thinking? If something evil really is going on in that village, like devil worship or whatever - then how the hell did a child survive if a grown man can't?"

"Ruby?"

He nodded. "Yes. She might be ill but she's not as ill as Jack!"

"I don't know. It's a damn good question."

"It's like, I don't know, like evil can latch onto people..."

Kristy walked towards them. "Sorry - I couldn't help overhearing. That's why we need to compare notes and keep open minds, Noel," she said. "Because I'm not sure any of us can explain what's happening. Look, I didn't want to say this in front of Isaac, but when I was driving home after my horrible encounter in Woodsend, a strange thing happened as I said. But it was a lot more than a compulsion..."

As she related her experience of the old woman appearing in her passenger seat on the drive home, and the feeling she was willing her off the road, Becky's eyes widened and kept on widening until she interrupted, "Yes! That's what it is - a hallucination that's a bit too real. You know it's real - that it's nasty, that it's evil personified...I'm getting it day and night. Thank God you were brave enough to share everything, Kristy, or we'd all just sit here going quietly mad, in case we got locked up and dosed with anti-psychotics, careers and family lives down the drain. Us - of all people! Of course we'd think it's psychosis! But this is the thing - *all* of us psychotic? All at once?"

Kristy squeezed Becky's arm as Callum and Martha finished talking and joined them. "I have a feeling that something or someone does not want us to uncover what's going on in that village," she said. "Here's something else - when I was driving home from Jack's I remembered Hannah saying to watch out for stuff on the road - something that might make me swerve off.

She'd obviously had it happen to her but I didn't really believe her, I have to say. Well I was at full throttle taking a bend, when suddenly there was this child just standing there in the middle of the road. I did an emergency brake and the car spun round and reversed up the embankment, but I swear to you - there was no one there when I got out. I walked up and down that road - and you can see for miles - not a soul. Nothing."

Callum frowned. "Are you sure it wasn't a dog that ran off or summat?"

She shook her head. "No tracks on the road, which was covered in sleet. On some level I was prepared because Hannah warned me, but it was still a shock. Just be aware of the unexplainable, the unusual, the downright scary. Because we are the ones who have to be here to help those most vulnerable - the victims - Ruby and Tommy, and whoever else is still at the mercy of whatever is going on in Woodsend."

"I believe you," said Callum. "I might not 'ave done if it weren't for what I saw with me own eyes all them years ago. Holy crap. Black arts - believe it or not - us lot do come across stuff like that now and again. It's the fear - very powerful is fear."

"I'm going to stay with friends for a bit," Kristy said. "Still in Leeds - but not on my own. Not for a long time do I want to be on my own at night again."

"That bad?" Noel asked.

She nodded. "Even keeping the lights on doesn't work - someone or something keeps switching them off!"

"Shit! Are you serious?"

"Yes she is," said Becky. "I didn't dare say - but that happens to me too."

***

Chapter 22
Cloudside, December 2015

Celeste opened the door to a small woman in a brown bobble coat leaning on a walking stick. The dyed auburn hair had been slept on wet because it stuck flat on one side, revealing Brillo-pad grey roots. She held out a paper-dry hand. "Martha Kind. We spoke on the phone."

"Oh yes. Come in, love."

The maisonette she and Gerry now had in Cloudside - an ex-mining village dotted with a Legoland of 1960's bungalows - was compact, warm and functional. It suited her with it being on the main bus route; having the added benefit of being in the heart of a friendly community.

The intervening years had taken their toll on them both. Gerry had type 2 diabetes and had to use an oxygen mask at night to help his chronic obstructive airways disease. He had a separate bedroom and Celeste was his official carer. Always on the plump side, she'd piled on extra weight, and her vision was not what it was. Peering over her glasses at Martha, she motioned for her to sit down in the small sitting room and flicked on a bar of the gas fire.

"Can I get you a cup of tea, Mrs—"

"Oh Martha - do call me Martha. That would be lovely, thank you."

Celeste busied herself in the kitchen with a teapot and biscuits, while she waited for the kettle to boil. Hmm, that Martha would be taking in as much information as she could from their photos and choice of reading material. Well she wasn't going to find, 'Witches Weekly' if that's what she'd hoped for!

Why was she here, though? Why now?

"Here we are," she said, placing a tray on the coffee table between them, softening as Martha automatically began to do the pouring and stirring. The woman was kind actually, she thought, and possibly close to retirement if the bandaged knees were anything to go by.

Martha caught her eye and smiled. "Arthritis. I've got it in my left hip too. Ooh it does give me gip."

Celeste nodded. "Sciatica as well?"

Martha's eyes widened as she took a sip of hot tea. "Ooh lovely tea. Yes - how did you know?"

Celeste's brown eyes twinkled. "Aha! Well there's some as say I'm a witch!"

The two women laughed.

"Well if you could throw a bit of fairy dust my way I'd not be complaining," said Martha.

"Any time. Spiritual healing can really help. But I only work through the church and never for profit. If you'd like to come to St. Mary's on a Sunday evening I'd be very happy to do some for you."

Martha nodded. "Thank you. Do you know I think I'll give it a go? I've had everything the doctor can prescribe and all I get is too drowsy to work and a sore stomach, which I then have to medicate for, and on it goes. I'd feel a lot better if something natural worked."

Celeste handed her a card. "You're welcome anytime."

Martha took another sip of tea, then set her cup down. "It's actually very good of you to see me and now I feel a bit awkward. I hardly know where to begin, to be honest. I've been a social worker since - ooh well before Eve took a bite of the apple. Actually the only time I wasn't working as a social worker was when I took time out in the mid-nineties for a back operation. But apart from that, this area's been my stomping ground my whole adult life. Ooh, you wouldn't believe the stories I could tell - I ought to write a book!"

Celeste dipped a digestive and waited.

Ruby. A whippet-thin girl with long, greasy hair and far away blue eyes... A washing line and a woman who turns to stare... a woman with black, gypsy eyes...

Their eyes met. "This is about Woodsend, isn't it?" said Celeste. The very image of the place darkened her thoughts and instinctively she drew a protective shield around herself: a strong, white light.

Martha pulled an embarrassed face. "I'm afraid it is, yes, and I have to tell you I wouldn't be asking if we weren't desperate - all of us…I'm part of the mental health team up at Drummersgate, do you know it?"

Celeste nodded. *A dark path winding through the woods…running hard now with footsteps pounding into the ground…moonlight glinting through the canopy of treetops…*

"To be honest I'm hoping against hope you can help us. If you can't that's fine, but…"

"Go on."

"Okay, deep breaths, Martha - look, I can't share any confidential information, but we have a couple of clients suffering from serious mental health issues and both came, or at least appeared to originate, from Woodsend. Now I never had any dealings there myself. But the colleague who covered for me in the late nineties when I was ill - Linda, her name was - well she did! Only she's no longer with us."

"Oh?"

"She passed away from a brain haemorrhage at quite a young age - it was all very sad - and one of the main reasons I was jolted back to work - I'd had depression for a while, you see…Anyway, she left some notes but they're very top line and don't tell me much."

"Try the husband," said Celeste. "I can see he has something…a book, maybe a diary…He's got more - the real story."

Martha blinked. "Oh. Funny you should say that. I was thinking about calling him, but I felt a bit nervous, like I'd be re-awakening his grief."

"Go and see him. He's waiting."

Martha blinked at the other woman's surety. "Yes, I will. Thank you." She took a sip of tea. "Anyway, you want to know why I've come here today and so here's my thinking - biting the bullet here - around that time there was a story in the papers concerning your practicing witchcraft in Woodsend. Apparently the locals - and indeed the church minister at the time - demanded you left your home. Now, I don't know what happened and I'm not here to pass judgement, please don't think I am, but here's the thing, Celeste - we have a young lady in our care who urgently needs help. Something happened to her in that village - something that made her go back there and attempt murder, not to mention disturb her mind so badly that... well I guess you could say I've got to start somewhere. Digging, that is."

"Ah!"

"Can you enlighten us? In any way at all? I mean - any information would be useful - anything! What was really going on in that village? Something you knew about or guessed? Because you moved out and have lived quietly ever since. Something went on, I'm sure of it...and I'm suspecting it wasn't anything to do with you at all. You were, I'm guessing, a threat in some way - am I right?"

Celeste nodded.

"Hmm. You see family backgrounds are often a source of complexity in mental health cases, so social services do get involved; but as I said, Linda - who was working in Woodsend at the time - passed away suddenly and by the time I took over the reins, all the at-risk children in the village had gone."

Celeste nodded, taking in Martha's pale yellow aura. "How interesting. To be honest it's not a place I'd care to ever go back to."

"Why were you there?"

"We'd been given a house. By the council - one of the ones backing onto the woods. I practiced Tarot readings as a way of making ends meet - had done for years. My husband, Gerry, was just beginning to deteriorate health-wise, and things were a struggle financially for us, so I also ran classes in Doncaster at the spiritualist church. I've been a medium for many a year now, Martha. I never asked to be, and I was as frightened as anyone else who finds themselves with the gift; but once you know how to protect yourself, how to open and close it off, as it were - you can live a pretty normal life. So that's what I did - and I tried to help other mediums develop their talent and control it too - always through the church and never making a show of it. But there were some who refused to understand that and made objections. Those in the village, that is. Particularly the local vicar - Reverend Gordon - I can still see him sitting there on my sofa telling me I was evil and it would be best if I left."

"So the local people were frightened by the fact you were a medium?"

"They still came for readings, though. And once word got round I was accurate - the real thing - there were some who didn't like it one bit. And it was them as hounded me out. Daubed red paint across my door with, 'Evil Witch' written on it. Got their kids to bang on my door and throw fireworks through the letter box. My husband had a heart attack with all the stress."

"Oh my dear - I'm so sorry. Did you call the police?"

"Yes I did. Over and over. But after that things upped a gear: a girl from the village came to one of my classes in church and started to disrupt it, telling the others I was a charlatan, a fraud. Although that wasn't the worst bit. The worst was her using my energy to draw up bad spirits. She came to my house with a different name - Natalie if I remember rightly - and practically told me as much: that she'd invited bad entities in using my psychic energy. After that I had horrible experiences, and a girl from one of the local farmhouses went mad, I heard. Anyway, apparently it was all my fault and I'd brought bad spirits to the village. They wanted me out."

"I see."

"I have to tell you, love, that I'm a committed Christian. And I always protect myself and my clients when I do a reading." She fingered the cross around her neck. "I always wear this, you know? If you work with spirits you have to be careful and you have to know what you're doing or you can be vulnerable to the worst kind of spiritual attack. Anyhow, one afternoon after a particularly unpleasant visit from Reverend Gordon, Gerry had a major heart attack and was rushed to hospital. During the months he was there I was left alone in the house, and I don't think I can describe the horror of it - those nightly terrors and how they wore me down. It was then I knew the stress of living in Woodsend was too much. Gerry and I left that spring after Natalie visited. I couldn't go through any more psychic attacks or one of us would end up dead. So you see - I was hounded out but not in the way you'd imagine, or in the way it was reported. I wanted to go!"

"What was Natalie's surname, can you remember?"

Celeste shook her head. "No, but I can describe her as if it was yesterday - black hair and pale blue eyes. Very, very pale blue eyes. Being in the same room as her had the same effect as an ice cube running down your back on a hot day. She'd come to warn me off, of course! Tell me to stop working with spirits because she and her ilk were suspicious that I knew what they were up to. Look, I've no evidence for what I'm about to say, and I could never tell the police or I'd be a laughing stock, especially after I've been so discredited and scorned in the papers..."

Martha said, "Go on."

"Well when Gerry and I first moved there we went for a walk round the woods at the back of the house, and it was a bit creepy. Me, being as I am - I felt an unholy presence there but you know, nothing definable. Well anyway, the light was going and so we decided to turn back. It was just after passing an overgrown cottage, and the path was petering out so we couldn't see where we were going. Then all of a sudden there was this stone circle - shining white, iridescent, in the dusk - and I knew there'd been rites carried out there. I could feel it. See it." Her voice tailed away slightly.... *Dark hooded shapes in a circle, the sky bruised, an eerie light...*

Martha waited. Took another sip of tea.

After a moment, Celeste seemed to flick back into the present day again. "I just wanted to get the hell away from there, but Gerry had walked on and left me. I could see dark shapes forming from the undergrowth, like faceless, hooded monks rising from the damp earth, and I started to back away, calling out for Gerry. I was already protecting myself because I knew. But the thing is, these events can be hundreds of years in the past and I have to keep telling myself that it's not real anymore. Pagan rites happened in the past and sacrifices were made - it's a fact. It's just that I can still see them!"

She shook her head as if to dispel the images physically. "Anyway, I digress…because when Gerry re-appeared he was ashen and not just from being out of breath. He was so shocked it was a long while before he told me what he'd seen. And I'd been so shaken I forgot to ask."

"What was it?"

"An old Victorian cemetery surrounded by white railings. And on one of the graves, as he'd wandered round the periphery, there was a black wooden cross, which had been snapped in two - recently - and left there. The vestiges of satanic rites, Martha. In the present day."

"And you believe the villagers thought you knew this?"

"Well they used every dirty trick in the book to get me out, so they were certainly freaked. Looking back now, I realise my fear may have made me overlook certain other matters, and for that I am profoundly and overwhelmingly sorry."

"Other matters?"

"Well again I can't be sure. And it's nothing concrete. But I can recall that around that time there was a little girl I used to see occasionally. Maybe about six or seven years old? I remember seeing her on the common with a dark-haired young woman in sunglasses, and the little girl was chanting from a book, rocking back and forth. At the time anyone witnessing the scene would have said it was a book of nursery rhymes or something, and maybe I'm putting two and two together and getting six - but looking back I realised that the woman she was with was a neighbour, a divorcee, and yet I'd done her a reading and there was no child. I don't know who the girl was, is what I'm saying. Those Dean children were a menace and running wild - she could have been one of theirs and. I didn't want any more trouble and so in the end we just left. Not a day too soon either."

"Dean?"

"A rough neck family who had one of the cottages down the track which runs around the back of the woods. You know - pick-up trucks in and out all the time, odd jobs, scruffy kids with no manners. Her, the wife, looking at you like she wanted you dead - fag hanging out of her mouth, hair scraped back into a greasy rat's tail, always in trackies. Just rough and rude and nasty - like the worst kind of travellers only they weren't travelling! I'm surprised you lot weren't involved to be honest."

Martha frowned. "Did you ever meet a girl called Ruby?"

"Ruby! Oh yes. I'll never forget *her*. It was much later though and not in Woodsend. No, she came here. Girl of about twenty or so, and very troubled. She was living or squatting I should say, with a gypsy chap over at Bridesmoor in the mill!"

"Why did she come to you, can you remember?"

"Well that's the odd thing. She said the mill was haunted and it was driving her nuts. I sensed immediately that she was a clairvoyant. Told her if anything bad had happened in the past, in that mill, then she'd be picking it up. It was all complicated by the fact she'd been on drugs and was going cold turkey - but there was no doubt in my mind she was psychic and way out of control. Poor girl was distraught! Going mad. Anyway, I taught her as quickly as I could how to close down the psychic channels and suggested she come to my classes at church, because she desperately needed help. Well anyway, she rang after that for another appointment but never showed up. I had the oddest feeling about her, so I drove over there."

"Where? The mill? When was this?"

"It would have been about six or seven years ago, I suppose, and what happened will be imprinted on my memory for as long as I live, I can tell you." She picked up her cup and drained the tea. Poured them both another. "That place had a really bad atmosphere, and I mean terrifying. Menacing. It would have been difficult enough for anyone trying to sleep there, but for someone mediumistic it must have been intolerable. Ruby. Oh dear how can I explain? She was little more than a fragment of a person. A worn out shell. And he'd upped and left - the man she was with - called her a druggie off the streets, which is what I believe she had been before she took up with him, and then taken a hike and left her there. When I found her she was lying on a filthy mattress in one of the bedrooms reciting a nursery rhyme…"

"Four and twenty blackbirds?"

"Yes."

"What did you do then?"

"I called Father Adams - a Catholic priest I know."

"Why?"

"What do you mean, 'Why?' Because the girl was in psychic trouble. I suppose I thought she was possessed. Sorry, I know people like you will think that's bonkers. But…if you'd seen her…"

"Well I'd have called a doctor."

"Yes, and I did. But first I called the priest. Only here's the thing - he died en-route - his car went across two lanes on the M1, and under a lorry. I waited and waited. The GP never came, by the way, and eventually I called an ambulance. When I finally went back into the mill she'd gone. I don't know how she left without me seeing, or what happened to her after that. I think a police report was filed because of the ambulance call-out."

On impulse, Martha reached out and squeezed Celeste's hand. "Thank you. Thank you for trusting me. I've got a much clearer picture now, and a few more pieces to the jigsaw."

Celeste closed her eyes for a few seconds. *That moment…the ambulance crew stumbling back into the twilight clearing, asking where exactly the girl was because there was no one in there. The impatient sighs. The glare of incredulity. How busy they were. A wild goose chase…*

A voice from far, far away cut into her thoughts. "Celeste?"

She blinked and looked into Martha's small, bluebird eyes. "Yes? Sorry. I'm feeling a bit vague…this happens…"

"Look. I'll level with you: we have Ruby in hospital with us. Only she doesn't appear to have any relatives and there is no surname, which is what I'm trying to find out. There's also, as I mentioned before, another client who's suffering a similar set of symptoms - the one my colleague was investigating back in the mid-nineties. On top of that we have some unusual goings-on with the staff who treated them both."

Celeste had half closed her eyes. "Yes, and it's all too late. You're going to have to be extremely careful. I mean it, Martha. None of you will believe in God but it would be a very good idea if you started. I know that will fall on deaf ears."

"I do believe in God. I was baptised." Martha showed her crucifix.

Celeste nodded. "Good. Keep the faith then and start praying. Be vigilant at all times. Something is going on in that village and I fear it's satanic rites. I can see them." She closed her eyes and slumped heavily back in her chair. "But they know you're coming. And there are things I cannot see. Hidden....I can't...it's worse than anyone could imagine...I feel terribly, terribly sick." Suddenly, tears spilled copiously down her pillow-cheeks and she doubled over. "Oh it's terrible what they've done. It's terrible. You have no idea. I had no idea. But now I see ...And you have to be careful. You in particular. Driving home."

***

Chapter 23
Woodsend
3a.m. December 2015

Callum turned off the Old Coach Road before letting the car freewheel silently down Ravenshill to the river at the bottom. There he parked and got out.

The night was freezing; an ice-fresh breeze rushed against his skin from the river, and slithers of moonlight illuminated the forest.

All the good souls of the world asleep…

Dead leaves crunched beneath his feet as he walked along the tow path into the woods, haunted by gradually emerging emotions. Well what else would he be doing? It wasn't like he could sleep. Not with Becky like she was, and worse - turning to Noel for help in her hour of need. Suppose she couldn't really turn to himself without arousing suspicion about their seemingly forever-in-the-shadows relationship? Even so…the guy had taken her hand, and looked into her eyes like he was her oldest, most trusted friend. Noel was a nice bloke, but that hurt. It did. It fucking hurt. God, why did he ever let her go first time round? Just a stupid argument as teens and he'd had to go and marry someone else, with the decades of consequences that brought. Just to show he didn't care. *Stupid, stupid…*

The shock brought him up short.

So incongruously as to seem absurd and out of place, the path ended and suddenly ahead lay a caravan site. 'Fairyhill Caravan Park,' announced an arched sign rusted by damp days and rainy nights. A large open field, bordered to the north and west by the forest, contained just four white caravans, opalescent in the dark. God, who on earth would want to holiday here? Mind you, it was probably ok in summer, what with the river running by it. No facilities though, and everyone wanted to plug in televisions and charge mobiles these days, not to mention take a hot shower. He smiled grimly, remembering some of the scout trips he'd taken as a boy - rubbing sticks together to make a fire - well this wasn't far off!

He flicked on his torch. May as well take a look since he was here. Got to start somewhere. If that Kristy woman was right - and he'd have tagged her as barking if it hadn't been for the call-out with old George Mason all those years ago - then there *was* something odd going on in Woodsend, although it was highly unlikely to be here in this derelict camping site. Usually if abuse was taking place you'd find it deep in the walls of a tightly-knit family home. And try getting into that without a warrant!

The first caravan he came to was an old Alpine Sprite. He grimaced, peering in through the window. Tried the door, then moved onto the next - a similar 1970's style two-berth with an equally unappealing interior. The beam of his torch picked out the murky image of a Formica pull-out dining table and a set of bunk beds. He shuddered, about to move onto the next one, which was nestling closer to the woods, when something caught his eye, and he swung the light back over it.

His heart gave a sickening thump.

Good God.

It took a second or two for his brain to process the information. He switched the torch off then on again, nose to the window. Slowly, oh so slowly, what he was seeing computed to his conscious mind. Nailed to the far wall was an upside down cross. And in the shadowy gloom other artefacts now began to take shape - the pull-out table, now he examined it closer, was dressed like an altar, with a draped dark cloth and two candelabras - one either end. His eyes strained to see more, while his pulse accelerated.

A feeling, just a feeling... of someone watching...

A shiver traced up and down his spine like icy fingers. Gradually he eased himself round to face the woods, and an impenetrable, silent wall of blackness.

Callum flicked off his torch and waited. His own breath came too loudly in the icy stillness. A barn owl skirted the outer length of the field, as eerie and unworldly as a spectre; the air so motionless that the vixen's painful cry, which ripped through the night, made his heart pump even harder. *A fox. That's all it had been. Just a bloody fox. Get a grip, man!*

Still with his back to it, he tried the door of the caravan. Locked. There was no one out here. He was totally alone. And spooked - he had to admit - just bloody spooked! After a few more minutes he walked around the caravan again, shining the torch in to see if there was anything else, any excuse to break in. Satanism might be deeply offensive but it wasn't against the law, he reasoned. He could hardly gain a warrant and bring a team of officers down in the middle of the night just because of an altar cloth and a cross on the wall. Even so, added to the weight of everything else he'd heard tonight, it was definitely worth investigating a bit more.

One more caravan - a longer, static one - remained. The chilly damp of early dawn began to permeate his jacket, filtering through to his back as he walked towards it. He'd have a quick look in the windows of this one and then come back tomorrow. Especially if someone was watching him. Right now, frankly, he'd donate a spare internal organ to be sulking sleeplessly under the cover of a warm duvet than be wide awake out here at this Godforsaken hour. *Whatever had possessed him? Lovesick, jealous old sod....*

Flicking on the torch again, he pointed it through a side window. Nothing. Walked round the back. Still nothing. Tried the door half-heartedly, ready to go now. Unexpectedly though, it was unlocked; and after a quick backwards glance towards the woods, he stepped inside.

Torchlight illuminated shadow shapes on the walls, of his own distorted silhouette, and objects not yet identified. He tugged open the wardrobe with a solitary click, and knelt down to check out the contents of a cardboard crate on the bottom shelf, tentatively pulling back the black cover. Except it wasn't a sheet, he realised, but a hooded robe like something a monk would wear. His brain tried to catch up as one by one, each item contained in the box was revealed: a brass chalice, a pack of syringes, incense…. and something nasty in a bottle - like dark wax. He opened the jar and reeled back from the unholy stink. *What the fuck was that?*

Looked like someone had got a disgusting little satanic cult going on here. One which had probably ensnared some of the local children over the years, guaranteeing they would never grow up to be sane, well-adjusted adults. Nice. Right, well it stopped here. Probably this had caused that girl's madness all those years ago too. What the hell did these people think they were doing? Were they back in the dark ages, or what?

He moved to pick up the box of horrors, intending to take it back to the station, when he glanced inside again, and put it back down abruptly. Was that what he thought it was? *Holy crap.*

He lifted out a small skull. And then another. *A wild animal's? A sacrificial offering? No, too big…too round…oh Lord… this was a baby's skull…a human baby's…oh hell, hell, hell…*

With violently shaking hands he reached for his mobile and took photos, then hurriedly threw the black robe over the lot and picked up the box; only then noticing the row of torches - about five - advancing from the woods outside.

Shit.

Fumbling clumsily, he pulled out his phone to speed dial. No signal.

Fuck, fuck and fuck.

He glanced outside again: the torches were closing in rapidly. *Shit - were they running?*

He backed out of the door, still holding the box. If he bolted across the field towards the river and along the tow path he could out-run them. He'd got the lead. He shot one last look over his shoulder.

They weren't torches. They were flickering. They were flames. What the…?

His breath caught tightly in the freezing air as he jumped onto the frost-hard ground. And then he was sprinting flat out. Picking up speed. Faster and faster and faster…

Thudding footsteps on the turf behind him. Holy crap they really were running. They weren't just scaring him off - they meant to get him.

Panic gripped his whole body. He dropped the box and powered forwards, his muscles searing with heat, heart jackhammering hard into his ribs as he ran flat out in a way he hadn't since being a boy chased through the local housing estate by a gang of school bullies. *Fuck, he was going to die.*

Ahead, the ebullient River Whisper glittered darkly in the moonlight - the tow path seemingly so much longer than an hour before.

The sprint was now a desperate chase. An evil game.

Oh God, help me, I'm going to die. Please not like this, not now, not now I've found Becky, and I love her...why didn't I tell her? Pride, stupid, stupid pride...

Think!

It would take a precious second to look over his shoulder... he couldn't risk it...instinct forcing him onwards, lungs gasping to full capacity, ignoring the screaming acidic pain in his legs...as he catapulted, lurched and stumbled in turn. Stitch crippled his side.

Where were they now? Behind him? Level with him? Minutes to the car. He fumbled for his keys. Yes in the right pocket. Keep them there til the last moment. Faster, faster...rasping breath tearing in his ears...not his own...*almost there though, almost there...*

Suddenly on the path in front, a dark hooded figure materialised.

Callum's glance flicked to the right - the woods were black - no choice...a split second's decision. He darted off the path. Brambles in his face, the undergrowth wrapping round his ankles - twisting, falling, grabbing helplessly at prickly leaves with bleeding fingers - as blinding pain abruptly shot up his leg, and a metal clamp clicked and locked firmly around his ankle.

Just before he lost consciousness, a curious hallucination hovered over him - a circle of hooded, black-robed figures looking down with hollow eyes, one bending down to smile widely with stubs where teeth should be. A man with a white widow's peak and the palest blue eyes imaginable. As translucent as glass. And older than time.

***

Chapter 24
Present Day

4 pm and Kristy sat in her friend's back bedroom, curled up against the headboard. The house was lit up like a football stadium with every light in the house switched on. Yet dark shapes skittered across the walls, the curtains twitched and billowed, and children's whispers echoed in corners.

Let us in, let us in...She isn't part of the gang...she wants to be...

Trying to shut her mind to the incessant chatter, Kristy picked up the book. The one Martha Kind had posted to her the day her heart gave out. The one Linda Hedge's husband had handed over to Martha when he knew what she was investigating. A post-it note had been stuck to the front:

'Kristy - urgent reading! I don't know why but I don't feel safe...as if there's someone following me, probably just tired... but we need to go to the police now - we have more than circumstantial evidence that something is wrong. Martha K.'

Poor Martha. She should have retired to that bungalow by the sea, she really should, and she - Kristy - should never have let her investigate a dangerous case like this at her age. No one had known about a heart problem, though. She frowned for a moment - come to think of it, Martha had never mentioned one either - only her arthritic knees and constant back ache.

Coincidence?

The very air in the bedroom seemed to crawl with an unseen presence. Who was here, watching, listening to her thoughts, waiting to skip like a shadow across the doorway, or blow softly onto her hair? Kristy's heart rate jolted up a gear as she scanned the room over and over, on high alert for the faintest flicker of sound or movement. The books on the shelves - still there...the alarm clock still ticking...What was real and what wasn't? A dream within a dream...or a nightmare from which she could never wake up? Put simply - there was no protection from whatever un-named, un-known force threatened her sanity. Doctors like herself - what could they do? Tranquilise the mad and the bad? That was it - there was no sanctuary from this special kind of hell - no respite and no cure. 'Put simply', she thought - 'something that could not be heard or seen lived and breathed the same air...try telling that to a shrink! '

And now D.I. Ross was missing. His car found burned out and upside down on Bridestone Moors that morning. Pretty much the whole of the local police force was out looking for him.

Another coincidence!

Kristy's hand shook slightly, a trickle of sweat running down between her shoulder blades, as she turned to the first page.

Linda Hedges. Diary. November 2nd 1995

'I'm keeping this diary separately from my official notes. The reason being there are things to do with my latest case and I'm scared. Of what? I don't know. I suppose I just want to document it all in case anything happens to me. Dramatic? Yes, and that's exactly why this is in a private diary. You'll find it, dear Rob, one day when you go through my things. If you aren't doing that then I survived and put the whole thing down to experience, or wild hormones or something. Time of life, you might say, and time to do something else - it's getting to me! Or maybe simply a story to tell when I'm old and grey - there's a book in me, ha ha! Anyway, I'm starting it and maybe it'll fizzle out or maybe one day it will explain things. Let's call it my 'Woodsend Diary' and DON'T give it to anyone else, Rob, because it's politically incorrect....
Well here goes...
A few days ago I was asked to go and see a girl in Woodsend, at the farmhouse just off The Old Coach Road between Leeds and Doncaster. This isn't my area - I'm covering for Martha Kind, who's off with a slipped disc - and I didn't know what to expect. The place is one of those forgotten relics - you pass an old mining village with the pithead wheel scarring the landscape to the left. Then there's a fork in the road down to Woodsend, which you go

past, until you see a long drive down to the farmhouse. I parked in the yard and was left standing by the door for a good ten minutes before this guy in a string vest eventually opened it. Because this is my private diary I'm going to say what I like - he looked like scum on the social! I really shouldn't say that, should I? Ha ha ... burn this, Rob! Really though - we're talking fag-ash breath, a week of stubble, stained trousers and greasy hair. Ugh! TV on full volume. Big dogs jumping round the kitchen going ballistic...you get the drift. Anyway - here's the thing - a teenage girl called Belinda Dean - he called her Belle - who apparently wouldn't go to school, said the devil was out to get her and had started locking herself in cupboards, chanting to herself. The GP had been and said she was depressed, prescribed Prozac (oh please...) and guess what - not even referred her to a psychiatrist...great! What he had done though, and thanks a bunch, was manage to refer her to social services because she wasn't going to school. So anyway, Mr Greasy, aka Derek Dean, asked me to 'sort it' because 'we've 'ad enough on 'er!' Nice!

Fast forward to Belinda's bedroom. No 'Take That' or 'Backstreet Boy' posters, no make-up, fairy lights or nice clothes. Belinda's room was stark. Dirty lino, a bare bulb in the ceiling, grubby bedclothes and one scuffed set of drawers for her stuff. The cupboard in the corner contained an ironing board and a few mouldy blankets - this being where she'd taken to locking herself in at night. The girl herself looked like she was a lot younger than the said fourteen - small and skinny, so pale she was almost grey, with huge colourless eyes and black hair that hung down round her shoulders. Hair she kept pulling and twiddling while I talked and she listened. I'd say she was distracted and distant, almost like there was no one inside. She couldn't recall ever going to school, she said. Couldn't read and write. Didn't have any friends. Hard going! I asked her about the devil preoccupation and she backed up against the wall as if she'd disappear through it if she could, hyper-ventilating. I'll be honest - the whole thing was way off beam. Confrontation followed with Mr Greasy, when I told him I was recommending she see the mental health crisis team with a view to being sectioned immediately. Suspect Schizophrenia t.b.h. Didn't go down well with Mr Greasy, who went off on a major rant, but I think his old mother looked relieved. Looked like Mrs Dean was no longer around - can't say I blame her except for not taking her daughter with her. Neither the old lady nor Derek would say where she was.

Anyway, you'd think that would be that...and the girl would be taken away within hours...but no! Turns out nothing happened. The crisis team came, made a judgement after speaking to the father, and left her in the 'care of her family.' Absolutely unbelievable!

I'm livid. Will be having a private word with her GP to see if a psychiatric referral can be arranged as soon as possible. These things take ages though. I've got a really bad feeling about the whole thing. That girl's room was stark! I mean devoid of a single personal object. And some of the things she said, in that vague other-worldly voice - about dark shapes in the night, a voice telling her to let someone or something 'in' seriously concerned me....she'd started wetting herself and pulling out her hair and nails too. Definitely psychotic. Definitely needs help! I'm going to dig further on this!

November 11th

November 11th

Massive case load (not an excuse but def a reason), which is why I've only just got back to Woodsend. Had a bit of a scout round the area - very deserted, dark and damp, reeks of misery although I can't say why or how. Spooky area at the back of the woods - an old cemetery and a pagan stone circle by the look of it. I didn't hang around. Anyway, I was on my way to Woodpecker Cottage down the track. It looked overgrown and uninhabited but as the light faded a lamp was switched on downstairs and so I knocked on the door. No answer. Thing is - a boy called Thomas Blackmore lives there - nine years of age and goes to the local school. He came to my attention because on checking the local school records the other day after seeing Belinda, I noticed only two children *were registered from Woodsend village - Belinda and Thomas - so I thought I'd pay the boy a visit to see if he knew anything about Belinda, or had seen anything unusual, that kind of thing. Out of order, I know, I'm not a copper - but I am a bit of a terrier when I sniff out a potentially abused child. If my superiors (!) knew how much I dug around off-piste they'd fire me quicker than a starting gun at the races.*

Anyway, I've tried several times now to find Thomas and can't! Consider myself on a mission....

November 13th

Spotted a small boy running like the clappers through the woods. He shot past my car on Ravenshill just as I was getting out, and tore past me faster than a hunted fox. Couldn't catch him - not a chance - middle-aged woman in trench coat and court shoes! Knocked on the door - no answer. I'll tell you what though, that child was small and very emaciated, pasty faced and running for his life! Something wrong here...

November 16th

Paid another visit to the farmhouse - this time unofficial. Confronted by Mr Greasy again. Very angry man, who kept looking me up and down trying to intimidate me. The whole place stank of dogs and re-heated chip fat. Old lady looked worn out and wary - beady eyes flicking nervously from him to me and back to him again . Mouth working itself up for a row! I asked to see Belinda and was told she was sleeping, but what had I done about getting her taken off their hands? Explained I'd handed things over to the GP and she should be having a visit from a mental health professional very soon who would treat her at home. He threw a blue fit. I promised to follow up, push things through. Meantime would he tell me about next door's boy because I was concerned there was a link between him and Belinda - i.e. it was a possibility that someone or something was scaring them both out of their wits. Mr Greasy went 'ape' and told me I was barking up the wrong tree and it was my job to get Belle 'gone'. She was ill and that was it!

U-uh!

Something odd - note - no furniture in front room apart from a table and chairs and dresser all at one end. The rest was barren. Bailiffs in? Big 4x4 truck in the drive though so they can't be that destitute...

Took another wander into Five Sisters Woods. Another scout round the cemetery...a lot of small graves with no markings. I don't know if I should tell the police about two scared kids and a spooky graveyard... not enough to go on...just a feeling. Got flu coming on...

December

Don't feel well - backlog to do...just heard Belinda was sectioned last night after two coppers were called out. Relieved in a way - hope she'll now get the help she needs. They had to take her to Leeds children's unit as she's under 16. Well that should be the end of it. She'll get anti-psychotics and hopefully recover nicely. Thomas is going to school each day, apparently, so between his parents and schoolteachers I shouldn't hear any more. Happy Christmas!!!!

January 1996

Decided to dig the Woodsend Diary out again.... bit of hearsay. Apparently Derek Dean's estranged wife, Kathleen Dean, has been allocated the end semi at Woodsend. Don't know where she's been in the interim, but seems she went to a friend's and just left her daughter to it!!!!! Wonder why she's come back if her husband was violent to her, which it's documented he was.

April 1996 - local invalided gentleman and his wife, Mr and Mrs Frost, recommended for re-homing on an urgent social basis. Mr

Frost has chronic obstructive airways disease and a serious heart condition. Circumstances at Woodsend are significantly contributing to the couple's distress. Alarm bells in my head. Local children and taunts of witchcraft. Nice lady - don't believe she's causing anyone a problem, more like the other way round. She's had media intrusion, her name trashed, and when I arrived 'Black Witch' had been daubed across the door only spelled incorrectly - 'Blak Wich!'

Recommended an immediate transfer on the grounds of their safety. Wish I had time to investigate further.

January 1997

Long time since I was called out to Woodsend, but Thomas Blackmore was reported as behaving oddly in school and the teacher asked me to visit his home environment. Fat chance. Can't get in for love nor money. No answers. Try again!
Tried three times. In the end I saw him at the school gates - gaunt, frightened child. Refuses to speak, just shakes his head and stares at the floor. Won't learn. Won't integrate with other children. Big question - does he go into care?

March....Thomas taken into care in Doncaster. Police made contact with parents who handed him over without a quibble. He'd told one officer he'd seen hooded black ghosts floating through the woods past his house, holding fire-lit torches. I only got to see him briefly. For the record he will not speak AT ALL. My curiosity is piqued again. Two kids now safely removed. But two highly disturbed kids with no explanations as to why! I wish I wasn't covering two posts, and had time to dig around a lot more on this. I always had a sneaky feeling there was something amiss in Woodsend but just no proof! Discussed with D.C. Ross. Shocked to learn that his Sergeant collapsed and died of a heart attack on the night they had Belinda Dean sectioned. Doubly shocked to hear about the circumstances in which they found the girl.

Anyway, all should be well now with the kids removed!

June 1997

I'm not keeping my diary very well but this is what I recall from this visit to Bridesmoor... Called out to Tanners Dell Mill. What a place - down by the river surrounded by thick foliage and hidden from view. You wouldn't know it was there if you hadn't sought it out. Tow path in front goes directly to Woodsend. Path behind trails up to Bridesmoor village through the woods. Carrions Wood to the West side.

Old guy - needs medical care but refusing to leave his home. Ought to have someone going in to him, says GP.

Hmm...all not as expected. Pale, unnerving blue eyes in an ancient, reptilian face, white widow's peak, leering, lechery in manner. Scary old goat! He sat there in a string vest and boots, dirty, stained trousers...stank to high hell - urine ineffectively veiled with Brut aftershave! Ought to try soap and water once in a while! Coughs phlegm up in front of you. No hanky, no tissue... Nice!

Seen some sights but this is one of the worst. There's a tree growing up the middle of the living room through to the floor above! Tin bath in the yard. Table in the kitchen covered with an oil cloth - milk bottle, loaf of bread, ketchup and brown sauce left out, sink full of greasy washing up. He won't go upstairs, says no one's been up there for decades. No heating. Sleeps on a dirty old blanket on the sagging sofa. If ever I've stepped inside a haunted house it would be this one. The walls seep with damp and the lights flicker on and off. You just feel relief when you get outside. Not a nice man, not a nice atmosphere. And here's the spooky thing - I was there to help him get nursing and medical care delivered, yet all he was concerned about was what I was doing snooping about! What did I know? What had Belinda or Thomas said? Like I know! Put my hackles up though...It was like he'd had me summoned!!

July 1997

Came back to Woodsend on a hunch - just parked up with a sandwich lunch by the river. Nice day. Walked along the river and discovered a caravan park. School hols, so bit odd no one was around, yet there was washing hung outside one of them. Took a walk up the forest path past Woodpecker Cottage, then on up to the stone circle. There are some odd carvings etched into the tree trunks on the path to the old cemetery. Rusted railings, once white. Odd place... even on a hot day with bees buzzing and the light full and golden, the air in the cemetery was bone cold. Not a single butterfly or bird - yet the woods were full of them! I took another look at the little graves - so tiny - children were smaller centuries ago I suppose - that's what I thought, was thinking, when this man appeared out of nowhere. Very similar in looks to the old guy at The Mill - same widows' peak and pale, glassy eyes - but younger, middle-aged. Same unnerving aura of mockery and menace, though. Asked me what I was doing. I said looking for a place for a picnic...Didn't like him - just a gut feeling. His eyes were on my back as I hurried away down the path into the forest. Felt like he was making sure I left, marking my card...

October 1997 -

Called out to the mill again. Old Mr Dean has taken a turn for the worse. Nurse refused to visit any more due to sexual harassment. Situation to be reviewed with regard to him being admitted to hospital. Won't listen to the GP. Ambulance told to clear off!
    On arrival I was greeted by a young woman with long black hair who was not exactly welcoming! I asked if she was related to Mr Dean and she said she was his niece, Natalie. She refused to let me in, said the nurse was 'a lying bitch' and they were considering suing for slander. Then she started laughing! Bizarre!
    I asked if she was taking care of him and she said they needed cough medicine if I wanted to help. I tried to ascertain if

they were refusing hospital admission. Mood changed. She looked me up and down before shutting the door in my face.

November 1997

First chance I got. Glorious blue-sky day. Crispy leaves and bonfire smoke in the air. Love it. Blackberries dying on the brambles now, but oh I don't know - there's a magic about this time of year. I just want to re-visit the cemetery - thing is, my curiosity is piqued again after doing a bit more research. There used to be a nunnery here, which also lends its name to the woods: Five Sisters Nunnery. That explains the ruins. I wonder if the cemetery belonged to them and the little graves were for orphans who were sent to the nuns? Infants who died in their care, perhaps?

Cutting to the chase because it's getting dark and I'm dog tired; anyway this is what I did - I decided to walk back to Ravenshill via the car track, which runs past a house on the right, instead of down through the woods again, as it was getting too dark. Met the man with the widows' peak. This time he was standing in the path barring my way. I could see a kind of trailer trash outfit over to the right, instead of the house I'd imagined was there - I'll call it the gypsy camp - and a woman with the blackest eyes I've ever seen was dead-eyeing me from the doorstep. Now she really did look like a baby-boiling black witch if ever I saw one! Had to sidestep the man, who laughed in my face. Rancid breath.

Ashamed to say I felt fear. Real fear in the pit of my stomach. Next time I'll be sure to come here in full daylight - if and when I get a chance. There's something I'm missing. Not enough to actually report though....

February 4th 1998

Cold, frosty morning. 9 am. Not what I expected to find - closer inspection reveals there are no dates on some of those tiny graves

- while the older ones have dates between 1649 and 1901. These are the weathered ones with Celtic crosses and may have been from the nunnery. But the whiter ones are relatively recent and unmarked. Maybe animals? Surely not children with no engravings on the headstones? What about the bereaved parents? No flowers, no grass growing round them.

Something else - ash. Fresh piles of ash.

Just let me check something…

<u>*February 5th 1998*</u>

No, there are no records of any infant deaths or burials in Woodsend.

***

Kristy closed the book. Linda Hedges had collapsed with a brain haemorrhage on February 6th 1998, and never recovered.

She looked up, mulling over what she'd read. So there was a possible connection with old Mr Dean and The Mill in which Ruby had been haunted so badly in 2008. Had Ruby really picked up what had happened there because of psychic gifts? Or had she been a victim herself and remembered the trauma? And now the matter of tiny graves in that ancient graveyard -one which had not been used for centuries yet contained relatively recent, unmarked burial plots. Maybe they were animals? The remains of sacrifices?

Callum hadn't known about either of those two pivotal facts before he went snooping, and neither had Martha. And now he was missing and she was dead - her desperately sad funeral held only a few days ago.

Kristy stared into the empty air of her friend's spare bedroom, her mind concentrating on the facts, trying to pull them all together. She had to get a report to the police first thing tomorrow morning, and hand over Linda's diary….see what could be unearthed…

Suddenly the ceiling light dipped, rendering the room gloomy for just a second. Before plunging it into total darkness.

Slow to react, Kristy stared helplessly as the door to the landing slammed shut at the same time, the breeze ruffling her hair. Downstairs, the sound of cutlery being clattered in the kitchen carried on, along with the soft hum of her friend's television set. She tried to call out but no sound came. Attempted to move, to throw off the quilt and walk to the door, yet her limbs remained leaden weights. Dully, her heart thumped in her chest and nausea rose like a nut kernel to lodge in her throat. As, gradually, so insidiously as to become almost acceptable to the mind, a figure materialised in front of her: a small girl with a bloodless complexion and blue, doll-like eyes, in a white dress.

"Be careful, Kristy," said the tinkerbell voice. "You're next."

***

Chapter 25
Leeds, November 2013

9 pm and it's fucking freezing. Still, it's work isn't it? The first car to slow down is a people carrier, so the hypocrite's got a family. Rolls of lard bulging over his waistband, stinking coffee breath and big open pores on his nose. Imagine the saggy, hairy arse on him! Puke! A disgusting old pig in an anorak. No wonder he's got to pay for it. We're the only women dirty old gits like him can get anywhere near. Anyway, he's offering me twenty quid and I've done worse. Helps when your brain's fucked with smack. Like, who gives a shit?

"Get in," he says, indicating the passenger side door.

His eyes dart to my crotch the minute I sit down. Garlic, stale sweat and unwashed flab make me want to vomit. I'm trying not to gag - but it's like I'm already on the way to getting my next hit. If I don't I'll die, it's that simple. Two minutes and we'll be parked down an alleyway and seconds later, trust me, it'll all be over and I'll get the smack.

Only it isn't seconds, is it? This is one of those nasty ones where he grabs the back of my hair and slams my face into his groin, calls me all the filthy whore names his pea brain can come up with and then does what he promised not to - comes into my mouth. All that disgusting, slimy scum. Only positive thing being on smack - you don't feel much. It's like it happens to someone else and that's fine - in my case, it actually does.

"There's a good girl," says he, zipping up and laughing as he pushes me out of the door.

***

When I wake up the light's changed to a kind of blue. The room is arctic cold, my breath steaming on the air. Through a gap in the curtains snowflakes billow round a streetlamp like fairy dust. It's night time again then - God, where did the days go? And how many? Because my guts are cramping and my mouth's dry.

He's silhouetted against the doorway.

"Getting up this week or what, you lazy bitch? You look a right mess."

Charming as ever.

"I need a hit."

"You need a fucking shower."

He's right. There's this woman in the mirror opposite, with hair that hangs like dirty curtains, bruises under her eyes, blood on her t-shirt. *Blood? Did something happen I don't know about?*

"We have to have a little chat, Ruby. Take the shower then we'll talk. You can have real coffee if you tell me what I need to know."

Now Jes isn't someone you can lie to. It's a struggle to remember stuff sometimes, though, and if he doesn't hear what he wants to hear you get a slap that'll knock you across a room and into next week. You've got to think on your feet, like, all the time because he'll smell a rat if you try to hide so much as a cigarette butt. He's got Romanian and Ukrainian girls here now - bit of language problem - lots of screaming going on…

So is it them or is it me? Screaming, I mean. Sometimes I don't know. All I know is, looking at him sitting on the stained sofa peppered with burn marks a few minutes later, is this - I'm in deep shit.

Think, Ruby, start thinking. Where was I?

"And?" He pats the seat next to him. Bares his teeth with the gold fillings. "I'll ask you one more time, Baby: what - the - fuck- do - you - know - about - the - guy - who - got - his - head - smashed - to - a - fucking - pulp?"

I don't know…

His shark grin dies in an instant. Then he examines his fingernails, stroking the knuckle-duster rings he wears. Another second and the back of that hand will slash across the side of my face. "Don't lie to me, Ruby. If we've got tracks to cover I need to know."

My brain sits like a lump of wet, grey concrete. Nothing. No memory. It can't be me. I'd never do that - I work, get the smack, sleep it off. That's it. God, I'm so cold, there's a sweat rising on me. I'm going to be sick.

"It was with a brick a few days ago. You were seen, Ruby. Katya saw you get in his car."

Lying bitch - just getting herself off the hook. There's a nerve in his jaw starting to twitch. *Seconds. Think!*

How the hell did this nasty bastard get into my life, anyway? The muscles in my face contract in painful concentration, trying to think through the fog - some distant memory of Jes from a long time ago…a swarthy but craggily handsome face looking down at me through a river, being dragged out and slumped into wet dirt, his mouth clamped onto mine, a huge swell of pain in my chest…Where? Where, though? There's rushing water and whispering voices in stone walls, and it's so very cold…I just can't…it's like there's a dream I can't quite catch…

"Ruby, wake up. Come on, wake up. Okay, I believe you - take this - hold out your arm."

As the syringe goes in, I'm shivering so badly my arm judders and his grip tightens round the tourniquet.

"I don't know 'owt about a bloke getting bashed, honest…" I'm saying, thinking, 'fuck he's good at getting the needle straight in - no skin pops from Jes - just an immediate highway to the stars'. Oh, oh, five, six seconds top and oh, oh God…like the best rush of warm, golden euphoria you could ever imagine. Exquisite bliss - heat filling my lungs, muscles melting into honey, arms wrapping me up safely like angels from heaven.

Thing is, you sometimes get this magical high but then you spend the rest of your life trying to get it again, because trust me it's like nothing on earth and once you've had it nothing else comes close. You crave and crave it, and if you do it right you almost get there again…And boy does he do it right.

God, that's good. So, so good…So safe, so sweet, so warm…

It's over though now - God, already - as fleeting as an orgasm - with a cold draft on my back to hasten the descent. Down and down and down… falling into the deepest water well, down and down to where it's dark and wet and hard. Oh please, not so soon….he should have given me more…I need more to stop the crazy dreams. But there's a dead weight climbing onto my shoulders now, pressing me down to the floor, legs crumbling under the weight, eyelids closing.

Numb. Anaesthetised. No more thoughts. No more memories.

"Better?"

I look up.

He smiles. Dark eyes. Black as glittering coal.

"Mmm."

"Back out tonight then, yeah?"

I shrug. Stumble to the door. Maybe got an hour before I need to get another fix. Hope there are a few punters out there, even with snow on the ground.

***

It's slippy underfoot. And sleeting sideways. Passing traffic sprays the pavements with dirty slush and people are rushing to cars with coats over their heads, groups of girls laughing and shrieking. Music pulses out from bars and oblongs of buttery light spread out across the pavement. That's a world that isn't mine.

People don't really see me - I am what I am - because once you've crossed the invisible line into a darker world then everything in that other world ceases to matter. So my coat's open to show what I'm wearing - stockings and a black pvc mini dress. Drifting down Chapeltown in a daze. Just need to be picked out in headlights, called over, climb in and do what I have to do.

A gang of lads stagger past on a pub crawl.

"Whoa - a prossie. What you charging, luv?"

"She'd have to pay me - look at t' state on 'er–"

A lucid moment. Looking sideways at my reflection in the window of a kebab shop, a cadaverous, sickly old woman stares back at me - a horror movie of mottled skin whiter than death, pockets of darkness under hollowed-out eye sockets, blood-red lipstick like an open gash. A woman of the night. Laughter snorts into the freezing air. A woman of the night…a vampire lady working the twilight zone…

Who's that? 'cos it ain't me!

"Fuck me!" someone says. "Fucking, fucking hell."

Doing a double take, there's another woman in the street staring at my reflection with her mouth open. A snapshot - that's me only years ago! *Look at what you could've had…* Next to me she's got colour to her hair and light in her neatly made up eyes, which are painted with liner and mascara. I look her up and down - taking in the sensible court shoes and dark wool coat, pink scarf, shoulder bag tucked tightly under her arm. Same height. Same features. Different world. What is she, then? Some kind of fucking social services bitch? Only, hang about - a foul mouthed one. How funny! She's just seen her doppelganger! Poor cow - imagine seeing what you'd look like if you were a drug-addled hooker! You'd curse like a navvy, an' all.

I stare back at her reflection. "Got a problem, love?"

"Ruby, I'm Marie!"

"And?"

Her hands fly up to her cheeks. Tears in her eyes. "I've been looking for you for ten years."

I laugh. "How do you know it's me? Even I don't know that."

Her reflection turns to stare at me. "Look at me, Ruby."

Ruby…

Something stirs.

A fragment. Whispers under the bedclothes.

"Marie?"

"Yes. Your sister, remember? Oh please say you know me! Ruby, listen to me - there are things you *have* to know. Do you remember Alice? Tell me you remember her! Please, please!"

I shake my head. "Gotta go to work." In the background there's a car slowing down and I whirl around. A punter. Twenty quid is life or death. It's like I got the worst kind of flu and it'll get worse and worse if I don't score soon. Stomach twisting already. Badly want to crash. I walk towards the kerb.

"No, wait!"

"Get off me, you mad bitch."

She holds on, though, fingers digging into my arm, her tone urgent and hard. "No, I'm not letting you slip away - Ruby you had a daughter when you were fifteen. Baby Alice. Shortly after the birth you left home, and I was told you'd taken her with you. I've been trying to find you both all this time. I've moved heaven and earth but—"

My heart lurches into my chest. "A kid? What the fuck's going on?"

"You got pregnant at fourteen. I remember you going into labour. But when I came home from school you'd both gone—"

"Fuck off lady - you're messing with my head."

"It's all true. I searched everywhere but Mum and Dad said you'd upped and left, and if I spoke about it to anyone official I'd be whipped to hide. I asked Nana Cora and she said it was your choice - you'd gone for a better life. I believed it for a while. I was thirteen. But later I knew they'd lied."

Nana Cora!

The pavement is rising up to meet me then panning away again.

The punter leans out of his window. "You working or not?"

I turn back to him, just as this woman, Marie's, words cut into a rare moment of lucidity, "Ruby, there are no records for your existence! Police can't search for you because you don't exist and neither does your baby. Ruby, I think he's doing to Alice what he did to you."

I spin round. Look into her eyes. My eyes. The palest blue. *He*.

I've never been so sick in all my life, and that's coming from someone who's been cold turkey more times than a Christmas leftover. Sick until my stomach burns in acid. Until someone, something else, takes over, and I can float away...

***

Chapter 26
Laurel Lawns Private Medical Home
December 2015

The others in here were bonkers. From those who paced across their rooms a thousand times, occasionally raging at the television with shaking fists, to the ones who tracked and ate spiders found in the skirting boards…

Jack rocked back and forth in his chair by the window, idly observing the reflection of fairy lights in the snow. Barking lunatics, all of them. What a strange mystery madness was when you really thought about it - not so much those with delusions and hallucinations such as in schizophrenia - which had a chance of being understood and treated - it was more the lost souls who hadn't a clue who they were - living out a human life in the shell of a body, which withered, festered and dried up before its time. Take Bertha down the hall, whose stomach protruded like there was an alien three stone baby in there waiting to pop out these last twenty years. She'd once eaten a snake, was the explanation. And that snake needed feeding.

Maybe their souls were living a perfectly normal life in another galaxy - after all, quantum physics suggested there were at least eleven parallel universes - but the body had been accidentally assigned to this one. Imagine the confusion! Did they have a body in the other universe? Or was this a duplicate? Maybe mad - truly mad - people were here to help everyone else appreciate their own sanity, or to induce compassion? God didn't cock up, did he? So there had to be a reason. Or…and here was a thought - because these souls were such easy meat for vengeful spirits when they'd no driver in the seat of consciousness - maybe they were possessed by evil spirits? And that was a good one - nicely played Satan - because there was not a chance in hell of a medic, even in their wildest nightmares, blaming a demon.

Frankly, once you'd been incarcerated, your only protectors were doctors, who in turn, had little in their armoury save a handful of drugs to sedate, lift depression or alleviate the symptoms of psychosis. That was it. And even that came at a price. Those anti-psychotics, the older ones for sure, made the poor sods look mad if they didn't before - gripped as they were by violent, uncontrollable twitches and tongue flicking. At least they had a chance though. The truly mad had nothing. And the possessed were fucked.

A chuckle (his own?) resonated around the room. Once a nice room with pale blue curtains, a television set, and a shelf stacked with books and films to watch. Now as barren as a padded cell. He'd been in that a few times too. Foaming at the mouth, kicking and biting, wondering why his body was convulsing and vile filth was spewing out of his mouth. They'd left him there for days. First strapped into a straight jacket and later restrained with padded cuffs to an iron bed. Dry food sat in his stomach like lumps of acid to be vomited straight back. Water ran through his body and seeped down his legs. Every muscle ached, his eyes blood sore.

He wouldn't be going back there. Had a word with the demons inside. It paid to be polite to the medics - to smile and agree with perfect, intelligent logic. That's what got you out and kept you out. The padded cell, with the accompanying rage to his heart, would kill him before he'd exercised maximum destruction, he'd explained to the demons inside. The Kingdom.. Hissing, sighing, they'd retreated for a while...but not for long.

You're not getting out, Jacky boy. That's not the point. We're in the last stages, you know that!

Damn voices. Why had he told the medics he heard them? Olanzapine would have done a fine job if he'd actually got fucking schizophrenia. Instead all it did was make him pile on weight and go to sleep a lot. What a joke. How come every single psychiatrist in here was a fucking atheist, anyway? Not one thought of a priest. There are loads of us in here sucking up demons - we need an exorcism not a fucking anti-psychotic! Mind you - he would have done the same. No way would he have thought about demons and priests. Fair cop.

A wave of depression washed over him.

No way out.

That's right, Jack. Biggest trick the Prince of Darkness ever pulled ...to convince the world he doesn't exist!

They'd assigned him to his old mucker, Isaac Hardy, on account of how he'd attacked his pregnant wife in the ambulance. So now he was a forensic patient dosed up on the full drawer of sedatives and anti-psychotics. All of which made it so much easier for the demon to hop into the driver's seat and have a high old time before writing him off as a car wreck.

Reasons to be fearful, part 1: take an agitated, well-to-do schizophrenic in relapse. A young man who had high hopes but now doesn't. Have a little chat about his particular brand of paranoia - someone on the television with a special message from The Kremlin, perhaps? And watch, from the recesses of your mind, as he breathes in your toxin. Swallowed and absorbed. Observe helplessly the change in the young face, as his pupils flicker lilac, the neck swells, and pulse points bulge…oh what strange hell to come...night descending then as lunatics, ever alert to the supernatural, wail from within their four walls, curling into balls, whimpering and calling out. Trapped souls. Watching black shapes lift out of a pile of clothes before crawling across the floor towards them. No one believing their stories next day - how a reading desk scooted across the floorboards in the blink of an eye, how their locked door flew open and they found themselves lying rigid and freezing in the corridor outside; or, worst of all, the choir of voices chanting the bible backwards incessantly through the night.

Yes, we understand - here's a bit more risperidone and something to help you sleep a bit better.

There had been four suicides since he'd arrived. All young. All temporarily out of touch with reality, left here in a salubrious private mental health facility to be rebalanced and returned to normality. Alas they never did. Three others had gone home to their middle-class, professional backgrounds where maximum damage could occur. With no one suspecting the quietly spoken doctor. His rages, sometimes heard from behind closed doors, were nothing to do with their son's increasing paranoia or their daughter's upturn in violent self harm. There was no connection. .All he ever did was listen, offer sensible counsel, and teach them chess.

Jack remained staring across the extensive lawns, at the frost, which spread like icing on a cake; at the grand, sweeping firs tipped with glitter as day sank into evening, and a crescent moon hung like a scythe in the lightly starred sky. This had once been a country estate for a wealthy family, whose parties popped and tinkled with champagne and music, whose furniture gleamed with beeswax while fires crackled in every room. Now the corridors echoed with wailing lost souls, and black shapes oozed under doorways.

So people who came here had money, which made not a jot of difference because a mad house was a mad house. Except they had wild salmon and asparagus on the menu instead of a gristly cottage pie. A knot formed in his throat at the thought of food. When had he last managed a bite of anything? Tracing down his ribs, each bird-like bone protruded like a toothpick.

Sometimes, increasingly rarely now, a flickering thought became his own, and panic set in. What had happened? What was real and what imagined? Was that really himself banging his head repeatedly on the floor - blood matting like jam on his forehead? His own body being thrown from its warm bed in the dead of night, smashing and crumpling against the wall like a broken doll? A far distant fragment played with his waking dreams, of trying to get his fists to stop hitting his wife in the ambulance. Yet those fists had continued pummeling into her soft, white face, her throat, her protruding belly - even as she lay on the floor and sticky dark blood dripped from her mouth and pooled around her thighs … A tear swelled and plopped down his cheek at the exact same moment a raucous cackle erupted from within. It was happening again. His eyes darted from side to side. It was coming…

As always, it started with electric shocks. No leaping around, more a kind of hot-whisky-burning-through-veins feeling, neuroceptors frying, sparks tingling all over his body; followed by a creeping, knowing intelligence easing its way under his skin, before sliding into his brain.

Above the sink, the crack in the mirror widened and groaned, and shadows crept along the walls. He pressed the emergency buzzer. By now the nursing staff knew what to do. He'd be tied to the bed again, sedated, put out of conscious misery for as long as it took.

Good-bye, Jack. See you later.

No way, pal. You've got a special visitor coming tomorrow and we're excited. Don't think you'll stand much of a chance of fucking her, though - not looking like that, buster.

***

At ten the next day, Kristy stood at the foot of Jack's bed. The man was unrecognisable. Blood rushed to her head and she leaned onto the metal frame for support. He could only be days from death.

After a moment she turned to Isaac. "Have his parents been informed?"

"Yes. His mother's asked for the priest. Last Rites, I suppose. Irish Catholics."

Kristy's eyes opened wide. "You suppose? Have you checked it's for the Last Rites?"

He sucked in his breath. "Why? No. But you can see…of course it is. To be honest I don't understand how he's gone downhill so fast. He complains of something in his throat preventing him eating, but we've had a full physical examination done - poor old chap's had scans, blood tests, tubes down the oesophagus - the lot." He shook his head. "And he's repeatedly pulled out his drip at night even though we've sedated him. I have to say this is the worst case of treatment resistant psychosis I've ever come across."

"Isaac - if this is psychosis I might as well train to be a beauty therapist. The man is possessed. I never thought I'd say anything like that in my life but he's bloody possessed by something - a demon - something terrible. I'm scared to death. If this can happen to an educated, strong man like Jack…"

He stared back at her in disbelief. "I don't believe I'm hearing this from a fellow professional. Dr Silver - Jack is suffering from psychosis secondary to depression, as you well know. He believes there is something in his throat and that's why he can't eat. We've had round the clock care and you can see the state of his arms from ripping out IV tubes! I suggested a life support machine but his mother won't hear of it. She's on about his soul too."

"Excuse me? Psychosis secondary to depression? Are you serious?"

"Yes - hallucinations, delusions, paranoia, almost no insight, need I go on?"

"Accepted. But you've talked to him - you know, you must, that he has an inexplicable knowledge of others' personal lives, that he talks with multiple voices, blasphemes every other word, and abuses himself. In addition, and verified by the staff, there are external phenomena such as solid objects moving round the room, foul odours out of nowhere, and the electrics blowing. Nor can you put the cadaverous frame, the black unblinking stare or the attack on his wife - down to schizophrenia. His total personality changes. And no drug regime works…There have even been multiple suicides here since he arrived."

"Oh you're surely not inferring–"

"Isaac - we are in a different league here - out of ours anyway - and it's one we know nothing about - this man needs a priest to conduct an exorcism or he's going to die and so is his soul!"

Isaac leapt back from her. "Oh, I hardly–"

He got no further. Both doctors turned to see the bed shaking as if it was in an earthquake. Then Jack's eyes snapped open, the pupils brilliant red.

"Dear God," said Isaac.

A guttural choir of voices erupted from his former colleague, the tongue flicking in and out like a chameleon. "Fucked any chambermaids recently, Dr Hardy - me old mucker? A Philippino for a tenner when your wife's at home wondering where you are? Don't think we can't see you, you sanctimonious twat! We know you very well - just how low down you really are…come closer my friend…we need to *verify* something, mother-fucker–"

A deep red flush burned its way up Isaac's neck, scorching the side of his face faster than a bush fire. He turned to Kristy, unable to form a sentence.

She looked hard into his eyes. "I need to know. Is he right - have you? Because–"

His sickened expression told her what she needed to know, while behind her Jack's emaciated form began to thrash violently from side to side.

Then stop dead.

His eyes locked with hers.

'Enjoying your dreams, Kriiiiiistyyyyy…?'

***

Chapter 27
December, 2015

Becky lay in crisp, white sheets staring at the skylight. In the circumstances there couldn't be a better place in which to wake up - Noel's flat was a modern loft conversion in the heart of Leeds, with pale wooden floors and white paintwork - lit today by the dazzling light of winter snow. A wedge of it shifted and slid down the glass pane. *Was it Christmas yet?*

"Is there anything else I can get you?" Noel asked, hovering in the doorway.

She shook her head slightly, unable to stop stinging tears from coursing down her cheeks. It was a good thing, she told herself, to feel this pain. Not to be numb anymore. A good thing. It meant she was human and would be okay.

"Are you ready to talk?"

It had been three days now. Three days since Martha Kind's funeral. Four since Callum had been reported missing, the burned-out shell of his car discovered upside down and abandoned on Bridestone Moors.

She nodded.

Noel drew up a chair, turned it round and sat astride it. "How you feeling?"

"Exhausted. Confused."

"Mark's been ringing. All he wants to know is if we're having an affair or not. I've put him straight but he doesn't believe me."

"Well this doesn't look good, you have to admit!"

"No. I've told him I'm as gay as a row of pink tents, but he just said people could change."

Becky smiled, almost laughed. "Yes, he would say that. He thinks it's a choice."

"Becks - first things first. Can we go back to what happened at the church because I'm still reeling? And scared. "

"So am I."

He reached across and squeezed her hand. "I know."

She closed her eyes, steeling herself. "Okay…"

"Start at the team meeting. When you asked me to take you to the church."

"The team meeting - my God, that was the last time I ever saw Martha! Do you realise I've known Martha for the whole of my adult life? She was the social worker when I got my first placement in Doncaster. I still can't believe it. She was really looking forward to retiring - to doing something other than working. She wanted to travel and do a cruise, bless her. I just can't believe it, Noel, I really can't."

"Me neither. I've never seen a funeral so well-attended either. She was loved by everyone, wasn't she? It was such a shock. Here one minute then gone - doesn't exist anymore - it's hard to get your head round." He reached out and took Becky's hand. "I wonder what happened to her, as well? I mean, it doesn't make sense. As far as I'm aware she'd been at home that day. Just popped out to the post office and never made it back. I suppose, just guessing, it was the strain of everything that had been going on? But she was fine at the meeting, wasn't she? What did she say last, can you remember? What was it she was going to do… let's take it from there."

"She said she was going to Woodsend to investigate the Dean family, and also to read her colleague's notes - the one who covered for her back in the nineties - what was her name, again?" She shook her head. "Didn't she say she was going to talk to the woman's husband? That she'd died suddenly and he was devastated?"

"Hmm….yeah, I remember now. Linda, I think."

"So she'd presumably read Linda's notes? Had she visited Woodsend? You see I don't know. I only know how ill I felt that night. Still, you know she was sixty-five and she'd had a lot of health issues. Poor Martha."

"I didn't think she'd had a heart condition, though. Just rickety hips and knees. So we've got another woman in otherwise good health, investigating Woodsend and suddenly she's dead as well! Another coincidence, Becky? It's like Kristy said - it isn't each individual story it's the whole picture! Almost every member of the team associated with Ruby has become seriously ill, which brings me back to you...I mean, do you still see this um...apparition...Chester? Because that's who you were speaking to that night - someone the rest of us couldn't see!"

Becky regarded her friend and colleague closely. He'd seen the worst and yet she was still here, not under lock and key doped out of her head. By rights she should be in the local psychiatric ward pumped full of anti-psychotics. "No. Not since that night."

"Do you remember anything after we left the meeting?"

"I've got a vague image of not physically being able to enter the church. I could see the soft red of the carpet down the aisle, and candles flickering on the altar in the distance, but I couldn't get my legs to move. I was focusing on the stained glass window at the back...but I just couldn't get there."

"You were screaming. Except it wasn't your voice. More like a teenaged boy, and you were saying the same thing over and over, 'Don't make me go in there, don't make me, I can't - I hate you, I hate you...'"

"That sounds like Chester!"

"So the hallucination spoke?"

"Oh yes - he was a tiny man in a sharp suit and black hat with a New Yorker accent, or maybe Chicago - I'm not good on accents. He was funny and charming, and then kind of wheedling and sometimes nasty. He first appeared after my accident, sitting on a chair at the side of my bed. I thought it was the head injury and didn't want to say anything to the nurses for obvious reasons ...but here's the thing - he followed me home! And then it just got worse and worse...and don't ask why I didn't confide in anyone! I'd lose my job, you know I would!"

Noel said nothing.

"Anyway, I got into the church so I must have managed to keep him out!"

"Keep him out?"

"That's what he wanted - he kept saying 'let me in, let me in,'....that's how I started to guess it wasn't my own madness but something external. All he wanted was for me to say, 'okay', but the more pressure he put me under the more I feared giving in to him. I had to keep my real self separate and strong if that makes sense? I knew Chester wasn't real...so I wasn't psychotic. But who'd believe me if I said he was an independent entity? What could I do? Noel please don't look at me like that - trust me - Chester was an obsessive, intrusive thought. A very real one, though."

"Okay."

"Actually, I don't remember how I did that - overcame him and got into the church - because I've got a memory of suddenly being at the front praying, but not of actually crossing the threshold!"

"I dragged you in, then I called to a priest, who was in there praying, and together we forced you inside, with me frantically telling him it's what you wanted even though you said you didn't. It wasn't nice. In the end, we sat you down in a pew with one of us either side of you, and we all prayed together."

She nodded, frowning. "Yes. And there was all this light streaming through the stained glass windows. I begged and pleaded inside my head. I thought of the days I went to Sunday school as a kid, and some of the hymns we sang... *Immortal, Invisible*...I thought of my old dad and he was smiling and beckoning to me to come and look at the sunflowers on his allotment. He played in a brass band, you know? How long were we there?"

"All night. All three of us."

"Who was the priest?"

"I don't know. Michael, he said. I went back to thank him but no one knew him."

Silence bathed them in the silvery, white room; snowflakes collecting wetly in a lower corner of the skylight.

"He saved me, you know? Because I feel cold and real and, I'm not sure how to put this, but 'alone' - like there isn't anyone watching me anymore. I can remember things, but it's like they happened to someone else in a very bad dream. It's weird."

"I understand."

They let the silence grow, as only truly good friends can, taking solace simply in each other's presence.

Eventually, Becky asked, "Noel - is there any news on Callum? Have they found a…a body?"

He shook his head. "No."

"Where did he go after the meeting? He didn't come with us to the church. I deliberately made it clear I didn't want him to in case he thought I was bonkers, but I wish he'd come now. Noel - I …I loved him."

"I know."

"How? How do you know?"

He smiled sadly, kindly, squeezing her hand in his. "I just do."

"Thank you."

"For?"

"For just being there. Not asking. It was an affair and it was wrong."

"That's okay - I'm not here to moralise and judge you."

"Thing is - we knew each other from schooldays. He was my first! We had a wedding planned, then I went out on a stupid, wild drinking night and someone told him I'd cheated on him. After that he went away for a while and when he came back he was cold, different. Joined the Police Force. He met someone else and the rest is history - two kids, divorce - then came looking for me when it was all way too late: my mother told him I'd re-married and so our paths veered off in different directions again and he never knew the truth. Until last year when we attended a case meeting about a patient we had. We sat staring at each other, unable to talk because of everyone around us. After the meeting he asked me for a quick coffee, no strings… and then it all came out - how the so-called friend who told him I'd been unfaithful had been someone he'd thrashed on the football pitch and wanted revenge. That simple."

"Oh Becky!"

"I'm not sure it would have worked out, to be honest: we both had issues, but well you know... there was no one who made my heart skip like him! Not before or since. And now he's gone."

"Not necessarily. I'm guessing he snooped around Woodsend after our meeting and encountered someone nasty, maybe that guy Kristy mentioned? Anyway, I'm sure he can take care of himself and he could be hiding out! Doesn't mean it's the end by any stretch of the imagination. And remember the whole Force is out looking for him. Woodsend is practically under siege."

"Is it?"

"Well there were police cordons round the caravan park and tape round a cemetery at the back of some houses."

"Did you go to look?"

"No. It's in the papers. There's a lot of talk about black witchcraft, dating back years to when a local witch was reputably driven out - funnily enough in the mid-nineties when Martha was off sick and Linda was covering for her. So maybe Callum happened on some kind of satanic cult and they wanted to silence him?"

Becky stared. "I bet that's it! And if those kids who were taken into care - Thomas and was it Belinda - had been subjected to it? My God, it's all making sense."

"Hmmm...I'll be honest with you though, Becks, I'm not happy about this evil spirit stuff - I'm easily spooked. After I watched 'The Exorcism of Emily Rose' I didn't sleep for a week!"

"And yet you took me to a church instead of a mental health unit! And that was after everything Kristy told us about Jack and her own experiences! You must have been scared witless? That must really have gone against your grain?"

He nodded. "Yes. But it was what you asked me to do and somehow I just knew I had to. That there was only me. And I'm glad I did because I kind of feel stronger now, if that makes sense? I'm not sure how to explain myself either, except that here you are

- back to health - so what happened in that church? Something good...that's all, something spiritual and good."

"We humans don't have all the answers, that's for sure."

Noel nodded. "Makes you re-think everything, doesn't it? About mental illness, and everything you've ever been taught, really?"

Becky blinked away another sudden rise of tears. "Noel - do you think Callum's still alive? What's your gut feeling?"

"I don't know..."

Suddenly the flat buzzer sounded, severing the conversation. They looked at each other, eyebrows raised.

"Mark?" Becky said.

"I'll get it."

Becky reached out and grabbed his arm. "No. You don't deserve his temper and he has no idea what we've just been through. Leave it. I'll sort things out when I'm fully recovered. Until then I'll message him and tell him it's nothing to do with you - that I'm ill and need some help. Leave it - please!"

The buzzer sounded again, a palm flat against it for a good twenty seconds. Followed by the sound of footsteps receding down the hallway.

"I think we need a coffee, don't you?" said Noel, standing up.

"Noel?"

He turned at the doorway. "Hmm?"

"Do you know what's happened to Jack?"

"They had the priest to him, according to Isaac. I think, only based on hearsay, that he's gone home to Ireland with his parents. I don't think he'll ever be the same again, though."

"But is he well? You know...sane? Okay - you know what I mean?"

"He was exorcised, Becky. I didn't want to tell you in case it freaked you out."

"Exorcised? Oh my God! So someone else thought he was possessed? How did that happen in a hospital? Oh my God, oh my God...this is a fucking nightmare. We're living in a horror movie.

Oh God, Noel, I'm so, so scared. That means…what happened to me too…?"

"Isaac was pretty cagey about the whole thing, but it seems Jack's mother got a priest in, and the resident M.O. agreed. I gather it was originally for the last rites but the priest ended up being there for two days. After that he was whisked off to Ireland with his parents. According to Isaac he was hours from death when he and Kristy saw him."

"The M.O. agreed to an exorcism? Really?"

"Things had been happening in the hospital - suicides. Isaac said it was a last resort and very hushed up. I gather he's okay in that he's alive, but you know - finished really - certainly as a doctor. Oh and Hannah lost the baby, too."

"Oh no. Oh that poor family."

"I know."

"Oh God, poor Jack! And that could have been me too…"

"Yes. But you knew to ask for help. You must have had your faith deep down, Becky - you must have! It's the only difference between you. But Jack had very clearly and publicly rejected everything spiritual - even argued against it on many, many occasions - I heard him myself! So I guess he didn't have anyone to ask for help…he couldn't ask God if he didn't believe he was there? I don't know - I'm just guessing. Poor bastard."

Becky turned to look at him full on. "You know, everyone who was directly involved with Ruby has been under psychic attack! And we've all been totally unprepared and unguarded because we're looking in the wrong direction - basically at the pharmaceutical industry to cure all ills! Shit, you know what this means? That now there's only me, Amanda and Kristy left on Ruby's case? And we've still not got to the truth. We don't know who she is, where she came from or what happened to her except she went after Paul Dean in Woodsend. Why? A satanic cult? And how come it's affected the rest of us all these years later? Frankly, and we've got to face it, none of us have any idea what we're dealing with or what to do about it!"

211

"Correction - there's actually only you and me left, Becky. Amanda resigned yesterday - she's apparently been taking a lot of time off anyway. And Kristy's disappeared."

"How do you mean - disappeared?"

"She's taken a month's leave to do some lectures, followed by an extended holiday."

"Oh great. I actually thought she was onside! It's not exactly a brilliant time to go swanning off again, is it?"

Noel shrugged. "She'll be back."

"I know, but a month! There's no one for Ruby now…I'm still off sick and you weren't even her case worker."

"I know. Lousy timing, I agree."

"So why did Amanda go? I can't believe it."

"She was shit scared, Becky. Let me get those coffees."

"Noel?"

He sighed demonstrably. "I'll die of caffeine withdrawal in a minute."

"Sorry, no but listen, Noel - is it Christmas?"

"Yes, angel. In three days time."

After he'd gone, Becky slumped back onto the pillows. If she didn't know better, she'd say there was an unwritten conspiracy to stop anyone from ever discovering what happened to Ruby.

And now there was only herself to do the job. Which she would do - for Ruby, for Callum, for Martha, and for Jack. Because there was a person at the root of this - someone who was getting away with the worst imaginable abuse anyone could inflict on another human being. And that someone had also unleashed an unknown, uncontrollable darkness on an unsuspecting world.

From deep within herself, an unexpectedly warm, honeyed feeling spread through her veins - a renewed strength, along with the realisation that if this was the very last thing she did, she'd find that person and drag them into the floodlights by the hair, for all to see.

She waited for an inner voice to tell her she was crazy - to jump ship now like Amanda had done, in the name of self-preservation. Only that voice never came.

***

Chapter 28
Cannes, Provence

Kristy stretched and yawned, reached for her mobile and clicked on, 'One New Message'. Amanda Blue!

She scrolled down, started to chuckle, then threw her head back and laughed raucously until the tears ran and her stomach muscles hurt. Ruby had apparently stopped in the middle of a drawing and told Amanda she was 'next'. Amanda was worried enough to resign: she was a single mother with a small child, and the pressure was too much. She hoped Kristy would take care. 'Only u & B left now who know full story - pls watch ur back! U know where I am if u need to chat.'

Kristy deleted the message, then tossed the mobile onto the plush cream carpet and lit a cigarette. Boy did it feel good to smoke - like a liberated, rebellious teen all over again! On the bedside table there were two empty champagne bottles. She emptied the dregs of one into a glass and looked at her watch. She'd to give a lecture in fifteen minutes.

Her suite was on the top floor of a luxury hotel overlooking the Mediterranean. She'd been upgraded after a contra-temp with the haughty, rather smug receptionist last night. Made a fuss to the manager, and ended up staying in the presidential suite, which came with glittering chandeliers, a king-sized bed, a black marble bathroom with a sunken bath, and a full sound system. How decadent, how thrilling - to listen to The Rolling Stones full blast while soaking up to your neck in scented bathwater! Rising naked from the steam she'd lit candles and admired her own body in the many faceted mirrors. Such, such….self-indulgent pleasure!

Room service had been even more satisfying...Champagne on ice, smoked salmon, cocaine...Kristy's mirth bubbled over as she pulled on yesterday's clothes and buffed up her hair a bit. *Fuck - where were the notes for this lecture? Oh well, piss it - winging it would have to do!*

In the cheval mirror there was an expression of shock, though, on the pinched, ashen face looking back at her. There were smudges of grey beneath her eyes, the pupils tiny as a pinhead. Something not at all right with that reflection. Was that herself? She peered closer, tracing her fingers down cheeks that seemed more bony than she'd imagined, avoiding eye-contact. Something not at all comfortable - almost, she thought, like looking at someone else instead of yourself. Someone you didn't recognise. How odd! Must be the cocaine...*Cocaine? Kristy? Cocaine??*

She stepped back in alarm, suddenly aware of the creased clothes, and the blood. *Blood?* Blood smeared on her smart, nude court shoes. Blood grouted into her nail-beds, and streaked in her hair.

You can't go out like that.

The woman in the mirror smiled then, the eyes glinting shades of lilac and purple.

No you can't. You mustn't. What will people think?

Again, the reflection ignored her. Shrugged. And grinned.

Please stop. No, don't do this. Kristy!

Watch me. Moments later she stalked into the marbled foyer, located the bar and ordered a double whisky before entering the conference hall and walking up the aisle, past hundreds of fellow psychiatrists and psychologists.

On spying her, the conference organiser visibly breathed a sigh of relief and rushed forwards with a microphone clip. "Ah. Dr Silver. Thank goodness. We thought you'd got lost. "

Kristy climbed the steps on the side of the stage, her footsteps cutting into the wooden floorboards as she walked towards the lectern. For a few silent moments the audience waited while she fiddled around with the laptop. Nothing seemed to work properly. And where were her notes? *Oh God, had she left them in her room?*

She stared into the darkness of the auditorium for several heart thumping moments. Tired, she was just tired.

Someone whispered in her right ear. A sharp, hiss of a whisper. "You have just been deconstructed. How does it feel?"

Kristy whirled around to see who had spoken, but there was no one behind her on the dark, empty stage.

She turned back to the lectern, trying to ignore the white faces staring up at her from the front row. *Think, think…*she could do this without notes, of course she could. This was about Dissociative Identity Disorder and no one knew more about this subject than herself, especially as the paper she'd had published was a case history she'd been working on for years. With or without a Microsoft presentation she could do this.

"You're being an arrogant, stuck-up bitch again!" said the nasty hiss. "Everyone hates you, did you know that?"

She twitched a glance over her shoulder, before examining the computer again, and re-checking the connections one by one. *Keep calm. It's okay. Nerves, just nerves…*Nothing worked, though.

Finally, she switched it off. Coughed and cleared her throat. She had to say something. Anything. She opened her mouth, but with horror realised a voice other than her own was speaking. Something low and foreign, syrupy thick and guttural was coming out. Mostly though, and here was the real shock of it - the voice was male!

She flushed hotly, sweat rising under her skin, sticking to her palms, oozing under her arms. From deep within the audience there came the sound of confused murmuring, rising to a droning hum.

"Dr Silver…"

Kristy peered into the dark auditorium. "Who's there?"

The voice now came from the side. "Dr Silver!"

She swung round to the left. "Who's out there?"

"Dr Silver!" The voice now to the right.

She swung around and around again and again. Where was the voice coming from?

You need to tell them what a whore you are! After your husband fucked that cunt in his office, tell them what you did…tell them how you got yourself fucked up the arse in an alleyway, you dirty fucking bitch…by a patient…

"What?"

"Dr Silver - are you all right?"

You're just a filthy, disgusting whore - a dirty slut - a pill-popping pig...not fit to be human. All we've done is give you what you really wanted - what you really want because that's who you really are...just a drug-addicted whore...

The strange thing was, these iron-heavy legs of hers wouldn't move and yet her body must be pacing back and forth along the podium because there were people trying to hold her, footsteps pounding along the floorboards, strong arms grabbing at her own, which were flailing wildly in the air, although they too felt dead and disconnected.

Who was shouting obscenities? Who was being so nasty and disgusting? Saying the worst imaginable things? Was this a breakdown. Was this what it felt like? Oh my God.......

A hot, pouring-out feeling exuded from between her legs. Crushing pain cramped her stomach. Loud giggling echoing in the black bowl of her head.

"Help her!" someone said.

"Get her off the stage."

"She's ill. We need to get her to hospital."

Jesus Christ - I've been stopped.

***

Chapter 29
Tanners Dell, November 2013

I've been here before, haven't I? Only it's a hell of a lot colder this time - freezing, in fact - with most of the windows broken or missing, and just the few damp twigs I could scavenge, hissing and spitting in the grate. Got to keep it together, though. It'll take a day. Less. For the right moment.

That's all the time I'll have anyway, because Jes'll know where to look. And looking is what he'll do when he sees half his stash missing - look I had to get it from somewhere! Anyhow, he's not daft - quick off the mark for a smack head pimp is Jes - and if it's a choice between a day without smack or a beating, I'll take the beating anytime, know what I mean? I've got just enough to see me through...just...if I play it right.

Night's closing in. It happens fast here in the woods. One minute smoky and grey, the next it's so black you can't see the hand in front of you. There are voices out there...getting a flashback...out of the window, coming out of the trees are torches flickering and floating in a long line....No, they're gone...What was that then? A dream? Or a memory? God, I don't know. My brain's shot to pieces.

From here you can lie low, really low, like no one in their right mind is ever gonna come here, especially at night. Maybe I shouldn't have lit the fire? Better stamp it out. How stupid am I?

I need it pitch black before I leave. Quarter to eleven now. Fog curling round the tree trunks, smoke and dead leaves heavy in the air. It's so, so cold in here and getting colder, damp sinking through my clothes, soaking into my spine. I wish I didn't have to hole up here of all places, but it's the only place no one's ever gonna see me. Even local teens don't come here to shoot drugs or drink lager or get a shag or whatever. You can hear the dripping damp, rats scratching inside the walls, and there's whispering in the corners, like bitchy girls snickering behind their hands giggling with malicious intent. It's seriously fucking creepy - like you're being watched from the shadows, fingers stroking your hair, a puff of breath on your cheek, silvery laughter…Even tramps don't hunker down inside these walls for the night. Not a living soul….

I can see things. Hear things. I know they aren't there. I know it…yet knowing that somehow makes it even more terrifying, because it's like…what the fuck's happening? What is this?

Just now I had to go to the bathroom, if you can call it that, picking my way down the endless gloomy corridor, and there on the floor was a cracked mirror. I picked it up. Staring up at me from behind my own jagged reflection was a woman, with wet, dark hair and bruised, hollow eyes. Eyes that moved around in their sockets to make me look at what she was looking at - in the bath…a child, more a baby really, having purple, mottled skin peeled off and the fat cut out with a knife. A woman with a coal-black stare looked over her shoulder and her gash of a mouth split open to show a toothless grin. I dropped the mirror, glass splintering on the floorboards, and ran back in here - an upstairs room with some dirty, damp blankets and a clear view of the woods below.

We know you see us. We know you're here. Ruby, Ruuuubbbbyyyy…………

It's just a place to hide out. Not long.

Lying here now, just waiting. Shutting out the whispers. Picturing the journey, going over and over how it's gonna be. There's this thing I have to do, because my mind floats off and when I wake up again whole days will have passed. So it'll be too late if I don't keep this together. *I am Ruby. I am Ruby. I am Ruby.*

Keeping it together. Blocking out the images. Images of the floorboards underneath me being pushed up, creaking and groaning, bloodied hands squeezing through the cracks…*Don't fall asleep. Don't drift off. I am Ruby. I am Ruby…*

They wake me, though, the spirits, rousing me into a half dream - fuck! I didn't drift off, did I? Heavy boots are clomping up the ladder that serves as a staircase. Clomp. Clomp. Clomp.

Footsteps moving down the dark corridor, each door being squeaked open, hinges groaning with rust.

My heart slams hard into my ribs, the beat pounding in my ears...I'm trapped. Is it Jes? What day is it?

The night now is a total blackout. But the moon's position hasn't changed...I could have sparked out for less than a minute.

The sound of breathing comes from behind the door, and the handle starts to turn. But Jes would be shouting, calling for me. *This isn't Jes.*

Is this real, though? It feels like someone else is living this. As if there's a distance between me and whoever's experiencing what's happening. No, it isn't real...Like I know the woman in the mirror wasn't real. This happened to me before - I saw stuff through other's eyes. Things happened here that I know about and can see and they know it. *They...* Like I know the man on the other side of the door has the palest eyes and the hardest stare I've ever seen. That the woman who was skinning the baby is without a flicker of humanity. That the children who once lay here in the dark knew what was coming.

I'm one of them.

I want to speak to those children - the ones who wet themselves long before gnarled claws reached down to snatch them from their beds, the ones whose tiny hearts gave out in fear, their faces now zooming close range into my own one after the other. I want to tell them they are safe now and not in this terrible place anymore - not trapped in this dark, hellish crypt. Their souls can dance freely into the light... But my body is floating across the floorboards as if in a trance, to open the door.

I'm staring into the face of a man older than my father - a man with an expression so chilling it cannot possibly be human. My body arches like a cobra, spitting venom, pushing past him, tearing down the ladder until a freezing rush of air blasts into my face and the roar of thousands of tons of water cascading in torrents over shiny, smooth rocks, drowns out the guttural rage of a man thwarted.

Don't look back. I am Ruby, I am Ruby. Keep running. It's time...

The track through the woods is hard and dry, tree roots covered in the slippy death of decaying leaves. But this is a nightmare well-rehearsed. Every venal fork in the path as it splits and veers off, is marked, if you know where to look, with elder signs carved into the bark.

Don't look back.

The towpath is lit with the faint silver light of a new moon, shaded with belts of fog and high cloud. Occasionally stars twinkle fleetingly, and shadows dance across the path. To my right the River Whisper gurgles darkly, lapping and glugging in the reeds. This is where I have to run like a hunted fox. Like hell. And vanish into the forest.

The second I'm in Woodsend things change without warning.

Uncle Rick's behind me. Another man steps out onto the path...no, it's not real. *Do not be distracted. I am Ruby, I am Ruby.* I need to score. I need to score. Keep running. Past Woodpecker Cottage, with the light in the window burning low just like always. This is where there's another path. You get scratched with all the brambles but keep down and soon there's a clearing, then the stone circle. Another flashback, something on the periphery of my mind like a flickering insect...black hooded figures and loud humming...Panic in my chest...But it's not real and now I can hear her. Marie.

She waiting, her voice faint from somewhere in the trees.

"Ruby, hurry up for Christ's sake."

We're kids and I've got stitch in my side. *"Hurry up, they'll see us."*

"What are they doing? What's that screaming?"

"It's a sacrifice."

"What's a sacrifice?"

The flashback's gone. I can't get it back. I can't see it.

But ahead is what I came for. This is real time and I've got to keep it together - just a bit longer - gotta do this one last thing.

Slumping against the old oak opposite the house, I fall onto the ground next to Marie. Getting my second wind as we skulk in the shadows, watching. Waiting. She passes me a bottle of water. "Glad you could make it."

The place is exactly as I remember. Like a travellers' camp with abandoned caravans, trucks, and half-burned bonfires topped with scabby mattresses. A Rottweiler's chained to the fence, a wisp of smoke spirals into the stars, and directly outside the front door stands a shiny black 4x4 bought no doubt, from her disability allowance - what a joke - its rutted tracks gouged into the track.

"He's home," says Marie.

"Where's Ida?"

"Not sure. Looking at the light downstairs I'd say he's watching TV. She'll be upstairs drugged up."

"What about Alice?"

"She's in there - I've seen her face at the window enough times. They're doing to her what they did to you, Ruby. We have to get her out of there and that's why I needed to find you. I'd say we need to wait til 3 am to make sure Rick or Derek don't turn up. And we've got to be positive the old witch is spark out."

"How are we getting in with that bloody dog outside?"

Marie whispers, never taking her eyes off the place, "Give it some of your stash. Got a syringe?"

Behind us the trees are cloaked in dank fog. While ahead the house squats darkly, one downstairs lamp glowing amber. All it would take would be one yap from the dog and he'd be out on the porch, scanning the area with a torch, while the witch fetches a knife. He can run like some kind of supernatural being, did I say? Oh yes he fair scuds through the trees, with feet that skate the ground and hands that grasp your hair and wrench joints right of sockets.

Clouds float across the scythe moon, and a fox barks throatily. This body of mine, the longer we sit here, is getting leaden, numb and bone-cold, with an aching lower back from pressing it into hollow bark.

I shiver and Marie says, "Do you want to know what happened to our mother?"

"I don't care. She didn't care about us."

"They had her too, Ruby. I saw her - down at the mill with his dad. That's where they did the murders. And she had those kids with him, and Rick and Derek. That's where the bodies are - the infants - they used the blood and foetuses for sacrifice, and the baby fat to mix with pitch so they could make candles for the black mass. She had to do it. They called her Natalie. After the old guy died they had her killed. I saw it. The old witch did it with belladonna at a ritual - she was a human altar and when it finished that's what they did. I followed them. There's a place underground, underneath the Mill…you keep on walking and it gets darker and darker, wetter and cavernous…"

The snap of a twig makes us stop dead, staring into each other's widening eyes. Waiting without breath or movement for the longest, longest time. Eventually our collective breath is released. It was a wild animal, that's all. There's no one out tonight. The night is dead.

"How do you know all this?"

"I've been watching them for years," she says. "About twenty of them. You wouldn't believe who they are!"

"I'm surprised no one saw you. You must have been shit scared?"

A caustic laugh catches silently in her throat. "Hate can replace fear, didn't you know?"

"Why haven't you gone to the police?"

"Because no one would believe me. Everything's brilliantly covered up. People like I said, who you wouldn't believe, are in this - police, the doctor, even a fucking priest. They're Satanists and paedophiles - they stay in the caravans at Fairyhill - and there is no one we can trust. Not one single person. You can't tell a doctor anything. You must never get into a hospital or a police station. We've got to do the job ourselves and save Alice. He knows we're out on the loose and he's looking for us all the time. All the time, Ruby. We are not safe and never ever will be. God knows how we've survived this long."

She glances at her watch. "Nearly the witching hour. Come on, Kid - let's get closer and dope out the dog."

***

We are stealthy as wild cats, our footfalls soft on the leaf-sodden turf. The dog sniffs, growls, then snaffles my remaining chocolate while Marie gives him a dose of smack. Sweet dreams, Pooch!

We stroke his head until he dozes. Or dies. I'm not sure which. But there isn't much choice - if The Bastard hears us we're dead, and it won't be painless!

A complicit nod, then like common thieves we flick the knife into the door lock. A chain bars us. We hesitate for just a second - the air still and silent - then creep round to the back and ease open a window instead. It's Ida's laundry room - where she washes things on a daily basis - we never knew why she spent so much time in there cos the beds were always rank, so it wasn't like it was our sheets she was washing. Thankfully the window lurches open on a looser catch than in the rest of the place, and we push our bodies through - plopping onto the linoleum below like slugs.

Snoring reverberates through the walls, followed by a creak of the double bed he shares with the witch we thought of as Mother, until we realised we don't have eyes like hers. Hate consumes us, the adrenalin of it making our hands shake, while our breath steams on the air. With backs to the wall, we climb the stairs we used to flee down screaming so many times, his stick cracking our arms, legs and backs until we crumpled against the locked door and our small, fragile forms took the full force of his rage.

At the top of the stairs there is a mirror. A child's face stares back at me, with wide blue eyes in a skin that never sees the sun. The child is holding a knife. She hesitates.

Alice...where is Alice?

The floorboards creak dangerously as another apnoeic snort signals one of them at least is asleep. But who?

Where is Alice?

We push open doors in turn: there are only four and one will be the bathroom.

The first, our old room, and most likely to be Alice's, is at the back of the house with a view of the oil tank and wood store below. That's where Marie saw her looking out of the window. She must be here...But the head on the pillow is wedged with rollers and a scarf, the body bulky. Sickly perfume and body odour cloy the air. So he and the old witch are in separate rooms, now!

Closing the door carefully, we move to the next room.

"What the fuck are you doing?"

We reel back. He's bolt upright in bed while her snores rattle on through the walls. Moonlight streaks across the room, glinting off the dresser onto his shock of white hair.

There is a fraction of a second.

He is reaching for something.

He isn't looking at me, though - he's looking at the bad girl screaming at him with a knife in her hand.

While I float away, to where there is a castle and a moat. Marie is beckoning to me. *Hurry, hurry*...Across the drawbridge...Pulling it up behind us...running quickly down a long corridor...then all at once, bursting out of French Windows into the full glare of daylight. There are lots of children here, and they're rushing up to us with crayons, books and games. Behind them tables are set with white cloths piled high with exquisitely decorated fairy cakes and dishes wobbling with coloured jellies. All laid out on sun-dappled lawns, where in the background a river glints invitingly beneath a weeping willow.

***

Chapter 30
Drummersgate
Christmas Eve, 2015

Becky looked through the porthole window at Ruby, now in Room 8. Claire stood next to her. "She's doing really well. Amazingly. Thank God."

"You look exhausted, Claire."

"I am. I can't tell you how grateful I am you're back. Noel's been doing double shifts and I can't remember when I last had a day off."

Becky inclined her head towards Ruby. "How have the other patients been with her?"

"Fine. She reads their palms and tells them what their auras mean and they love it. I have to say she's pretty accurate too - she got my grandma's name, told me what she looked like and described where she lived - quite incredible! And if the old lady really is watching over me then I'm pretty happy about it, to be honest. Ruby seems to know stuff she couldn't possibly know, it's incredible - she just blurts it out while you're doing something else. I think she's got trouble controlling it, though…Now look - she's got me believing this stuff as well!"

Becky smiled.

"She also said you were 'on your way back'! Oh and that my mum had a health scare coming up but she'd be okay. Funny thing is - Mum's booked in for a breast scan the first week in January."

"I don't know where her knowledge comes from either, Claire, but she's spot on, all right, so hopefully you won't have to worry too much about your mum!" Becky swallowed hard, then took the plunge. "Did she um…say anything about the police officer who went missing? D.I Ross? He was working on her case, you see, investigating Woodsend village."

"It's odd how everyone working with her has had something awful happen to them, isn't it? She didn't mention him, sorry, although she did say Martha should never have read a diary or something."

"A diary?"

Claire shrugged. "It doesn't make too much sense."

"But Martha had a heart attack, didn't she?"

"Yes, I know."

" This is the thing, you see. We all had something happen - Jack had a mental breakdown after a hypnosis session with her. I tripped over nothing and ended up in hospital. Martha's dead after reading a diary about Woodsend. D.I. Ross has gone missing. And now I hear Kristy's had some kind of breakdown too? None of it makes sense as you say, Claire! None of it."

"What exactly happened to Kristy? I have to say I'm really shocked - she was so cool and right at the top of her game. She was my idol, really. I wanted to *be* her!"

"I don't know. Something about collapsing on stage at a conference. Another coincidence anyway."

Claire frowned.

"The thing is - taken in isolation, as Kristy said, everything can be explained, but look at the wider picture and it's distinctly odd. It's like everyone who was trying to uncover the truth about Ruby has, one way or another, been stopped - even Kristy herself, who I have to say I thought was pretty invincible."

"You know Amanda was freaked out, don't you? She had this weird session with Ruby before she resigned - where Ruby was painting a cave with black shapes on the walls. Suddenly Ruby turned to her and told her she was next! Amanda went into melt down. I didn't think she'd react like that but I suppose in light of the fact we'd just got back from Martha's funeral and everyone was talking about Jack...well she literally packed her case there and then, wrote out her notice, the lot!"

"Really?"

"Ruby is way too accurate to ignore and we all know it! Even the dinner ladies ask her stuff and she's spot on -doesn't know them from Adam but she'll be able to list their grandparents' names and who their childhood babysitter was; tell them who should see a doctor and if one of their kids is up to no good - and she's always, always right. You'd have to be tough as camel hide to brush off a warning like that from Ruby. Even Isaac's taken extended leave. We've got a locum next door now!"

"No wonder you're shattered, Claire."

"It's odd how she hasn't got to me, isn't it? I mean - I'm ok so far!"

"Ah well you're not involved in her case, are you? You aren't researching anything that might uncover a few unpalatable truths about Woodsend village for example?"

Claire's brow furrowed in puzzlement.

"I know - it's hard to get your head round."

For a moment the two women just watched Ruby lying on her bed. Without turning to look at her, Claire said, "What about you? Are you going to be okay, Becky?"

"I hope so. I'm scared to be honest, after what I went through, but I'm damn well going to find out what happened to Ruby if it's the last thing I do. For all our sakes."

Claire nodded silently. " She survived, though, didn't she? Ruby, I mean! Which is more than we can say for our colleagues."

"Survived what, though? And how did she do it?"

Claire's beeper sounded and she glanced down. "I'm going to have to go - there's been a lock-down next door!"

***

Ruby looked up and smiled when Becky walked in a few minutes later.

"Don't worry, he's okay."

The blood rushed to Becky's face. She stood with her back to Ruby, gazing out of the window across the wind-flattened lawns until her heart steadied.

"How do you know?"

She shrugged. "I just do."

"Tell me–"

The words gushed out with rapid speed, devoid of punctuation. "I can see him on a dark road - shiny and wet with rain - moors on either side - oh no he wasn't supposed to get out -

he was put in the dark place - left deep inside on the stone floor - his fingernails are bleeding and his head's cut - blood down the side of his face - there's a swimmy feel about him - like he was drugged - but now it's all cold and wet - outside -he'll get picked up soon, though." The monologue came to an abrupt end. "I don't know anymore."

Becky whirled around. "Ruby, there have been some very bad things happening to the staff here - all of us who've tried to help you. Why? What have we done?"

Ruby's far away smile faded slightly and Becky immediately regretted her tone. None of this was the girl's fault. She took a deep breath and tried again. "Sorry, sorry. It's been hard on us - all of us."

Ruby stared back at her.

"The thing is - Kristy's now very ill. And your doctor, Jack McGowan - he'll never be the same again. Martha Kind died of a heart attack and I…well, I just don't understand, Ruby. I saw terrible things too…I wasn't myself at all. In the end I persuaded Noel to take me into a church. Since then I've been better. I just don't get it. What on earth is happening to us? You're the link, don't you see?" Against her better judgement she slumped onto the edge of her patient's bed, head in hands.

Ruby's face settled into a worried frown, her gaze focused on something deep inside her mind.

Eventually Becky looked up. "Sorry. I'm sorry, Ruby. The thing is we really need to understand where this is coming from. What's at the heart of it all. I know Amanda did a lot of work with you. I've seen the drawings of trees and a house with caravans with washing strewn outside. Is that where you lived? In Woodsend? There's no record of you there but there is of a boy called Thomas and a girl called Belinda - both still in psychiatric units, by the way. Kristy was helping Thomas before she heard about you, and she went out there. On the way back she had a nasty experience, and of course, it's where D.I. Ross vanished from. Maybe you could tell me more about Woodsend - did you grow up there?"

Ruby's demeanour remained unchanged.

"There's no record of it, as I said. No record of you being there, at all! And yet that's where you were found before you came here!"

No response.

"It's odd about the children actually. None on the birth register according to Martha's research, for the last thirty years except Thomas Blackmore and Belinda Dean, who I've mentioned and who are mentally ill. And there were no children born to Paul and Ida Dean at all, yet there's a lady called Celeste Frost who recalls lots of children running wild around their place in the mid-nineties. Gypsy children? Did these people travel? Do you know anything? Anything at all that might help?"

Ruby's head jerked up, her expression now one of quiet contemplation, her lips tightened into a prim line of disapproval .

Was this still Ruby? It looked like her and yet something infinitesimal had changed.

"Who am I talking to?"

In response, the voice was small and tight. "Marie."

"Marie? Hello Marie."

"Hello. I'm very worried about Alice, that's the problem and I've been trying to tell Ruby to do something. "

"Who's Alice?"

"Ruby's daughter, but we don't know where she is. We tried to find her once but we got him instead."

Becky nodded slowly, carefully. "Him?"

"Dad. Ida was there too, and she woke up and came in, started screaming."

"Who's Ida?"

"The witch."

"Not Ruby's mother?"

"No. Natalie's Ruby's mother, although she looked after his father down at The Mill. Did stuff for Ida, as well. Some of the little kids were Uncle Derek's and some were Uncle Rick's, but mostly they were his and Natalie's, or Kath's."

Becky swallowed her disgust. Tried to focus on the worst of it. "Hang on a minute, what little kids? Where are they now?"

"Sacrifices. In the cave, mostly, or buried in the cemetery. They moved them after that woman came snooping round so mostly they're in the cave."

"I beg your pardon?"

The politely spoken young woman sighed. "I can't find any documents for any of us children - probably there's hundreds. Sometimes the gypsies take them, but mostly they're skinned before or just after they're born."

The colour drained from Becky's face, bile rising in her throat. *Fuck!* "Satanic rituals!"

"Yes. I've been trying to catch him and find evidence but I'm always on the run, hiding, using different names. Years go by and the next thing I know I'm looking in a shop window at myself in Leeds and I've got a drug problem. I don't know - I keep blacking out."

"Marie - hang on a minute - are you the host or is Ruby?"

"Ruby. Me. Shit - I never thought of it like that. We all work together. We are 'we', I suppose."

"Yes. Oh my God. Look, we can help you Marie, we really can. But here's the thing - our entire team is in serious danger - we're all getting sick. Or worse. And now there's only me left and I have to track this man down. Are we talking about Paul Dean? Did he do this to you?"

She nodded. "There are more than him but he works for the father. The father of lies…"

"The father? Is that what you call him? Good God. Who else is involved?"

"His brothers - Derek and Rick - they're in the coven. And Ida. Then there's the doctor at Bridesmoor, and the local copper, although he's retired now, and the Reverend Gordon. There are men they bring in from outside too, who stay in …" Her voice trailed off a little and her colour faded…

Becky squeezed her hand. "It's okay, it's okay. I need to know this. You're safe, Marie. You're quite safe."

"They stay in caravans. And there's Natalie and Kathleen. Witches."

"What do you mean? I thought Natalie was your mother?"

"Yes but they used to read us the Satanic Bible on the common. They told us we were bad children and deserved to be punished. I saw them at the Black Mass. I saw it - underground - I saw them. I watched. Natalie was a human altar. Everyone fucked her afterwards."

"Underground? Marie - stay with me. Who is this father of lies?"

"The gatekeeper."

"Can you explain?"

"He's left us now - he got out that day - you saw him! But now he's not here anymore we can talk to each other in the system - there are hundreds of us - but we're piecing it all together cos he's not here to stop us now and scare the little ones. And that's how I can tell Ruby about Marie - because the Gatekeeper has gone...the father of lies - he kept us all locked up in here.... Down long, dark corridors imprisoned with iron bars and locks. But he's gone to your friends now, I'm sorry, I'm sorry, he's everywhere...he got out–"

"Marie, just stay with me okay? Priorities now - where is this little girl we should be looking for - Alice?"

"We tried to find her, I told you."

"On the night you attacked Paul Dean?"

"We couldn't find her. She wasn't there."

"Do you think Alice is in that house?"

"She was at the window. Sometimes."

"Marie - are you telling me that you, I mean Ruby, had a daughter and she's in that house? We have to tell the police."

Ruby's expression began to fade, the eyes staring into a distant place.

"What? Marie - please don't go. Not yet."

Ruby's blue eyes lost their light, leaving her face as vacant as a plastic doll's. A minute passed.

"Ruby?"

Slowly Ruby's eyes registered recognition. She leaned forwards clasping her head between her hands. "Oh God, my head."

"Headache?"

"Oh God my head hurts. Jesus!"

"I'll get you something." Becky prepared to stand up, but then held back. "Ruby, think -can you remember anything you've just told me?"

Ruby had bent over on her bed, whimpering with the pain. "Oh God, I don't know. I get fragments of stuff–"

"It's okay, we'll get there. I promise you - we'll get there. Now, please, do you think we are looking for a young girl? Alice?"

Ruby's eyes widened, the pupils dilated to black ellipses. Then slowly she shook her head. "I don't know the name."

Becky left the room, unlocked the drug cupboard to get a couple of paracetamol for Ruby, and returned deep in thought. Next thing would be to contact the police, in the hope they would take Ruby's information very seriously in connection with Callum's disappearance. *A cave underneath the mill…*

Ruby washed down the tablets, then looked straight at Becky, her eyes glittering. "I need to see someone - Celeste," she said, in her strong Yorkshire accent again. "She lived at Woodsend when I were at that mill. They're saying I should be working…but I'm scared to. If I'm not in control he might come back and get in me again - get us all."

Becky nodded. How clever Ruby the child had been - the Dissociative identity disorder had saved her soul. "Hmmm, I'm sure Martha visited a lady called Celeste Frost before she died - wasn't she driven out of Woodsend by local people for being a witch?"

"Yes. I need to see her. Urgently. Please."

"Okay, I'll find her phone number.

***

Chapter 31
Christmas Eve, 11.30pm

Callum woke with a dull sickly headache, the chill of a crypt at his back. Slowly he sat up. It looked like he was in a cave of some sort - certainly underground: the place was coal-face black and oozing with damp. He rubbed the base of his skull, wincing with the pain, and listened intently. Nothing but the echoing drip-drip-drip of water onto a stone floor. Alone then…

Gradually, as his eyes adjusted to the dark, he rose to his haunches, then carefully to his feet, feeling for a wall to lean on. The surface behind was glistening, slippery and rough. A mine shaft? A cave? A crash of blinding, oppressive pain nearly knocked him down again, but he remained standing, concentrating solely on breathing regularly and stilling his fear. There had to be a way out.

How much time had passed? Days? Hours? His watch had been taken. As had his phone, wallet and car keys. The only course of action was to start walking in case whoever had attacked him, came back. Perhaps he was supposed to just die in here? A rush of bilious nausea rose without warning and he stopped to vomit, the acid burning his throat leaving a metallic taste. Some kind of drug, then? A blurred memory surfaced - of a circle of faces shrouded in dark hoods staring down at him, swirling tree tops, flickering stars…and then nothing: spark out as if anaesthetised. Instinctively he surveyed his inner arms and sure enough the puncture marks and bruises confirmed his suspicions. Someone knew what they were doing. And yeah - he was here to rot.

Without a compass, or a single shard of light, it was difficult to know which direction to take. Blind faith then. Just start walking.

As he did so, his brain began to gather facts, permeating a fog of pain and fatigue, and the irresistible urge to sit down, close his eyes and drift away. *Keep walking. Don't go to sleep. Keep walking so they can't find you…*

The question was, if this was underground then was he walking towards Bridesmoor Pit? Or further into a network of caves beneath the moors, in which case he'd be below Carrions Wood by now and west of the old mill. Where would it end? If ever? He could wander underground until he dropped and no one would ever find him. At least towards the mine there might, just might, be a way out - a vent, a shaft - something!

The thought of going the wrong way pumped a new wave of claustrophobic panic through his veins. Endless, frequently forked corridors beckoned - each blacker than the last, the darkness ever thicker, and less and less oxygen with every footstep. While overhead sat the mighty weight of sodden moorland, the insidious dripping of rainwater trickling through the peat and down the cracks, seeping into the caverns below. He kept on walking... *I'm a dead man walking...* palms flat to the slimy walls, footsteps cautious on the slippery floor. The dripping was becoming louder. The blackness blacker. *He'd gone the wrong way. Shit. He'd gone the wrong way.*

His heart lurched heavily, the terror of being buried alive screaming in his head. Should he retrace his steps and go back the way he came? Start again on a different route? But how many hours had passed? What if this was a maze and he'd never get out? There was nothing he could do! Nothing!

Sanity, must keep his sanity. Breathe in and out. In and out. Start counting out seconds and minutes.
Think! How long had he been here? Try to think!

His stomach was turning in on itself with emptiness and his throat was sore and dry. His head banged and his limbs were trembling. Low blood sugar. He ran fingers down his ribs. Two days? *Okay, so start counting. As from now. And get water...Don't lose it you stupid bastard. Don't lose it!*

Ahead there was the sound of a more solid trickle. It would be a fresh spring, and he picked up pace as best he could, eventually turning a corner into a huge cavern. In front of him an icy spring splashed onto the stone floor and he sank to his knees, crawling towards it until his clothes became soaked and his whole body lay prostrate beneath the gushing water - as pure as nectar and startlingly, brilliantly cold. He splashed it over his face and scooped it into his palms to drink, gulping and gasping. Whoever had left him here had stripped him of all but his shirt and trousers, leaving him without a coat or shoes. Men in hooded robes. A woman. A woman's laugh as his head hit the floor with a nauseating crack. Faces lit by flames. Faces he would remember to his dying day.

He would not die.

More images came - skulls on the walls, dancing shadows, a low humming sound. He closed his eyes for a moment, reeling from an unexpected and vivid flashback - there'd been an altar like one in a church, except the candles were black and the cross was upside down. A putrid, acrimonious stench hit his nostrils - like decaying flesh and old blood....

A sudden cramp gripped his stomach with colicky pain. He doubled up, breathing hard, breaking a sweat. Then stood once more. *Keep walking man! When in hell keep walking...*

The stomach cramp brought him down every few steps but he forged ahead, feeling along the walls, and praying. Praying like he'd hadn't prayed since he was a child. Was this what all mere mortals did in their hour of need? With no emergency services to call, and no one to hear their cries? Call on God? Did he believe? Callum rubbed angrily at the hot tears coursing down his cheeks. Was it a weakness to call on God? Again he stopped, bent over with the pain, weak with exhaustion. Was this the end then? Was it time to make peace with himself?

The urge to sit down was overwhelming yet somehow he kept on walking. Kept on counting. Kept his legs moving.

It would be better to die of suffocation deep underneath a mine than in some kind of satanic cult. Not to give them the satisfaction of finding his dead body. God, it would have been good to bring those bastards to justice, though. They had abused those kids, hadn't they? The girl, Ruby? The boy, Thomas? And how many more?

His body was shivering violently now, teeth chattering so hard they banged his jaws together, fingers and toes numb. But he kept on walking, losing count at a thousand before starting over again. He'd know those faces…know them...every single one of them…if he ever got out of here…he'd know them.

And he'd marry Becky.

***

Chapter 32

Christmas Day

Becky handed over the keys to the night staff just as the phone rang in her office. Her hand reached for the receiver, but then she hesitated: in some ways it had been a good day. Celeste had very kindly come in that morning to see Ruby, even bringing her a small gift of chocolates and soap; and the two of them had got on well, promising to keep in touch. It had been a good start to their relationship, and although it was far from conventional, Ruby was going to need friends because one day she'd have to fend for herself again. Yes, she'd done the right thing calling Celeste.

Mark had changed the locks when she'd shown up last night and who could blame him? Probably it was for the best, and besides, how could she cope with his pain and his questions when she had so much else on her mind? Hopefully there would come a day when they could talk and he'd listen, possibly never understand, but listen - to her story.

She stood looking at the ringing phone. Should she answer it? The last bus was in ten minutes but the night staff consisted of one senior staff nurse and two orderlies, and the new patient in room 10 was already screaming down the walls. In the corner the tinsel tree flickered with coloured lights and a box of half eaten chocolates sat on the desk. That was the extent of Christmas in a place like this!

What if the call was urgent?

She sighed, leaned across the desk and picked it up.

"I've been told to ask for Becky - this is Sergeant Hall."

Becky's breath caught tightly in her throat, her voice coming out in a squeak. "Yes, it's me. I mean, yes–"

"We've picked up D.I. Ross and he's at the D.R.I. He's asking for you."

Quickly thanking him she phoned for a taxi. No chance. She rang Noel.

"I'll be there in ten," he said. "Grabbing my keys as we speak."

Later, sometime in the early hours, as she sat stroking Callum's hand in the blue-grey light of dawn, the only sound the bleep of a cardiac monitor, Becky wondered about the fate of her colleagues: Jack had apparently spent Christmas with his parents, playing chess and reading in front of the fire. He said he couldn't remember a thing yet he slept with all the lights on and a bible by his bed. His mother said he kept busy, but looked 'gaunt'. 'I'm feeding him up but well, you can imagine…We'll get there," she said to Becky, before thanking her for calling. "We'll get there…"

Kristy had been transferred to Laurel Lawns and according to the nurse in charge - a woman she'd worked with many years ago thank goodness or she'd never have been given the information - had, in a lucid moment asked to see a priest.'

"Get the same priest who helped Jack McGowan," said Becky.

"He's ill," came the reply. "On indefinite sick leave. Actually, I understand he won't be returning at all. To be honest, our current M.O. doesn't agree with that sort of thing."

"Current M.O.? What happened to the other one?"

"He left. Struck off by the GMC for professional misconduct."

"You're joking?"

"No. No, I'm not. Under his watch there were several suicides and more relapses than we've ever had in the history of Laurel Lawns. Other members of staff weren't at all happy when a priest was brought in."

"But–"

"Look, sorry, Becky. I have to go. You can come in and see Kristy any time you like - just give us a call first, okay? She has good days and bad days."

After the call had ended, she could only hope and pray for Kristy Silver. Meanwhile, Callum had been saved. By something. Or someone. Please God he found something to get to the root of all this evil, the ripples of which were devastating and seemingly never-ending. He couldn't be left alone though, not for a minute - because sooner or later they, whoever they were, would know he was alive. And talking.

At Six-thirty, one of Callum's colleagues poked his head round the door. "Do you want to go get a coffee? I'll sit with him for a bit, if you like - let you know if he comes round."

She smiled faintly, reluctant to leave, living for the moment his eyes opened again, and the corner of his lips lifted in recognition.

"Okay. I won't be long, though. Any news on where he'd been? He isn't speaking to me yet - did he say anything to Sergeant Hall?"

The young officer shook his head. "Only that when he were picked up on Bridesmoor, he were covered in soot and delirious. We think he'd found a mine shaft and somehow scrambled up. We don't know - it's a bloody miracle."

"So he'd been underground?"

"Aye. And we've got his phone - it were in't woods near the old mill - must 'ave dropped out of his pocket. I've just heard there were pictures on it - of skulls and stuff...they're being examined now. There were shots of dark shapes and trees, all upside down, but on one of 'em there's this girl of about nine or ten... in a nightie. Standing there in t' woods....just watching in t' background."

Becky's hands flew to her face. "Oh my God, that's Alice! She's real then? That's Alice! He found her."

"Alice?"

"Ruby's daughter. I wasn't sure if–" She looked at the puzzled frown on the officer's face and shook her head. "Look – all that matters is you find her and then get that child the hell out of Woodsend, because she's in serious danger."

"What the hell's going on down there? Is it Satanism or something?"

She stared back at him.

"Shit! You're going to 'ave to be interviewed, Becky."

"Yes, I think we all are." She nodded towards Callum. "And let's hope he can remember what he's seen because…" Despite the heat in the hospital unit, she shivered visibly. "Well, let's just say they have powerful help on their side, and my guess is when they know he escaped they're going to come looking."

As she spoke, the fluorescent lights flickered and a dark shadow began to spread across the walls.

Or was that just her imagination?

***

Acknowledgements
Glossary of Terms

The author of this book would like to add that a considerable amount of research was undertaken in order to broaden her knowledge of Dissociative Identity Disorder (DID), which affects many people, and in 90% of cases can be attributed to child abuse. Thank you very much to those who helped with this research.

RSA: Ritual Satanic Abuse
DID: Dissociative Identity Disorder (previously known as multiple personality disorder) is thought to be a complex psychological condition that is likely caused by many factors, including severe trauma during early childhood (usually extreme, repetitive physical, sexual, or emotional abuse).
PTSD: Post Traumatic Stress Disorder
Dystonia – A syndrome of abnormal muscle contraction that produces repetitive involuntary twisting movements and abnormal posturing of the neck, trunk, face, and extremities. (Farlex Partner Medical Dictionary © Farlex 2012)
Haloperidol – an anti-psychotic agent.

***

<u>Tanners Dell – Book 2</u>

Now only one of the original team remains – Ward Sister, Becky. However, despite her fiancé, Callum, being unconscious and many of her colleagues either dead or critically ill, she is determined to rescue Ruby's twelve year old daughter from a similar fate to her mother.

But no one asking questions in the desolate ex-mining village Ruby hails from ever comes to a good end. And as the diabolical history of the area is gradually revealed, it seems the evil invoked is both real and contagious.

Don't turn the lights out yet!

*****

Magda – Book 3

The dark and twisted community of Woodsend harbours a terrible secret – one tracing back to the age of the Elizabethan witch hunts, when many innocent women were persecuted and hanged.
But there is a far deeper vein of horror running through this village; an evil that once invoked has no intention of relinquishing its grip on the modern world. Rather it watches and waits with focused intelligence, leaving Ward Sister, Becky, and CID Officer, Toby, constantly checking over their shoulders and jumping at shadows.
Just who invited in this malevolent presence? And is the demonic woman who possessed Magda back in the sixteenth century, the same one now gazing at Becky whenever she looks in the mirror? Are you ready to meet Magda in this final instalment of the trilogy? Are you sure?

***

Out April 26th, 2018

The Owlmen

Pure Occult Horror

If They See You They Will Come For You

Ellie Blake is recovering from a nervous breakdown. Deciding to move back to her northern roots, she and her psychiatrist husband buy Tanners Dell at auction - an old water mill in the moorland village of Bridesmoor.

However, there is disquiet in the village. Tanners Dell has a terrible secret, one so well guarded no one speaks its name. But in her search for meaning and very much alone, Ellie is drawn to traditional witchcraft and determined to pursue it. All her life she has been cowed. All her life she has apologised for her very existence. And witchcraft has opened a door she could never have imagined. Imbued with power and overawed with its magick, for the first time she feels she has come home, truly knows who she is.

Tanners Dell though, with its centuries old demonic history...well, it's a dangerous place for a novice...

http://www.amazon.co.uk/dp/B079W9FKV7

http://www.amazon.com/dp/B079W9FKV7

***

Also by S. E. England
The Soprano: A Haunting Supernatural Thriller

'It is 1951 and a remote mining village on the North Staffordshire
Moors is hit by one of the worst snowstorms in living memory.
Cut off for over three weeks, the old and the sick will die; the
strongest bunker down; and those with evil intent will bring to its
conclusion a family vendetta spanning three generations.
Inspired by a true event, 'The Soprano' tells the story of Grace
Holland - a strikingly beautiful, much admired local celebrity who
brings glamour and inspiration to the grimy moorland community.
But why is Grace still here? Why doesn't she leave this staunchly
Methodist, rain-sodden place and the isolated farmhouse she
shares with her mother?

Riddled with witchcraft and tales of superstition, the story is
mostly narrated by the Whistler family who own the local funeral
parlour, in particular six year old Louise - now an elderly lady -
who recalls one of the most shocking crimes imaginable.'

http://www.amazon.co.uk/dp/B0737GQ9Q7
http://www.amazon.com/dp/B0737GQ9Q7

***

If you enjoyed reading Father of Lies, please would you leave a review? It would be hugely appreciated by the author. Thank you.
http://www.amazon.co.uk/dp/B015NCZYKU
http://www.amazon.com/dp/B015NCZYKU

***

Printed in Great Britain
by Amazon